**He had chosen his next victim—now all that remained
was the pleasure of the kill…**

Dexter asked Debbie out, and she gleefully accepted.
Rome's face went a hideous shade of scarlet, Dexter noted cheerfully. He looked hard into Debbie's playful eyes
and could almost see her used up and on the brink a few
months from now. Dexter knew how to wipe out a woman's soul. When their mind had gone, and you were left
with a blithering wreck, then Dexter got tired of them,
and it was time to kill. Death would be either slow or
quick, the manner of it depending on how much pleasure
the specimen had given him. In Debbie's case, he saw
endless hours of pleasure in front of him as his mental
torture made her steadily unwind. Because of the joy
she'd give him, he wouldn't make her suffer at the end. A
knife to the jugular, a gunshot to the heart, the choices for
a quick kill were endless.

He ignored such thoughts and decided to spend the
rest of the afternoon trying to wind Rome up. Rome had
no idea what he was dealing with. He would never have
had anybody play with his mind like Dexter could. Dexter was the best. The problem was nobody on this movie
set knew it yet. Paul Rome and Debbie Duncan were
about to find out how fucked up they could become at the
hands of an expert. Dexter was the ultimate drug, alas,
Debbie Duncan was soon to find out it was a drug of the
lethal variety.

The movie set of the Regal Films post-war drama, *The Valley of Dreams*, is a place of dark menace and evil, where everything isn't as it seems. Cameraman, Peter Rivers, has a hidden past. Under many different identities, this serial killer has left a trail of victims behind him, a fact the cast and crew of the movie are blissfully unaware of. Charming and confident, he chooses Debbie Duncan, the movie's co-star, as his new soulmate/submissive, but she isn't as easy to manipulate and subdue as he expected. Then Detective Inspector Sarah Machin shows up at the movie set in Wales with questions about his former girlfriend's murder, and things spiral out of control for Rivers. He knows he should flee, but he can't settle into a new life while one of his intended victims is still alive, resulting in an all-consuming need for him to come after Duncan. Even though she has police protection and the close attentions of friend and confidante, Director Clay Thompson, Rivers will not be denied, leading more than one participant to confront the dark side of their souls…

KUDOS for *Soul Mates*

In *Soul Mates* by Paul Howard, Peter Rivers is a man with a dark and secret past. When he joins the film crew of the movie The Valley of Dreams, he sets his sights on the film's co-star Debbie Duncan. Rivers expects things to go as they always have and that Debbie will fall under his spell. But Debbie hasn't read that script. While she thinks Peter is charming, to her, he is just a fling. Her career is just taking off and she refuses to allow a man to get in her way. When the police begin to investigate Peter in connection with his old girlfriend's murder, things start to spiral out of control, setting off a chain of events that leave everyone with their own demons to face. Expecting a romance by the title, I was pleasantly surprised to find a well-crafted, exciting, and fast-paced thriller that I couldn't put down. A really great read. ~ *Taylor Jones, The Review Team of Taylor Jones & Regan Murphy*

Soul Mates by Paul Howard is the story of a film crew making a movie in Wales. What none of them realize at the start is that there is a serial killer in their midst, and he is targeting one of the stars. Peter Rivers hires on as a camera man for Regal Films on their new movie. The director Clay Thompson has a new starlet, and he is excited to be directing her in this film. Debbie Duncan the co-star of the movie was discovered by Thompson at an amateur play, and she is smart enough to know this is her big break. When Peter helps Debbie out of an awkward situation, she is charmed and agrees to go out with him. But Peter isn't quite as charming as he thinks he is, and instead of worshiping him, as he expects, Debbie tells him after a few dates that their relationship is over. Peter is outraged. He can't start over without breaking and killing her, and now he may not have the chance as the film is almost done. Debbie doesn't realize the monster she has unleashed with her rejection, but she is about to find out. Howard tells an incredibly complex and intense tale of murder and intrigue, one that will have you up late at night turning pages and saying "Just one more chapter." I highly recommend *Soul Mates*. *~ Regan Murphy, The Review Team of Taylor Jones & Regan Murphy*

ACKNOWLEDGMENTS

Once again, I'd like to thank Faye for her patience and Faith, Lauri, and all those at Black Opal Books for their support.

The introduction of DI Sarah Machin, is the start of a series of books involving the police inspector that I hope the readers of *Soul Mates* will enjoy. Again, I'd like to thank Jack Phillips for his help in my early writing years.

SOUL MATES

Paul Howard

A Black Opal Books Publication

GENRE: CRIME THRILLER/MYSTERY-DETECTIVE

SOUL MATES
Copyright © 2018 by Paul Howard
Cover Design by Jackson Cover Designs
All cover art copyright © 2018
All Rights Reserved
Print ISBN: 978-1-626948-51-8

First Publication: JANUARY 2018

Published by Black Opal Books **http://www.blackopalbooks.com**

DEDICATION

I dedicate this book to my deceased parents, Mike and Hilda, and all my love and thanks to my partner, Anna-Maria, for her continued support.

CHAPTER 1

It wasn't the door slamming that told him Carol was leaving. Nor was it the constant arguments or learning that she didn't play on the darts team she was supposed to every Wednesday night. The day that Dexter finally realized Carol was planning something, that he'd lost control of the situation, was the day he went to withdraw some money out of their joint account and discovered Carol had cleaned it out.

Dexter fumbled with the wrapper of the plastic tasting cheese he'd taken out the fridge. The invention of polythene—that was the moment. The invention of polythene was the moment when all dairy products started to taste horrible. Dexter originated from Somerset, could remember the real cheese he'd been brought up on, the wonderful succulent childhood product that bore no relation to the muck he was about to grill.

As he cut the cheese, it fell out of his hand and slid under the cooker. Dexter knelt on the hard, tiled floor, tried to reach it using a knife blade. As he stretched toward it, he could smell burning, he sprang up, banged his head on the worktop. In a daze, he managed to retrieve the wheat inferno before the grill completely incinerated it. He blew out the flames, decided the edges were blacker than coal. He dissected it with a table knife as the middle still had a chunk of cheese that was slightly singed but edible. He cut out the middle then doused the rest under the cold tap before throwing it unceremoniously into the overflowing rubbish bin.

He studied the dirt and dust coating his trousers, evidence, if any were needed, that his filthy kitchen floor was not a place to crawl around on. He shook his head, there was nothing to say. He'd been confused for weeks since his Carol discovery. His job was suffering, the house was a pigpen. He rummaged in the bread bin looking for bread that could be salvaged, but all he found was a green spotted roll with an exclusive art deco mold pattern on it. Through recent experience, Dexter was an expert on the intricacies of mold and fungi in relation to food, so much so that he decided if he tried to eat the roll, it could kill him.

It was desperation time. He pulled off the bin lid, rummaged inside the bag, and found the third piece of burnt toast he'd thrown away. It was salvageable. He scraped the coal-black crust off it and smeared the toast in a mountain of butter to counteract its repulsiveness. The first crunch was the hardest. The act of willing the brain to bite into something that you wouldn't feed a stray dog was the hardest act of all. The horror was soon over. He washed the toast down with a cup of putrid coffee that had been left far too long on the damp windowsill.

He grabbed his mobile phone and rang work—told them the usual lies. He explained that he felt slightly better and might be back later in the week. It was always best to give his employer hope. His boss, Croucher, grumbled. He was a miserable sod. Croucher had been a bachelor all his life, used to bachelor ways. Being used to bachelor ways meant he could never understand the complications of women. He wore the same shirt two days in a row to keep down the washing. It saved money, didn't save him from being nicknamed the skunk by those who worked under him.

Dexter had seen pictures of young Croucher. He hadn't always been dirty. In his youth, he looked like a model out of a suit commercial. It was only after he'd clawed his way up the promotion ladder that things started to go wrong. There was often a matter of debate among the juniors as to what had made him stop caring? Some of the boys said he was gay and the sudden change to a skank was brought on by a lover's rejection.

Once, at a conference, Dexter had been cornered by a drunk Croucher at the hotel bar. He had told Dexter his secrets and unburdened on a disinterested Dexter a sordid tale of lost love. She'd left him for his best friend. Croucher's friend had been a man that he trusted—a man they'd spent holidays with. Regrettably, a Judas in the making. They'd moved to Portugal to set up a bar and had left Croucher behind to pick up the debris. After his experience, Dexter wasn't surprised that Croucher was a confirmed bachelor, and had an intense hatred of women.

Dexter had never been fooled by a woman. Carol had thought she was clever, had tried to play games, treated him like an idiot. The money she'd stolen from the joint account was only a tiny part of their assets. For months, Dexter had been diverting money from their joint account to his secret one. He smiled—stupid woman, he was always in control.

Dexter finished his feast and decided he needed to lie down and give himself time to think. He stared across the living-room at the newspapers piled up by the sofa. He'd been meaning to clean them up. He didn't want to turn into a slob. His mobile phone rang. He would let his voicemail handle it.

In the kitchen, he dropped his cup on top of the mountain of dirty plates, balancing precariously at the corner of the worktop. He'd do the washing up soon—it was only a matter of time until he sorted himself out.

At the top of the stairs, he made a detour to the bathroom. He stared at the sorry sight in the mirror. He hadn't shaved for days and was starting to take on the remarkable resemblance of a spaghetti western villain. As he shaved, he suddenly felt fresh and invigorated. He towel dried his face, a face that now didn't look like a hobo. He yawned, hadn't slept much the last few days. He'd been kept awake by the pressure of planning his next move.

The bedroom was cluttered, clothes scattered to every corner, clothes hangers like booby traps awaiting unsuspecting toes. He trod on one, cut his toe, limped over to the bed, and sat on the edge, commiserating. He was too tired to take his clothes off—he'd slept in the same clothes for days now. He lay down next to her, touched her cold, stiff flesh.

Her skin now had a blue-white sheen, discoloring her once vibrant warmth. It had been over a week. He'd followed the same routine he'd followed with Samantha.

"Good night, darling," Dexter said, kissing her cheek.

Carol Barnes didn't answer. Although she said nothing, the kitchen knife that was wedged in her blood-strewn stomach, Dexter decided, said more than any amount of words ever could.

CHAPTER 2

The fire alarm shrilled. Didi couldn't believe it. Why did the alarm always go off when he had a winning hand? He dropped the four aces upright on the table. Clements laughed, the laugh of a man who'd just lucked out on a losing hand. When they were racing east in the fire engine, Clements said, "Remind me never to get on a plane with you, Didi. With your luck, it's sure to go down."

Didi simmered all the way to the fire scene. Clements was a lucky bastard—a fact that, from the smug look always locked on his face, Didi was sure Clements knew.

The biting east wind whipped the flames into a frenzy at the fire. The house fire rampaged through the terrace it had started on, now engulfing the properties on either side of it. Didi, wearing breathing apparatus, cautiously sprayed the house with his hose. To his right, another hose from the second engine doused the neighboring property, toward which the wind was whipping the flames. The intense water pressure was taking a toll, as, slowly, the orange-red flames were beaten down to extinction.

"Was anybody in there?" Clements asked a young dressing-gowned couple sheltering behind an engine.

The man wiped spray from his face with his sleeve. "Another couple live there. I've no idea whether they were at home or not."

They'd better have not been inside, Clements thought. *The smoke alone would've choked them long before their bodies were burned.* Clements, the chief fire officer at the scene, moved toward the house while his men doused the dying embers. The dense-black smoke made any assessment of cause impossible in the dark. For the fire brigade, the real investigation would take place in daylight.

Fire Officer Jackson, standing in front of him, meticulously studied debris. "I don't like it, sir."

"What don't you like, Jackson?" Clements had learned to listen to the opinions of all members of the crew.

"When I was posted at Southend, there was a similar fire to this, same ferocity, turned out to be arson, sir."

Clements didn't comment. It was too early to say. With him being in charge, he had learned never to express an opinion until there'd been a proper investigation. After the fire was extinguished and mopping up operations were being carried out, Didi joined him.

"I could murder for a cuppa," Didi said. He grabbed a cup from a passing tea tray produced by a kind woman from along the street.

As Didi stood and drank, Dexter, wrapped in a muffler and Parker coat, observed the scene. He'd kept well back in the shadows as the fire raged for fear of being recognized.

Carol had gone to Valhalla, cremated in Viking fashion. The paraffin Dexter had doused the house with ensured the house was a shell and Carol's body would be completely incinerated. It would take the Emergency Services a long time to piece together what had happened here, and, by the time they did, Dexter would be long gone.

Dexter had no idea now where his future would take him, but he knew one thing—a great certainty—and that was that he needed to get out of town. He slipped away in the general kerfuffle, headed to the local bus station. It was time he started again. This time it would be different, this time he'd control himself. Ten years was a long time, though relatively short for Carol, Samantha, and Helen. Helen had been his angel, the one he liked the most. The first one you lost your cherry to—the one who made you realize what you were capable of—now there was always going to be a woman who was the memorable one.

He wouldn't dwell on the past. Now was all about his future. There were plenty of women waiting out there. It was the woman who, in the end, decided her own fate. Dexter knew how to abuse them, treat them rough, there could be no quarter given in his own personal war of the sexes. Controlling a partner wasn't something that came easy. It had to be worked on with extreme skill to achieve total domination.

This wasn't how you started. Dexter always started with the basics. First, you had to sucker your target in and, over a period of time, drain them into subservience. Once you dominated, things began to happen. Domination meant you could use them, abuse them—never give an inch with no need to show any sympathy for their problems. Their problems weren't your problems.

Helen had come close to being the model wife and had taken the beatings and the mental torture without complaint. Then there was that day—Independence Day. She'd questioned his judgment when he'd left his job at the car factory, told him it was unwise to leave a job in this recession. Helen had paid the ultimate price for her rebellion. Dexter had held her head under the water for several minutes. He still had a scar on his hand where she'd bitten him in her futile fight for life.

Samantha's efforts to please him were pathetic. Samantha only lasted two months.

The first month, she'd tried to nag him, had turned from sweet princess to a banshee barely hours after the marriage service. Dexter had warned her—every woman deserved at least one chance. When she'd ignored his warning, and the nagging started again, he'd been forced to kill her. Dexter wasn't a man who believed in idle threats. He was the model of Nietzsche's Superman, a man who stood his ground, always followed through with his threats.

Dexter boarded the London bus, carrying his meager bag of possessions that consisted of a few hundred pounds and a hotchpotch of clothes. The money wouldn't last him long. Under a new identity, he'd have to get a job quickly. He studied the passengers around him. All were engrossed in their uncomplicated sad little worlds. He opened his holdall and took out his forged passport and insurance documents. They were good forgeries, the best that money could buy. You had to know where to go to find these things, be as comfortable as Dexter outside, as well as within, the law.

He slid the documents back in the holdall and took out his tiny silver tobacco tin.

In the seat opposite, a pretty girl smiled at him, Dexter smiled back. He was always at his beguiling best around beautiful women. He studied her face, tried to search for something in her eyes that told him she was special.

At the moment, she was a maybe, would at least give him a chance to practice some of his pickup techniques if she was alone when they arrived at Victoria Bus Station.

He made sure nobody on the bus could see inside the tin. The tin was his special place where he kept all his treasures. He fumbled inside his pocket, felt the cold metal ring lying waiting there. The ring was waiting to join its brethren, to become one of the family. He slipped the smooth ring between his fingers, stared at the sparkling diamonds in the sunlight streaming through the window. It was a sparkle no longer attributed to Carol Barnes, the ring's former owner. The other two rings in his tin no longer seemed to have the same luster. Carol's ring was definitely the prettiest of the three. The tin clanked as Dexter placed the ring inside.

A shadow appeared over him as an old man tottered past, heading for the toilet at the back of the bus.

Dexter quickly snapped the tin shut and put it back in his bag out of sight. After zipping up the holdall, he closed his eyes and leaned back in his seat. Through his mind, apocalyptic thoughts darted, thinking about what lay ahead in the capital. City girls had an arrogant way about them, an independence that would be hard to grind down. Dexter would find a way to bend them to his will. Didn't he always?

He tried to sleep. It was four hours to London, four hours in which he wanted to avoid conversation with other passengers. Never to be noticed was his golden rule. Before he fell asleep, he picked up the holdall and lodged the bag inside him by the window. There was one undeniable thing that he'd learned in all his travels—there were some very strange people out there.

CHAPTER 3

The stage lights flickered and died. A murmur of discontent rippled through the audience. At the front of the stage, a glaring white torch suddenly clicked to life. Under the haunting light beam, the spectral figure of the play's director, Jacobs, could be seen. "I'm sorry, ladies and gentlemen, the maintenance man is going to replace the fuse. The rest of the play will continue shortly."

Jacobs left the stage to address the problem. The pianist near the stage played what he thought was soothing music to quell the rumblings of irritated punters. Clay Thompson found it hard to suppress his laughter. For his wife Jodie's sake, he somehow did. She'd looked at him with those cornflower-blue eyes, pleading to be taken out for a night of culture. She'd suggested the play at the town hall, amateur night, away from all the glitz and glamor. Thompson had readily agreed, deciding it might be interesting.

"Not a good start," he said.

"Give them a chance," Jodie pleaded.

Thompson shrugged, his bulk leaned back in the uncomfortable seat, and he patiently waited. Why Jodie wanted to see this rubbish was beyond him. Thompson had seen a few amateur plays in his life, all of which were piss and no substance. How could a man who'd worked with Hopkins, Caine and De Niro over the years see anything worth watching here?

The lights flickered a couple of times while the maintenance man fiddled—as he worked he was accompanied by cheers and groans until finally the hall was bathed in light.

"Thanks for your patience, ladies and gentlemen, the play will start in five minutes," Jacobs said briefly before disappearing behind the curtain backstage. The play was Macbeth, the Scottish play—a play that was supposed to be dogged with bad luck. Thompson didn't subscribe to that point of view. Thompson had made a modern film version of the play setting it in a South American dictatorship. One look at his elegant, graceful wife sitting next to him and Thompson would definitely say he wasn't unlucky.

When the play finally got going, it was the usual amateur dramatics' fare—dreary and dull until Lady Macbeth appeared. The girl playing Lady Macbeth had a presence. You couldn't explain it to the uninitiated. There was a quality about the girl that lifted her above the mire. It wasn't looks. She was good-looking, but she certainly wasn't a Monroe. It was her clarity of voice, her pristine movements, things that the untrained eye wouldn't notice, things that Thompson's eyes did.

Thompson wasn't arrogant. He didn't subscribe to the media suggestions that he had a star-making super quality about him. Thompson just knew how to spot winners. It was why he was king of the movies, why he was where he was today. Directors weren't naturally brilliant. The true geniuses were the ones that could spot the winning scripts on first perusal, who could quickly assemble the right cast to nail a movie.

Thompson's script-filter system was immense. Because he was a success, his office was saturated by scripts from wannabes. According to the writers, they were all original ideas. Thompson found, after a run-through, that they were usually somebody else's.

Writers were prima donnas, couldn't accept that their movie ideas weren't original and their scripts were crap. Thompson could tell after a few pages. If you couldn't grab a cinema audience's attention within a few minutes, you were doing something wrong.

Apart from the beacon of Lady Macbeth, the stage was becoming a cold, lonely place for the mediocre acting of the rest of the cast. At the end, there was muted applause. Each cast member stepped forward, the audience barely summoning a ripple. When Lady Macbeth stepped forward, she was greeted by cheers and loud applause. Thompson smiled as he looked at his wife.

"You've got that look on your face," Jodie said.

"I want to go backstage and see her," Thompson said. "I might offer her a screen test for one of my movies."

Jodie nodded. She had seen it all before. Her husband was a man who went with his gut instincts. His success spoke for itself. Jodie decided they could be headed for a long evening.

"What about dinner?" she asked.

"It won't take long," Thompson said.

Jodie smiled—the eternal lie. Whenever her husband said he'd be a few minutes, he usually took hours. She wanted to eat. "Ask her if she wants to come out to dinner with us."

Thompson kissed his wife on the cheek. She always understood—understood that his wasn't a nine-to-five job. He weaved his way through backstage people, Jodie close behind.

When he realized it was Clay Thompson, the famous director, Jacobs became nauseatingly accommodating. "I think Debbie's nearly changed." He knocked on the cloakroom door. "Debbie! There's a guy here to see you."

Through the frosted glass, Clay saw movement. After a few moments, the door opened, and Debbie Duncan stood there wrapped in a pink dressing-gown. When she saw it was Clay Thompson, she was momentarily awestruck.

"Hello, Debbie, I'm Clay—"

"I know who you are, Mr. Thompson."

Thompson smiled. If she knew who he was, then it meant that he could cut out a lot of waffle. "I want to talk to you about your career, Debbie. We're going out to a restaurant. If you've got no other plans this evening, would you like to join us?"

Debbie had plans. She was meant to be going to dinner with Gerry, a member of the cast. She was getting tired of Gerry's puppy love and their tongue-tied conversations over the main course. "I'm free, Mr. Thompson," she said.

"We'll wait in my car out the front. It's a green BMW."

Debbie nodded. Thompson and Jodie left.

Jacobs hovered by the door after Thompson and Jodie departed. "You know what this means?"

"No, what does it mean?"

"He only talks to actresses he's interested in. Don't mess this up, darling, this might be your one and only chance to break into the business."

Debbie laughed. "Do you really think I'm going to mess up something I've been waiting for all my life?"

Jacobs knew she wouldn't. Debbie was a go-getter, an actress who always gave a hundred percent in all her endeavors. In the plays Jacobs had directed her in, Debbie had always been the standout performer. He admired her confidence, but confidence could also be a weakness, make you unable to admit to any flaws. The arrogance that could make an actress a star could also lead to their undoing, he decided.

"Make sure they take you somewhere nice. Stars have got to get used to the best," he joked.

Debbie smiled.

Jacobs believed in her. He was convinced Thompson would offer her a screen test. If Jacobs could spot that Debbie was star quality, then he was convinced a star-maker like Thompson would certainly be able to.

At a stylish French restaurant, the Thompson party was shown to a quiet corner table.

"I hope you're not offended by my being forward like this, Miss Duncan," Thompson said after they'd ordered.

"Please call me Debbie. Miss is a title that should only be used by old spinsters," Debbie said.

Jodie laughed, quickly deciding she liked Debbie's straightforward nature. Usually, the young starlets that Thompson tried to get in his movies were sycophantic vamps. Debbie was different. She was refreshing and direct.

"Well, Debbie," Thompson said, as a waiter in a starched uniform poured the wine. "If you know anything about me, you'll know I'm a man of action, not words."

The waiter finished pouring, and Jodie admired his tight bum as he left.

"I want you to screen test for a part in my new movie," Thompson said.

Debbie was dumbstruck. She was starting to think

this was a dream—any minute now, she'd wake up. "This is all very sudden, Mr. Thompson."

"That's what the movie business is like, Debbie. If I like somebody, think they've got the ability, I give them a screen test and see where it takes us." Thompson studied her profile. She had marvelous high cheekbones and a porcelain-white complexion that a lot of Hollywood leading ladies would die for. She had the type of face that, as a director, you could mold into whatever you wanted.

"Thank you for giving me the opportunity, Mr. Thompson," she said.

"Just remember that I'm no knight in shining armor, Debbie. I'm just someone who's better at recognizing talent than most."

"Even I can see you've got talent, love," Jodie said.

Debbie smiled warmly. She was trying not to say too much, in case she said something that broke the spell. When the meal arrived, she decided that she was going to enjoy it. Whatever happened, dinner with two Hollywood A-listers such as Clay and Jodie Thompson would be an experience.

When she got home, sleep would be impossible. She'd resist the temptation to call her widowed mother. She'd wait until after the screen test when, hopefully, she would have something concrete to tell her mom.

The acting world was full of disappointments. She'd had promises of bit parts in Blackpool summer shows by lesser directors before, all of which had come to nothing. This time, she'd say nothing until she'd secured a role. This time, she'd wait until her screen test was a success and her new life was waiting to begin.

CHAPTER 4

Dexter sat in the crowded Plaistow bar, not sure where he was going or what he was going to do. The showy waitress with the tits kept clearing tables near him, making sure he got a good look down her blouse at her cleavage. She was there for the taking. Dexter didn't want her. Straight and uncomplicated wasn't how he liked it. In his eyes, sex without the mind games wasn't an experience worth having. He paid his bill, didn't leave her a tip. The waitress smiled as he passed her at the door, Dexter ignored her. He had a wonderful knack for being able to turn cold with people in an instant.

He moved along the street. The chill east wind ripped through him, reminding him of those freezing winter Somerset nights as a child. His father was a teacher. The only thing Dexter learned from him was that he was a pathetic little man, so tired of his own inferiority that he beat his son regularly. His father's love was saved for Dexter's younger sister, Becky.

Becky the perfect, Becky the wonderful, Becky who always got new clothes bought for her while Dexter had to rely on hand-me-downs. He was always made to feel inferior. His mother was no better. Although she tolerated Dexter more than his father, she still didn't show him the love he craved. He smiled, thinking about it. Reminiscing could be beautiful, especially when it concerned his beloved Becky.

He jumped on the Piccadilly bus—he had a job interview in under an hour. He took a Polo mint from his pocket and sucked on it to take away the smell of alcohol on his breath.

The dirty steam-smeared window meant looking out was virtually impossible. He contented himself by closing his eyes and thinking about Becky. He pictured her summer profile, her strawberry blonde hair fluttering gently in the breeze. Becky was stunning, a real beauty. It was a shame that it had to end the way it did. For Dexter, there could be no other way.

He'd worked on his sister over a matter of years. Little things—her favorite ornaments moved around her bedroom to confuse her, the odd item stolen or hidden. Dexter knew how to play his games, just like Becky knew how to turn his parents against him.

Becky broke a window, and Dexter's football would quickly appear—by way of Becky—at the crime scene. No protests of innocence on his part were ever accepted. They always fell on deaf ears.

His parents decided that he was lying and that their little angel Becky was incapable of such vandalism.

Dexter was thirteen years old when he killed his sister. Officially she'd fallen from the cliff edge into the gorge, a little push and then a fall. The vision was locked in his memory—Becky's ocean-blue eyes staring at him at the end as, too late, she realized what he was capable of. He'd run for help, like any caring brother would. He'd told the inquest that she'd slipped, and he'd tried to save her but failed. Dexter's mother never recovered from the shock of losing her favorite child. In Dexter's remaining childhood, she'd barely uttered a word to him. It was the perfect solution—Becky's murder had resulted in the killing of two birds with one stone.

He jumped off the bus at the Haymarket, feeling uncomfortable among the bustling shoppers and tourists. He walked slowly, eying each passing woman. Dexter went through his mental list of prerequisites—too short, too thin, a smoker, he particularly hated smokers.

Whenever he saw a smoker, he couldn't help seeing the vision of his father sitting next to a burning log fire smoking his foul pipe.

He reached the building just off Piccadilly just before two. On the second floor of a modern three-story, he found the Harvey Lomax Employment Agency. He'd spoken to Harvey Lomax over the phone. For the usual fee, Lomax had been keen to take Dexter on his books.

Dexter needed a job badly. If he was going to start a new life, then he needed the empowerment to control his life that a job would give him. His money was running out, the bedsit he was staying at was clean but expensive. He liked things clean and antiseptic. None of his wives had understood, when he'd murdered them, that they'd led him to a life of mess and confusion.

Sympathy was impossible for such skanky bitches. If only one of them could've been bothered to understand his nuances. Dexter had hated, with a vengeance, the dark world of filth that his murder of Carol had forced him to step into. On the agency's frosted glass door, he rapped gently. In the glass, he could see a woman's blurred image approaching. A dumpy middle-aged brunette opened the door.

"My name's Peter Rivers, I've got an appointment with Mr. Lomax at two," Dexter announced.

"Mr. Lomax is expecting you," dumpy said. She showed Dexter through reception to another office at the rear. The offices were furnished with bland Scandinavian furniture.

He liked the decor, it was neat and efficient, qualities to be respected.

Harvey Lomax was a slick-haired man in a Pierre Cardin suit. They shook hands, Lomax's grip was weak. Dexter stared into his green, bloodshot eyes, he could see warmth and understanding. Lomax didn't avert Dexter's gaze, he wasn't as easily intimidated by his piercing hazel-eyed stare as others usually were.

"Glad to meet you," Dexter said. He was offered a seat opposite Lomax. He sat down while dumpy left to make coffee.

From where he was seated, he discovered that he was looking slightly up at Lomax—Lomax was obviously a believer in office psychology, the notion that his raised chair would mean that he always retained dominance.

"So, you want to join the agency, Mr. Rivers. I've explained about the five-hundred-pound sign on fee. There's also another two-hundred-pound fee if any job we send you to proves to be successful."

"The money doesn't bother me, Mr. Lomax, your agency's ability to find me a job is all that matters."

"We have a very high success rate. If you ask any of our clients—"

"I'm not asking your clients, Mr. Lomax, I'm asking you."

Lomax rested his chubby hands on his belly. He believed in honesty. "Looking at your qualifications, finding a job for you will be quite simple. At the moment, I have a few jobs on my books suitable for a man like you." He took a file out of a filing cabinet behind him and studied it.

"I don't just want any job, I want a job with prospects," Dexter said.

"Don't we all, Mr. Rivers?" Lomax smiled reassuringly. "In all the years I've run this agency I've never had a dissatisfied client."

From the folder, Lomax took out a computer printout and handed it to him. Dexter looked at the jobs on the printout. There were five jobs on the sheet, and all of them paid between thirty and forty grand. He noted there were no company details on the sheet. Being a shrewd man, Lomax was only going to show the company names when Dexter had paid the agency.

"Not bad," Dexter said.

Lomax didn't comment. He knew the jobs he listed for his clients compared favorably with other agencies. "With your qualifications, if you go to any other employment agency in London, you won't find anything better than this."

"Maybe not, but at other agencies, I wouldn't be paying such a high sign-on fee."

"You have to pay for quality, Mr. Rivers. If you don't like the jobs—"

"I never said I didn't like them." Dexter took his wallet out and handed Lomax the sign-on fee.

Lomax put the money in his desk drawer. "Do any of the jobs on the sheet interest you?"

There was one—a trainee cameraman for a film company. The money was the lowest paid of the jobs on offer, but it had prospects. Dexter had once been to art school, had diplomas for photography and some A levels. He didn't look his age. Through regular exercise and vitamins, his thirty-seven-year-old face looked more like twenty-seven.

He had to retain his youth, as women didn't want beer-bellied slobs. All that bothered him was women—

his quest for women was endless. Life-consuming.

"I'd like to apply for the trainee cameraman job," Dexter said.

Lomax smiled. "After reading your resume, I thought you'd go for that one."

Dexter was annoyed. He was becoming too predictable. Things would have to change. He didn't like grease balls like Lomax being able to predict his next move. He nodded to Lomax. It was best not to comment while he could feel the rage inside him.

Dexter took the name and address of the film company, and Lomax arranged an interview. Dexter was happy. After Baguley, he could feel his life was turning around. A job with prospects would complete that transition and give him scope for the future. He smiled as he descended the steps of the nearby tube station. He always felt exhilarated like this at the start of a new beginning. The moment was almost upon him, doors were opening, new women would soon be on his radar. The camera never lied, so they said. But Dexter knew *his* camera would, or maybe it would just lie about the man behind it.

CHAPTER 5

The barroom was smoky and uncomfortable. Debbie wrapped in a mink stole sat on the edge of a gleaming wood piano. A brawl broke out around her. She picked up a whiskey bottle off a nearby table and cracked it over the head of an unshaven lumberjack who was unlucky enough to fall within the range of her swinging arm. The lumberjack toppled forward and crashed onto a table that immediately folded beneath him. As he hit the dusty floor, he was trodden on by two blue coat soldiers involved in a brutal fist fight. The pianist had long since stopped playing and was nervously sheltering behind the bar with Louis, the ramshackle owner of the Lazy Goose. Escape was looking grim. Debbie picked up another bottle, prepared to slug another guy—

"Cut!" Thompson shouted from his position just off set, seated in his black director's chair. When the chaos subsided and the debris settled, he called a half-hour break.

Debbie jumped down off the piano. She was fitter than she'd ever been in her life.

The moment she was signed up by Thompson on a

five-film deal was the moment she started working out at the gym. She'd changed her diet, spent most of her spare time studying her lines. Debbie was the model starlet. She wasn't going to let her big chance escape. If the western, *El Dorado Pass*, was going to be a success, then Debbie was going to make sure that her brief role in it was noticed.

She was actually in the film for a half hour of the film's two-hour running time.

It was longer than she'd expected. When Thompson told her he had a part for her in his next movie, she'd assumed it would be a brief walk-on. She couldn't have been more wrong.

Today's filming was the ninth scene she'd been involved in. She ambled toward a refreshment table laden with every snack or drink you could desire. Thompson was a great believer that a happy crew was an efficient crew, and everybody working on the film, from humble messenger to leading actor, was welcome to tuck in.

Cowboy Jake, alias Quincy Hooper, the leading man in the film, was an egomaniac. Hooper had decided long ago in his acting career that everybody in the industry should adore him, particularly the female members of the cast. With Debbie, his vanity had not impressed, his come-ons were ignored—a fact that annoyed him. It was an irritation he couldn't mask in his aggressive attitude toward her every time they spoke.

"Hello, doll," Hooper said as he sauntered up to the drinks table picking up a diet Coke.

"I stopped playing with dolls when I was seven, Mr. Hooper," Debbie said.

Hooper ignored her wisecrack and walked over to Thompson standing nearby.

Hooper had thought about getting the hard-faced bitch dropped from the film, but had decided against it. It would be a sulky admission that Debbie was immune to his charms. Debbie swallowed a mouthful of juice and then walked off, followed by Hooper's stare.

"I wouldn't bother," Thompson told Hooper.

"What's her problem?" Hooper asked.

Thompson laughed. "Nothing, apart from not worshipping the ground you walk on."

Hooper ignored Thompson's quip and shuffled over to an impressionable young starlet, the twinkle in her eye making it obvious that *she* was susceptible to Hooper's charms.

Thompson knew the signs. His situation had been similar to Hooper's—that was before he met Jodie. Jodie changed everything. Love changed everything. When Thompson reached Debbie, a makeup artist was touching up her face with a brush.

In the mirror's reflection, Debbie suddenly saw Thompson's bulk blot out the light. "How am I doing?" she asked.

"Not bad. Getting used to the camera takes time. Your timing is out in a couple of scenes. We might have to shoot them again," Thompson stated.

He was always honest in his appraisals. The big stars didn't like it. The up-and-coming appreciated it, until they made it, and then they suddenly found his honesty irritating.

Debbie had thought her scenes were good. Thompson was the expert. She'd bow to his experience. "Was I bad?"

"Of course not, just inexperienced."

Thompson moved off to talk to a production manager. Debbie was one of his favorites. On set, he tried not to show it. Thompson believed in equality among all the people who worked for him. If Thompson had been around in Governor McCarthy's Communist witch-hunt-time, he was sure he'd have been blacklisted as a Communist. Back in his chair, he spoke to Jodie for a few moments on his mobile phone then called the break over.

They'd restart the filming from the moment the scrap between the soldiers began. Thompson knew what the public wanted—action was their god. A story-line these days was a bonus. Hooper was one of Hollywood's top action stars. A Quincy Hooper movie was big box office, up there with Stallone and Statham. Although Hooper was successful, he had a problem. His ego had told him to diversify.

Hooper had decided he wanted to be taken seriously as an actor. His next film was going to be a Shakespearian production, Hamlet. There was a big budget being set aside for it by the studios. There was also talk of leading British thespians taking support roles.

Thompson wasn't impressed. Thompson had worked with Hooper on many films, enough films to conclude that Hooper didn't have the acting range to do Shakespeare.

That was Hooper's big problem—it was what separated him from actresses like Debbie Duncan. Debbie had started acting in Shakespearean roles, playing in Dickens dramas and small-time repertory. By following this route, Debbie had learned her craft. American actors didn't have the same pungent flare for the bard as the British. Most had a stab at it, Heston came close, Brando was impressive, all were good, but none of them a patch on Olivier.

When everyone was settled, the camera started to roll. In front of the camera Thompson noted that, for a beginner in movies, Debbie was impressive. She showed a complete lack of nerves, was open to criticism, everything that Quincy Hooper was not.

Thompson sighed as Hooper butchered yet another

line, made a note not to work with him in future movies. Debbie was a different story. Thompson would try to sign her on a longer contract after this movie was over. After her performance in *El Dorado Pass*, Thompson was convinced that her star quality on film would mean that all the agent vultures would start to circulate.

Hooper strayed in front of the piano in a continuation of the fight scene—a big mistake. Debbie clubbed him with the fake bottle, hitting him much harder than necessary.

Even though the bottle was fake, the force of the blow caused Hooper's legs to fold. Thompson smiled, Hooper would go loopy when he came round, would want Debbie thrown off the movie. Thompson would refuse. He could see that Debbie was shortly going to be a star in her own right, and also, he could never get rid of someone who made him laugh so much.

CHAPTER 6

The lights flashed in Dexter's eyes, he was blinded for a few moments. He blinked, adjusted the shot, slowly moved in closer. His timing was perfect, just as he reached the center of the stage, Zane Socrates pranced on stage wearing one of the dazzling silver suits he was famous for. Socrates nodded to his six-string orchestra and smiled at the audience, revealing his wonderful teeth that were a glowing tribute to the power of money and modern dentistry. The crowd roared, the big Wembley event of the rock calendar was about to begin, Socrates, the legend, started to sing.

Dexter liked Socrates. There was no pretense about the man. Socrates treated women like pigs, always cheating on his vast array of partners. A man should never be ashamed to assert himself, Dexter had long ago decided. Dexter was dating again. He'd met Tracy Sparshot in a local library. She wasn't much to look at. She was plain looking, wore glasses. Whenever you tried to talk to her, she always seemed to have her head stuck in a book and never listened to what you told her.

For all these character faults, Tracy had one redeeming feature—the one feature that Dexter prized above all in his women, she was easy to manipulate. With Dexter, she'd met a man who knew how to press her buttons. At the moment, his current project was to work on curtailing her freedom. It wasn't an easy process. First, you had to alienate her from her friends. Such alienation was easier with people like Tracy who had few friends.

Dexter had noted over the years that if there were too many people around who cared, then there was a danger that someone might notice his abnormal behavior.

He hoped he was almost at the stage where she worshipped him. Frumpy girls were easier to maneuver. They couldn't afford to be choosy, particularly when they were over thirty like Tracy. Dexter moved his camera in closer as Socrates stepped on the walkway, thrusting his gleaming guitar like a weapon at the audience. He managed to capture every moment perfectly, and Dexter was fast getting a reputation for perfection in his camera work.

The gig droned on for a couple of hours. Socrates appeared back on stage for several ego feeding encores. Socrates wasn't embarrassed at the adulation and thought the public should get what they wanted. As the stage cleared and the satisfied crowd moved away, Dexter was given the signal by the director to stop filming. As Dexter was packing his stuff away, Eddie, the other more experienced cameraman, arrived by his side.

"Fancy going for a beer, Rivers?" Eddie asked.

At this point Dexter usually excused himself, enhancing his reputation as a loner.

Eddie looked shocked when Dexter said, "why not?"

Dexter had promised Tracy he'd be home straight after the show. This was a good moment to teach the woman the lesson that all his prospective partners needed to learn, and that was that there was only going to be one boss in Dexter's household. The quicker she understood how things were going to be, the better life would be for everybody. He was already getting tired of her dull company, and, as soon as possible, would push her toward their relationship's logical conclusion.

Dexter needed a challenge. Tracy was too easy to mold for a man of his abilities. Within half an hour of packing everything away, Dexter and Eddie were sitting in a pub in Sudbury supping ale.

"What do you think of Socrates?" Eddie asked.

"A poser, but his heart's in the right place," Dexter decided.

Eddie smiled. "The guy definitely loves himself."

Dexter didn't blame him. When you were in a position of total power over women like Socrates, who wouldn't? He was finding Eddie hard to talk to. Since they'd been assigned the job of filming the Socrates tour by MTV they'd barely spoken to each other.

Most of their working days they spent alone filming the concert from opposite corners of the arena. Judging by how boring Eddie was Dexter looked at that separation as a relief.

"If you were in Socrates' position wouldn't you have an ego, Eddie?"

Eddie knew he would. It was jealousy that made the average Joe talk down about rock stars. Dexter looked at him, Eddie was an average bloke who was never going to amount to anything. Dexter was different, he had every intention of climbing the promotional ladder and leave the boring Eddies of this world behind him in his quest for the top. As Eddie mumbled on about work-related subjects, Dexter was getting bored.

He'd decided that Eddie was a working class bore. Just as he was going to make his excuses and go, Eddie said, "Have you thought about moving on from MTV, maybe working in the movies?"

"Who hasn't? It's just getting a break," Dexter said.

"That's just it. I've got the break. Regal Pictures was impressed with the portfolio I sent them. A couple of people I know who work there have put in a good word for me—I've been offered a job there."

"That's wonderful news," Dexter said. Inside he was fuming. How dare Regal Pictures offer a talentless prick like Eddie a job when someone as multitalented as Dexter was out there?

"There's more. They asked me if I knew any other cameramen at MTV who were interested in making a career switch. I mentioned your name to them, told them I'd talk to you."

Dexter wanted to scream yes. Trying to remain cool, he contented himself with, "What sort of money are they offering?"

"More than we're getting at MTV."

"And how long's the job for?" Dexter asked.

"The Production Manager, Jimmy Murray, said there was at least a year's film location work."

Dexter didn't need to think about it. He didn't want to spend the rest of his working life filming rock stars. "When would they want us to start?"

"I'm not sure," Eddie said. He was getting irritated by Rivers's questions. To get a big movie company interested in you as a cameraman was an achievement in itself, something Rivers didn't seem to understand.

"Before I give up my MTV job, I have to have something concrete," Dexter said.

Eddie told Dexter everything he knew. "I'll be looking at the contract next week. Before I mention you, I need to know if you're interested."

"I'm interested," Dexter said. After Eddie had done all the donkey work, it would be impolite not to be.

They drank another pint and then Eddie had to go.

Dexter stayed and drank some more. The landlord had decided on an after-hours lock-in, something that suited the celebrating Dexter just fine.

Tracy was supposed to be cooking a meal for him when he got home, and he was already two hours late. He got on the last train after midnight, stared at his own reflection in the dirt-smeared window as he approached his station.

Tracy was going to be fuming when he got home. Dexter would make no apologies. He was tired of her presence in his life, decided she could only make him happy after he killed her.

CHAPTER 7

A Sparkling Performance!" *Film Monthly* said. "A girl with a big future!" a respected TV critic announced. Debbie took it all in her stride. Critics didn't concern her. She had always had supreme confidence in her acting ability. She was being offered a lead role in Thompson's next movie. Regal Pictures was impressed with the reviews, so much so that they'd offered her an improved contract. Whatever role they threw at her, she'd take it. Only the big stars could afford to be selective. Once you had figures with several zeros in your bank account, that was the moment you could worry about artistic credibility in any of the roles that they offered you, she'd long ago decided.

She sat in a chair and studied the script that Thompson had asked her to look at. It was called *The Valley of Dreams*. The story was set among Welsh coalminers just after World War II. It concerned the fight by a man to readjust to civvy street after two years as a prisoner in a Japanese Prisoner of War Camp. Thompson wanted Debbie to play the returning prisoner's wife. It was a part heavily laden with scene-stealing opportunities, a fact that some of the other more established members of the cast were sure to notice. She didn't care about their jealousy. Thompson had promised her a leading role in his next film. The fact she was reading a script for that film showed he'd delivered.

She read her lines with relish. The more she read, the more certain she was that the script was a winner. Thompson had arranged to meet her for lunch to discuss the project. She was so engrossed in the script she read it right up to a few moments before she left.

A smiling Thompson greeted Debbie warmly at an overpriced restaurant just off the Strand.

When they were seated, he said, "Don't get carried away by the positive reviews, critics are fickle."

"I won't," she said.

"That's my girl. There are a lot of pitfalls, some of the youngsters make a good film then think they're the business."

Debbie wasn't arrogant. Whatever the critics said about her films, she'd stay adjusted. In all the movie magazines she'd trawled through over the years, she'd noted that the stars that lasted were the ones who kept their feet on the ground.

"Don't worry about me, Clay, I'm Miss Boring, you won't find any stories in the gossip columns about me."

Thompson hadn't met any actress as well-adjusted as Debbie in a long time.

It was a refreshing change to have an actress you could talk to, rather than one who'd throw a tantrum at the slightest criticism.

"The boring survive the longest," Thompson suggested. "Look at me, I'm boring, and I'm still at the top."

Debbie tried not to laugh, could remember all the tabloid scandal stories about Thompson. There was a time before he married Jodie when he seemed to be swapping partners every week. If he was expecting Debbie to comment that he wasn't boring, in order to massage his ego, then he'd have to wait a long time, she decided.

She got straight down to business. "I really like the script, Clay. When are we going to start shooting?"

Thompson finished a mouthful of veal. "I'll be ready to start in three months. I've just got to finish off another project first." His current film was going to run over budget. The bigwigs at Regal wouldn't hassle him, had too much respect for him as a profit-making director to argue.

"So, I should carry on learning the role then?"

"Always learn the role, darling," Thompson said. "If you've learned the role, and the studio doesn't want you, then, under your contract, Regal will always pay you something for your trouble."

"I have been reading it," Debbie said, hurt by the fact that Thompson might think otherwise.

Thompson sensed her irritation. "I'm not talking about you, Debbie darling. I know how dedicated you are to the cause."

Thompson filled their glasses with Chablis. Debbie sipped the wine. She was driving so this would be her one and only drink. She didn't know what to make of Thompson—Clay and Jodie seemed happily married, yet, sometimes Debbie noticed Thompson's eyes wander lustfully over the young girls on the set. The meal came to a close with an outrageous calorie-laden chocolate dessert.

When it was over, Debbie said, "Thanks for a lovely meal, Clay."

Thompson smiled, a warm smile, an unnerving smile. She could see how easy it must've been for Thompson to charm a young starlet's panties down.

Outside the restaurant, Thompson walked her to her

car. As she got into her car, he caught a flash of her stunning legs. "I really like you, Debbie—"

"Don't spoil it, Clay," she replied, "I like Jodie, and you two are great together."

Thompson kissed Debbie lightly on the cheek. "I'll call you in a couple of weeks."

She nodded and sped away, tooting her horn. She didn't get involved with married men. She liked Thompson. He was a very attractive man, but he was married to Jodie, and that marriage commitment made him untouchable as far as Debbie was concerned.

She wasn't a marriage breaker and wanted Thompson to understand that fact from the very beginning of their friendship.

Thompson stood at the curb, watching Debbie's Volkswagen slip through the traffic. He was always attracted to ballsy women, a characteristic Debbie Duncan had in abundance. Life could be a bummer, Thompson thought. After a string of box office successes, his movie career was at an incredible peak. He had a stunning wife, all the money and charisma a man could ask for, and then along came a Debbie Duncan to completely knock your equilibrium out of sync.

Thompson grabbed his mobile phone from his pocket and called his driver, Aston, to collect him. His burly chauffeur arrived ten minutes later. Thompson had let Aston visit nearby family while Thompson dined. He treated all his staff with respect, treated them as friends, which was why they worked hard and didn't take the piss in return. Respect was a two-way street.

On the drive home, Thompson wondered if Debbie just respected him, or whether there was more. One thing was certain. When they filmed *The Valley of Dreams*, Thompson intended to find out.

CHAPTER 8

After Dexter's drunken return the night of the Socrates concert, Tracy had stormed out early the next day, fuming at his insults and the fact that he'd told her that the dinner she'd made him was garbage. He'd thrown the dinner on the floor as the ultimate protest.

In her fit of pique in leaving, Tracy had left it where it landed. The result of her neglect was a stinking pile of bolognaise sitting in the middle of the carpet. If she thought that would upset Dexter, she was wrong. It didn't bother him that she'd gone. He had plenty of other things to be angry about. His departing girlfriend was pretty low on his angry list. What really bothered him were the breakages. In a fit of fury, Tracy had broken a couple of Dexter's favorite mugs and a signed picture of Socrates. He picked up the broken glass and the shattered frame that had held it.

There was a time and place to get even. Revenge—"payback time," as the colonials said—would temporarily have to wait. He would bide his time. For the moment, Tracy Sparshot would be forgotten, stored in his memory—something to be dealt with at a later date.

He started clearing up the mess. Dexter hated messes. His second wife had been untidy. Even in death, she didn't mend her ways. After he killed her, he'd had to clear a pile of dirty clothes off the bed so he could wrap her body in a sheet for burial. He'd buried her in a peaceful place. It was a beautiful, flower-strewn, tidy meadow. It was much tidier than anywhere she'd inhabited in life, as Dexter had made one final effort to make her change her ways.

As he cleared up the picture frame, a fragment of glass cut his finger. He rushed to the bathroom to wash his hand under the tap. Wrapping a plaster around the throbbing wound, he shouted in a fury. He could feel the start of one of his intense black moods. He sat down, in a bid to calm down and control himself. Now wasn't a time for a burst of uncontrolled rage. He couldn't afford to go wild like the last time. The last time had been the rage, shortly followed by the fire. In his new life as a cameraman for Regal Pictures, there was no place for rage.

Control was his new mantra, his byword. It was a word that his strict adherence to would stop him from committing any further craziness like the house fire.

He needed coffee, a caffeine lift. The monster hangover from his previous night's drinking now engulfed him. Alcohol was a weakness. Dexter didn't like feeling weak. If you showed any sign of weakness it gave a woman the edge, an edge they never failed to use against you. If Eddie got him the job with Regal, then a new Dexter would appear on the set.

It was time for him to become less of an introvert. If he was going to find the perfect subject to work on, then he had to make himself more accessible. Steady and reliable was the key.

Dexter knew he was good-looking. Women fancied

him. It was now time to channel the energy from that positive into finding a woman worthy of his skill. As he sat and contemplated what lay ahead his phone rang. He let it ring for a few moments. He had a sixth sense about such things and wasn't surprised when he answered and it was Tracy.

"You're a pig, Peter. It's over between us, and I'm sending my brother over to move my stuff out of the flat while you're at work. Don't come near me again!"

The phone was slammed down by the bitch before Dexter had time to say anything. He smiled to himself, pleased that he'd upset her. It was now that he had regrets, regrets that she hadn't stayed around long enough for him to work on her.

Those few seconds on the phone—that one violent outburst—and Tracy had shown more promise as a subject than at any other time in their brief relationship. It was too late for Tracy. Her time—regrettably, in light of her newfound spirit—was done.

The phone rang again, and he thought, *Then again, maybe it isn't.* This time he was ready for her and was surprised when it was Eddie.

"I need to see you today," Eddie said.

"I'm busy today—"

"Make time," Eddie said. "There's a film starting next week. Regal wants us to start work with them a week early."

"You said two weeks," Dexter said, irritated that he was losing control of the situation.

"That's how movie people work, Peter. They tell you one thing, and it ends up being another. It's the way they are. If you're going to work for them, you'd better get used to it."

Dexter would find this hard. He liked everything orderly. With MTV, his assignments were given to him weeks in advance. It made it easier to plan his schedule, made it possible to work to a game plan with women like Tracy.

"I'll meet you in an hour," Dexter said.

"You'll be meeting me and a production manager called Murray. We'll meet you at the Savoy at noon."

"I've got appointments. I don't think I can get there by noon—"

"Don't mess with me, Peter. Regal Pictures can pick and choose cameramen in the industry. If you can't make it, then I can't guarantee you the job."

Dexter was starting to think Eddie was a control freak. It was the first time Dexter had ever felt any animosity toward him. "I'll be there."

"Wear a suit. Murray likes smartness, professionalism."

"You've seen my work. I am professional."

"I'm not criticizing you, mate. I've worked with you at MTV. I know your work is good. The problem is that Murray doesn't." With that, Eddie hung up.

Dexter went to the wardrobe. He opened it and found a new horror. Screwed up on the wardrobe floor were his two best suits among a pile of other clothes. Tracy knew Dexter liked his clothes neatly hung up on the rail. She had left no stone unturned in her attempts to piss him off. He picked up the less crumpled gray suit. It was salvageable, but only just. He set up the ironing board, ironed the suit on a low setting. Tracy was going to pay for this. If he went after her, he'd have to be careful. He wanted to keep the identity of Peter Rivers. If he did so, there would be a record of his involvement with her in any ensuing police investigation after her murder.

After he finished ironing, he put the suit on. He grabbed a flowery gray-black tie from a drawer and studied himself in the mirror. It wasn't perfect but, because of time constraints and as the result of what the bitch had done, it was the best he could do. This wasn't how he liked things. Preparation for the meeting had been far from perfect. If he failed to get the job because of Tracy's sabotage, then he'd make her suffer when he killed her. In his mind, he was already considering the gruesome tortures he could subject her to. All of that would depend on the circumstances. Now that she'd left him, his ability to carry out his plans became more limited.

Outside in his Renault, he sat for a moment to compose himself. It was just after eleven, under an hour until his meeting. Central London would be murder to park in at this time of the day. Dexter was sure he was going to be late. He angrily thumped the dashboard with his fist.

Damn Tracy for her destruction, Eddie for changing appointments, and most of all Murray for being a pain in the arse.

Tracy had made a big mistake—she didn't know what she was dealing with. To be fair to her, neither did most of his victims—and, alas, by the time they did, for all of them, it was always too late.

CHAPTER 9

Jodie plunged into the icy water, swam underwater for a few moments before splashing to the surface at the end of the pool. She loved swimming. It kept her in better shape than any other exercise seemed to. The pool was specially designed in the shape of a movie camera. Its stunning black-and-white mosaic made it unusual, a stand out in the crowd.

Although Jodie and Clay didn't flaunt their money, they didn't hide it either.

She lay on her back, floating. It was early September and the crisp morning was starting to take on that end of summer feel. She heard clicking footsteps at the poolside and looked up to see her husband dressed in a suit, carrying a briefcase and ambling toward her. Clay was a scruffy man. Even wearing an Armani, somehow he managed to look like a hobo. She'd spent some of last evening getting his clothes ready, what should have been elegant somehow now looked cheap on Clay's massive frame. She'd stopped getting annoyed about it, as he was attractive in his own way, and his brilliant directing and artistic genius made you overlook his other flaws.

"I'm leaving for town. I don't know what time I'll be home," he said. "I'll ring you when I'm nearly finished."

Jodie nodded, didn't ask what he was working on. Clay was his own man, and she had learned during their marriage that movie people were a law unto themselves. "Don't work too hard," she said, knowing that he would.

He kissed her lightly on her dripping wet cheek then left. Jodie swam for a few more lengths then went for a sauna. On the way, she told her maid, Silky, that she wanted a masseur. Silky went to ring Claudia, the masseur who was a regular visitor to the Thompson household. As Jodie sat on the pine ledge in the sauna steam, she thought about how to arrange her day. She owned a clothes shop in Guildford, which ran at a good profit as she had an eye for up-and-coming fashion.

Jodie was still paying off the loan she'd taken from her husband when she started up the business. Generous Clay had offered to give her the shop as a gift, but she had refused. Her strict one-parent upbringing meant that she believed in paying her way and wouldn't take—no matter how well-intentioned—any handouts. She had a simple philosophy in life. A person only respected something if they'd worked for it. Her mother was a single parent, and Jodie had never known her father. He had abandoned them when she was a baby. Jodie didn't want to know the bastard. Any man who could leave a mother and baby like that was not worth knowing, she'd decided a long time ago.

The timer pinged, telling her that her sauna time was up, and it was time to stop mulling over the past.

She wrapped herself in a fluffy towel and headed for the massage couch where gorgeous Claudia and her perfumed oils awaited.

"Good morning, Mrs. Thompson," Claudia said, in her sexy Swedish accent.

"Good morning, Claudia, I haven't got long, could you make it quick please."

Jodie wanted to get into Guildford early. She had a local clothes designer coming in to see her at eleven. The designer was meant to be an up-and-coming talent. She would give him a chance, but if she didn't like what she saw, she wouldn't be shy about telling him.

Claudia's supple hands got to work, kneading Jodie's back into shape. It was worth every penny of the hundred pounds an hour Claudia charged. She was definitely the best—Scandinavians seemed to have a knack for massage the British masseurs that, Jodie had at various times experimented with, didn't. In thirty minutes, it was over.

Jodie quickly changed.

"It wasn't a full hour, Mrs. Thompson, I'll only charge you fifty," Claudia said.

"I asked for an hour, I'll pay for an hour," Jodie thrust two fifty-pound notes into her hand. "It's not your fault I have to leave early."

Claudia thanked her and left. Jodie liked Claudia's honesty. Her decent character shone through. She was that rare commodity in Jodie's life—a woman that she could trust. Silky had introduced them. Silky was a good judge of people, and Jodie classed her more as a friend than a maid. Jodie checked with the shop that Max Spinner, the designer, hadn't canceled his appointment, then she sped off in her black BMW. Jodie didn't believe in appointment books, tried to keep everything in her head in the mistaken belief that she had a good memory.

When she arrived, the shop was busy, and, rather than disturb her stretched workforce, she went straight to her office to do some work on the computer until Spinner arrived. Jodie had some big ideas. She wanted to do something different, create a breath of fresh air in the fashion industry. The mistake fashion traders made was to idle along, not looking to the future. She wanted to market her own clothing line. Before she could make such a dream a reality, she needed some good designs from an innovative designer.

She'd seen a couple of designers in recent weeks, neither of whom impressed her. She was hoping that maybe Spinner might be different. One of the shop girls said he was brilliant. Jodie listened to her workforce. They dealt with fashion for a living, saw what sold and what didn't.

When Max Spinner walked into her office, she was surprised to find that he was a short fuzzy-haired guy wearing glasses. With the name, Max, Jodie had been expecting at least a German count.

"Thank you for seeing me, Mrs. Thompson," Spinner said nervously, "I realize how busy you are."

Spinner had a deep voice, deeper than she expected. "If I wasn't interested in your designs, I wouldn't have invited you here," she told him.

Spinner stared into the eyes of his prospective partner. What he saw was an intelligent woman who didn't suffer fools lightly. He reviewed his strategy and decided that straight talking was his best approach. He accepted the offer of coffee, while Jodie browsed through some samples from his collection and a sketchbook of drawings.

She could see there was a classy feel to his work, and she liked it. He showed her a selection of summer dresses off the rail.

"I can arrange a modeling session if you want to see the rest of the collection, Mrs. Thompson."

Spinner was gaining in confidence. The positive way that Jodie was looking through his work was increasing his expectations.

Jodie called in Janice, her ex-model shop manager.

"Janice is an ex-model. She can model some of your dresses for me."

Spinner let Jodie take charge. He wasn't a fool, knew of Jodie Thompson's connections in the movie and fashion industries. Spinner would give this woman anything she wanted. Janice reluctantly modeled the dresses, even though she'd promised her live-in lover, Gemma, that she was finished with the sexist fashion industry. Her reluctance wavered slightly when Jodie offered her extra wages for her improvised fashion show. Jodie also promised that Gemma wouldn't find out about it as the modeling would only be for Spinner and her in Jodie's office.

As Janice modeled the dresses, Jodie could see that she still had the knack.

Models never lost it, she decided. With Janice wearing them, Spinner's creations looked fantastic. Spinner was also impressed, knew that catwalk models could make a potato sack look sexy. It was why clothing companies employed them. The plain fact of life was that catwalk models sold dresses. He studied the effortless way Janice walked in his clothing. She had style and charisma. When she appeared in an exclusive tartan mini and Spinner noted Jodie's broad smile, it was then that he knew that he'd hooked her.

After five dresses and a couple of miniskirts, Jodie had seen enough.

"Thanks, Janice. You can get changed and go to lunch."

Janice left to get changed in a fitting room. An uncomfortable silence filled the room.

"Did you like them?" Spinner asked.

"I'm not sure," Jodie said. "There are things I like about your work, Max, and things I don't."

Spinner decided Jodie Thompson should go into politics. During the improvised fashion show, Spinner had seen that look of recognition in her eyes. It was recognition of talent, a look that showed she wanted his creations, a look that told him that, at last, he was staring the prospect of success squarely in the eye.

"Are you interested in stocking anything?" he pressed.

Jodie wanted to sign Spinner on a contract to market his clothing line under her label. It was going to be difficult. She decided her thrilled expression when she'd seen his dresses had given too much away. If she raved too much about his work and praised him too highly now, then there was a danger that his ego would take hold, and he'd be stubborn with the contract.

"Are you free for lunch?" Jodie asked. Spinner was. "I'd like to discuss a proposition with you."

Spinner was free to discuss anything with this woman. This was his big chance, and nothing was going to stop him from taking it.

At Jodie's favorite Indian restaurant, they ate a quiet meal accompanied by Kingfisher beer. Jodie decided she had to get this right. When she left the restaurant, she wanted him with her. Spinner was impatient, desperate. Now, Jodie would feed on that desperation. It wasn't negotiating with Spinner that worried her. He was a pussycat compared to her husband. Clay was going to be the big problem. She had a brilliant idea on how to market the new label. The problem was that she was relying on the co-operation of her husband to make the marketing program a success.

There were a couple of scenes in Clay's new movie, *The Valley of Dreams*, where the elderly couple in the present day looked back at their past. It was these scenes where Jodie wanted some of the cast to wear Spinner's designs. The big question was—would her husband go for it? Clay wasn't known for his ability to compromise, especially when the compromise involved his movies.

But Jodie was not going to miss this opportunity. This was her chance to break into the world of fashion, a chance she had no intention of letting slip by. Spinner was hungry for success, knew what doors working with Jodie could open. She crossed her shapely legs, giving Spinner a tantalizing glimpse of her stocking top. All men when making a deal could be distracted, some easier than most.

As they finished their dessert and the check was brought, Spinner was the only person around the table that didn't realize he was moments away from agreeing to a long-term deal with Jodie. She would soon make him realize, she could be very persuasive when needed. Later that evening was when the real work would begin when she had the problem of persuading Clay—persuading her husband was the hardest task of all.

CHAPTER 10

"Not dingy enough," Thompson suggested, slumping his bulk down in the uncomfortable white plastic chair located beneath a Heineken umbrella in the pub's beer garden. He picked up a pint of cider off a well-worn table and drank some of it.

"It's the best one we've viewed today," the film location manager, Clarkson, said.

Clarkson took his large-rimmed glasses off and rubbed his tired eyes. Finding a pub for the film in the area that could pass as a post-war pub was proving difficult. He was the best location manager in the business. Thompson used him for all his films. He liked the village, north of Neath but just wasn't sure whether he liked it enough. Thompson was a hard to please perfectionist who wouldn't say yes to anything until he was certain it was exactly what he wanted.

"We'll look at a couple more pubs in the area," he said, "I'll make a decision tonight, James." He could see the look of exasperation on Clarkson's lined face.

"I promise."

"It's your film," Clarkson said matter-of-factly.

Thompson shook his head. "You know that isn't how we work at Regal, James.

When I'm making a film, if you're not happy, I'm not happy."

Clarkson liked Thompson. He was the best director he'd worked with. He was brilliant at actually directing a movie, a feat equally matched by his ability to carefully handle the people around him. Clarkson drank up his beer, went inside the pub to get them both another drink. Thompson used the opportunity to ring his wife. Jodie was pleased to hear from him. He told her about the locations they'd been looking at, and she listened intently, knowing that her husband liked his ego massaged now and again. Thompson was the important director on location, her husband enjoyed this image, though he'd deny it if Jodie ever confronted him about it.

Clarkson returned with their drinks. Thompson decided he'd better go, "I'll talk to you tomorrow," he told her.

"Before you go, darling, there's something I want to ask you about," Jodie said. "It's to do with the clothes shop, I want to branch out. When you get home, I'll cook you a meal, and we'll talk about it."

Thompson ended the call smiling. When Jodie wanted something, she always asked for it wearing a sexy gown and during a candlelit supper.

"Something up?" Clarkson asked.

"Nothing important," Thompson said. Not important, but knowing Jodie, it was probably going to cost him a fortune.

Clarkson left it alone. If it wasn't to do with the film, he wasn't interested. "How much over budget do you think you'll go on the film, Clay?"

"Way over. This film is going to need a lot of location work."

Clarkson had read the script and agreed. Although they were constantly scanning the budget looking for ways to economize, sometimes it wasn't possible.

Setting up the location and making sure that Clarkson paid off the right people to make that happen, wasn't one of them. Clarkson laid the map on the table and studied it. On the map, marked in red pen, were all the locations that he and his team had decided were possibilities for the film. The last one they were going to look at in the afternoon was a village next to an abandoned coal mine. It was just north of Ebbw Vale, a village called Rockall. Rockall was situated in a quiet valley and had an old world feel about it. Up until the sixties, there'd been a thriving colliery at Rockall. It was then that the coal seam had run out and since 1968 the once proud pit machinery had sat idle.

They arrived at Rockall late afternoon just as the sun was setting, bathing the valley in a dazzling orange-purple glow. Thompson smiled at Clarkson as they stepped out of their chauffeur driven Mercedes next to a pub that on the outside looked perfect.

Inside was even better, the décor and fittings reeked of the post-war era. Thompson was a man used to making quick decisions, and here he quickly made the decision— the post-war scenes of his new movie, *The Valley of Dreams*, were all going to be filmed here in Wales at Rockall.

CHAPTER 11

Somehow Jodie looked more sexually stunning than usual. She must've spent hours on her makeup, Thompson concluded and was probably wearing a titillating suspender set under her stunning McCartney gown. When she asked him if he'd use Spinner's designs in his new film, Thompson could see why she'd made such an effort.

"No, darling. You know I don't do that sort of thing. It's the reason why I stayed with Regal and refused the bigger Hollywood offers. Regal allow me to keep my integrity and don't push things on me. I couldn't carry on making films and retain my integrity if I showed flagrant nepotism."

"I'm not asking you to lose your integrity," Jodie said.

Thompson sighed. "What else would you call it when your wife asks you to put clothes from her new clothing line in your movie?"

This was going badly, Jodie thought. It was time to pacify. "I wouldn't be asking if I didn't think Spinner had talent. I know how much you value your reputation. If I didn't think his designs would enhance your movie, I wouldn't ask."

Thompson downed a glass of wine. He knew he was drinking too quickly. He always drank too quickly when he felt pressured. He had a bad ulcer, a doctor had warned him. Thompson had ignored the doctor—life was for fun and merriment, but only if you didn't tell your voluptuous wife no. He decided to compromise and at least give Jodie the courtesy of viewing the designs before he refused them. He told her that he wasn't promising anything, but he'd view the designs in the morning.

Jodie left it at that. Clay was not a man to be pushed into a decision. If you pushed him too hard, tried to assert your position, then invariably his decision would go against you. She'd managed to get Spinner to sign a contract, all his clothing line would now go under the banner, Pattern PonMax. She'd promised him that she'd get his designs in Clay's new movie. That promise had been the main reason why Spinner signed the contract. That was a promise she thought she'd easily be able to fulfil—that was, until Clay decided to be stubborn.

The clothes stood up for themselves. They'd sell, regardless of whether they were used in the movie or not. Hollywood exposure would quicken the process. Seeing Spinner's designs in the new Clay Thompson movie would make sure the clothes were an immediate success. She knew what to work on. He was an exponent of new ideas and could be swayed by the opportunity to break out of the film company clique of only using popular, recognized designers.

Jodie slipped into the bathroom when Clay had finished. She slipped off her dress and looked in the mirror, in her black bra, panties, and suspenders she looked like one of those chocolate-box women who once adorned glamorous forties movies. As she entered the bedroom, she dimmed the lights and put on some soft music. She slipped on top of Clay's hard phallus and gently rocked up and down, realizing how much she loved this man.

Thompson, even before sex, had come to a decision. He loved his wife, wanted to make her happy. If Spinner's designs were any good, then he'd use them in the movie. Since meeting Debbie Duncan, he'd been plagued by those urges for other women that almost destroyed him in the past. He felt a bond with Debbie, the type of bond he'd only ever felt with Jodie. On the set of the movie, he decided, he might have problems. As he shot his manhood inside Jodie, Thompson decided his wife was everything to him and that she was a woman worth making compromises for.

CHAPTER 12

Debbie gunned her sparkling new red Porsche over the brow of the hill and then screeched on the brakes. Below in the valley, she could see the location crew busily at work like ants. In the distance the set was starting to take shape, it looked every inch the post-war Welsh pit village that it was supposed to be. She tried to memorize this scene of her first leading role in a movie. When she was old and gray, she wanted to look back at her memories and remember the set just the way it was now.

The wind gently ruffled the valley's flowing grass, trees on the hillside swaying to the rhythm of the buffeting wind. The sound of a crane grunting into action down below broke the calm. Only man could spoil such an idyllic scene, Debbie concluded. She stepped out the car and leaned against a rusting signpost. She closed her eyes and pictured past movies: *Ryan's Daughter*, *How Green was My Valley*. Any of those wondrous movies could've been filmed in a magical time-locked setting such as Rockall.

She glanced at her watch. She was due to meet Thompson in a few minutes. She got back into her car and drove into the valley. It was like stepping back in time. Clarkson, the location manager, gave her a brief nod as she drove by before going back to the sketches he had folded out on his camper's table. Everybody was busy. In her brief time at Regal, Debbie had noticed that everybody who worked for Clay Thompson was always busy, continually striving for perfection.

Regal paid good money. In return, they expected a loyal workforce that worked like slaves to make good movies. As Debbie parked and turned off her engine, Thompson spotted her. Debbie looked over her sunglasses. Thompson was wearing a loud Hawaiian shirt and white slacks, looking every inch the stereotypically brilliant, but eccentric movie director.

They walked and talked. Thompson said, "We'll be filming from September twenty-fifth. I want you to be fitted for your costumes and start going through your lines with the cast."

In his trailer, Thompson shut the door to cut out the noise of hammering from a carpenter working nearby. He made them coffee, and they sat on a slumping sofa.

Everything was easily accessible inside the trailer. Debbie decided that Thompson had planned the inside layout as meticulously as he did his films.

"This trailer's the perfect workstation," she complimented.

"It took me long enough to get it together. it was only after I made it big that I could afford it," Thompson told her. "Anything I need to know is in my files or on the computer, all easily accessible in this trailer. When I need a break, it's also a good place to come to get away from nagging actors and a moaning location crew."

Thompson thought back to his early years directing Dutch porn films in loft apartments in Amsterdam, he decided that the public didn't know the half of it. Thompson had kept quiet about those early years. He'd been paid in cash and never listed on the credits, which meant at least his past, unlike some other porn directors, hadn't come back to haunt him.

Debbie looked at some of the posters of Thompson's past films that were plastered around the walls of the trailer and asked, "How long have you been in the movie industry, Clay?"

"It'll be twenty years in August, the last ten spent at Regal." The Regal years were the golden years as far as Thompson was concerned. Working for Regal was like working for your family, from the moment he'd stepped through their studio doors he'd known there was nowhere else that he wanted to work.

Thompson took Debbie's copy of the final draft of the script from the drawer, on the front of it was emblazoned the legend: *THE VALLEY OF DREAMS—DEBBIE DUNCAN COPY*.

Thompson handed Debbie the script. "I'm sorry the file is so thick, I like my actors and actresses to know every facet of the movie."

Debbie said she understood. In Thompson's experience, most of the actors and actresses who said they understood usually didn't. He had a feeling Debbie was different, that she would read up everything in the file so she could get completely inside the movie.

Paul Rome, a former member of the Hollywood brat pack, was playing the film's lead role of John Foster. Thompson hadn't wanted to use Rome. Rome had baggage. In the end, Thompson hadn't been given a choice. There was a subheading in Rome's contract with Regal Pictures that said he could have the pick of starring in any of Regal's films awaiting production—a clause Rome's notorious, publicity-mad agent, Morty Schultz, had insisted was honored when he chose *The Valley of Dreams* for Rome to star in. Movie star contracts were a mine-field, as far as Thompson was concerned. Regal had signed Rome on a contract for several movies, which tied up the star for years. It was a mistake, Thompson thought. Rome was a heavy drinker. Earlier in the year, there were reports of him losing a million dollars at a Las Vegas casino. Rarely a week went by without Rome appearing in the newspapers involved in some kind of scandal. He was the perfect movie star for the tabloids but was not the kind of man Thompson wanted starring in his movies.

"Paul Rome is due to fly in tomorrow, he'll be attending a meeting with me tomorrow morning, I think it might be a good idea if you were at that meeting," Thompson said.

"Is it true what they say about him in the papers?" Debbie asked.

"I'm afraid so. I've never met him, but I've heard rumors in our profession."

Debbie opened her file and looked at her opening lines. There was plenty in the file to look at. She'd read her character, Megan Foster's lines, from her first draft copy.

She now fully understood how Megan would react in every situation. They left the trailer and had a walk around the set. He regularly looked at how the set was progressing. If there was a problem, he wanted to know, and he wanted to know fast. The hills were stunning in this part of the world. When the American studios tried to persuade Thompson to fly to Hollywood and ply his wares, Thompson remembered days like this. He looked at Debbie walking beside him. Who wanted to live in some Californian dust bowl when you could be filming and living here? As he strolled around this lovely valley with a stunning English rose by his side, he decided the

Americans could keep Hollywood with all its fake bravado, Thompson was staying put. They edged past some busy workmen and came to the top of the fictional village where a stone cottage surrounded by sweet smelling pansies stood.

"The cottage looks wonderful," Debbie said, "it's like stepping back in time."

They entered the cottage where the craftsmen had been busy, the kitchen looked like the setting for a fifties Bovril advert. This was going to be Megan Foster's home throughout the film. The cottage had a warm feel to it, looked like a family home, the type of home moviegoers could relate to, Debbie thought. She could see herself acting in here quite easily.

Thompson told her to stay there on her own a while and get a feel for the place. After he'd gone, she walked around the cottage touching and feeling things.

This was Megan Foster's world, Debbie's world, a world she needed to get inside of. When she returned to Thompson's trailer an hour later, the look on Debbie's face told him everything. It was a look that said that she understood Megan Foster and that she, Debbie Duncan, was going to be a success in the role.

CHAPTER 13

Dexter's neck ached. He was damp and wet. Dew soaked his feet. He was getting too old to be hanging around in dank-smelling bushes like this, although his time in the bushes had been productive. Tracy had arrived home after midnight. Dexter was still in shock that the bitch hadn't been alone. She hadn't pined away in her bedroom, staring at old photos of him. The bitch had done the last thing that Dexter had expected. She had tarted herself up and gone out on the pull. Considering the fact that she had arrived home with a man, she had obviously been successful. Upstairs in her flat, Dexter could see the bedroom light flick on. It was a room he'd known every crevice and corner of when he'd first met her—the room in her flat where Tracy and Dexter had spent most of their time before she'd moved to his flat.

Moving into the flat with Dexter had been paradise compared to this shit hole. The bitch should have worshipped the ground he walked on after he took her away from this.

Instead, instead of that, she'd let loose with that virulent attack the night he'd come home drunk. She'd somehow wormed her way back in with the landlord and gotten her old flat back, Dexter wasn't surprised. The landlord probably hadn't been able to get anybody to rent it since she left.

Dexter gripped the thorn bush tightly as he saw Tracy kissing HIM through the lace curtains. Soon the light clicked out, and Dexter was left with his imagination. He felt the cold trickle of blood running down his hand and released his grip on the thorns, gently pulling his hand away. Out of his pocket, he took a hanky and wrapped it around the wound. Sometimes the dark mood took hold of him, made him just as dangerous to himself as his victims.

He checked that the coast was clear, slipped out of the bushes, climbed the rusting railing fence, then jumped back into the street. He went back to his Toyota and sat inside a moment to think. A man on the scene so soon after the bitch had left him was unexpected. Maybe it was an opportunity. Maybe the new man was an opportunity to turn this situation in Dexter's favor. It would take a colossal amount of planning, but he liked planning, planning was how he got his buzz.

He had no friends, made sure his contact with work acquaintances was limited. Friends got in the way of things, didn't understand about life's necessities. His night out with Eddie Malpass had been a mistake. Eddie now seemed to look at him as a friend. It left a distasteful feeling in his mouth. From the glove compartment, he took out a notebook and scribbled some notes. His mind was continually active. He had an IQ that supposedly brainy people would die for.

At school, Dexter—because he'd physically been a late developer—had been bullied. The architect of his misery had been Simon Craven. By the age of fourteen,

Craven was a towering boy and had regularly tortured Dexter in front of Craven's gang in their hangout behind the school bike sheds. Dexter noted that Craven hadn't looked intimidating when Dexter had run him down in a hit-and-run on a quiet side street years later. Dexter had considered going after the rest of the gang but decided against it, concluding that Craven's gang had probably been just as scared of Craven as Dexter was. Fear could be productive, but only if used in the right way.

He thought about Tracy and her new boyfriend. They couldn't have been seeing each other long, had barely got into a couple's routine.

Dexter would wait until the lovebirds were comfortable with each other, and the boyfriend was recognized along with Tracy as an item. It was when they were looked upon as an item that Dexter would strike. HIM was going to spend the rest of his life in prison, framed for Tracy's murder. Dexter hadn't worked out where or when. He just knew for certain it was going to happen. He smiled, thinking about HIM spending the rest of his life in prison framed for a murder that he knew he hadn't committed.

Dexter drove slowly past Tracy's bedsit then parked at the corner of the road. He studied the street, the location of each car, how many streetlights, trees—little details the average man never noticed. Attention to detail was the thing that kept you one step ahead of the police.

The police had long ago lost touch with Dexter. His frequent changes of identity and his ability for anonymity would confuse even the most diligent copper. When Dexter was sure that he'd mentally noted everything in the street, he restarted his car and drove off. He would sleep easier tonight than he had in a long time. Knowing that Tracy was living on borrowed time was enough to sustain him for now.

Now was the time for distance. It was time for a new girlfriend, evidence to the world that Dexter was long over Tracy and so couldn't be considered as a suspect in her murder. He had always found mental games were the best. Some men got their kicks from perverted sex and torture. He wasn't a freak and always played things straight down the middle, only resorted to torture if his subject led him in that direction. In the bedroom, Dexter was a normal middle-class three-position man.

At his flat, he poured himself a large whiskey then slumped in the chair. After his second drink, he felt more relaxed. A plan was formulating in his head. First, he had to find out more about HIM. Once he'd established HIM's pattern, then Dexter could make a move.

He would remain in control. Staying in control meant you didn't make mistakes. If you didn't make mistakes, then you couldn't be captured, and, because he didn't, he wasn't going to be.

CHAPTER 14

I like the script, Clay, I can see it as a smash hit." Rome took off his Paco Rabannes and fixed Thompson with a stare from his legendary hazel eyes. "The film's great. I just don't see this Duncan girl as the leading lady. Surely, the movie needs a big player to push it through at the booking office."

Thompson had known Rome would be difficult. This conversation was proving how much so. Thompson was a superb diplomat, knew how to feed a star's ego. "You're missing the point, Paul. If I explain where I'm coming from with this movie, maybe it'll help you understand my reasoning."

"I'm listening," Rome said, though Thompson thought he was more interested in a cow-breasted makeup girl wandering past the trailer window.

"The movie is about John Foster, Paul. All the other roles in the movie are cameos. This film is all about the problems John Foster has adjusting to life after years in a prisoner of war camp. The film will be carried by John Foster. It's why I insisted on a great actor like you to play the role," Thompson lied. "No leading Hollywood lady would play Megan Foster's role. It would be too much beneath them."

Rome smiled, his gleaming white teeth a stunning advertisement for the bleach work of Californian dentistry. "I'm sorry, Clay, now that I've spoken to you, it's much clearer. I told Morty it was something like this. You know what Morty's like—good at cutting deals but an old mother hen sometimes."

Thompson had never heard of a veteran movie agent shark like Morty Schultz described as an old mother hen, but you lived and learned, he decided.

"I'm glad we've got it all cleared up, Paul. Debbie's a fine actress. Hopefully, she can learn from you."

"I'll teach her what I can, Clay," Rome suggested arrogantly.

Thompson knew he wouldn't. Rome was an egotistical bastard who did everything in his pictures to make sure he hogged all the limelight. The fact that he was making such an offer obviously meant he didn't look at Debbie as any kind of threat, a mistake Thompson knew he'd regret.

"I'm glad you're like that, Paul, a lot of actors forget where they come from."

Rome sipped some beer then stood up. "I've got to go, Clay. I've got an interview with the BBC in Cardiff in an hour."

Thompson shook his hand, and Rome was gone. There hadn't been time to call Debbie in to meet him. As the Bell helicopter carrying Rome whirled away, Thompson thought about what a prick he was. Rome always tried to make out that his time was precious and he was in constant demand. Thompson knew differently. Thompson recalled the lean spells before Rome went to the rehab clinic when the movie companies wouldn't touch him. Although he had the drugs under control now, he still liked the booze, but at least these days he restricted the booze to just a few beers. Until he'd checked into the clinic, Rome's career had been almost over. Unreliability was a star's death-knell in Hollywood. The clinic had straightened him out, and being a reformed drug-addict seemed to revive his career as the American public showed their penchant for a survivor story.

As the helicopter disappeared over a distant hill, Thompson returned to his trailer.

His answering machine was inundated with messages, the first one being from Morty Schultz checking on his client. Schultz, like the rest of the Hollywood hustlers, viewed Rome as an investment. Some stars had their lives ruled by them, wouldn't give you the time of day unless their agent gave them the nod.

Thompson sat back in his chair after listening to the other messages. None of them would divert him from the cause. The cause was the movie. The movie would receive his undivided attention at the start of October when the filming began in earnest. He shut his eyes and thought back to past movies. His thoughts were always drawn back to 'Sirocco,' his only movie that had flopped at the box office. He'd made many mistakes on that one. Filming it on location in Sudan was one of them. Sudan was a country alive with gangsters, people forcing you to pay over the odds for everything. Thompson had paid over the odds, in order to complete the movie. He had learned much from making this movie. By learning from all his mistakes with that film he had never made a flop since.

As he contemplated the past, there was a rap on the door. When he answered, it was Patsy, one of his set designers. If Patsy was disturbing him, it had to be important. He stood and followed her out the door. As Thompson well knew, when you were on set, you had to be prepared for everything.

CHAPTER 15

Johnny Douglas hid behind the lamppost. He stood there quietly watching and waiting. He'd heard footsteps, and yet, every time he'd looked behind him there'd been nothing. This time, the footsteps were louder, more tangible. This time, they were almost on top of him. When he could hear his pursuer on the other side of the lamppost, he leaped out of the mist and bundled the man to the floor. When he saw the copper's blue uniform lying beneath him, Johnny's mind regaled in horror. He leaped back up apologetically, "I'm sorry, Officer, I thought someone was following me, I thought that I was about to be mugged."

The cop wasn't amused. Dusting himself off, he rounded on Douglas. "Can you think of any good reason why I shouldn't take you in, sir?"

Douglas couldn't think of any, contenting himself with, "Please, constable, I'm not a violent man. I thought I was in danger."

The policeman considered the problem a moment, demanding to see some ID. The cop looked at Douglas's driver's license, gave him a warning, then moved away.

Douglas hurried to his apartment block, stepped through the trade door, and was relieved when the door locked behind him. He stared back out into the clammy mist, convinced there'd been someone following him. He waited in the foyer, staring out for five minutes, finally deciding he was wasting his time as he'd never be able to see anybody out there in this pea-souper.

It was as he started up the stairs that he was sure he saw a movement out there in the shadows. He thought about running outside and confronting them, but the thought of them being armed or bigger than him soon cooled his ardor. When he reached his apartment, he rushed to the window and stared out into the night. All he could see was hazy orange street lights and pinprick yellow headlights. He locked the window then bolted and locked the front door.

He was secure. Whatever was out there was probably just a random mugger chancing his arm on a cold Jack-the-Ripper night. It still didn't explain why the mugger was still out there, or why the mugger hadn't been scared away by the cop. None of it made any sense. Douglas had no enemies, and his job at the pharmaceutical lab wasn't exactly international espionage.

He poured himself a rum and coke to steady his nerves. He was meant to go to Tracy's later. Should he ring her and cancel? What was he going to tell her if he canceled? Did he dare show his new girlfriend he was a wimp by telling her that he was too scared to go out in the mist? All those Marvel superheroes that Douglas had read about in comic books as a child wouldn't sit here skulking, afraid of the dark. He decided to compromise. Instead of using his car, he rang for a taxi. When it arrived, he quickly rushed outside and jumped in.

"The Devil after you, mate?" the driver sarcastically remarked as Douglas fastened his seat-belt.

Douglas told the taxi driver where he wanted to go and then ignored him. He looked out into the dark as they left his road but could see nothing. He decided that, in thick mist and fog, the mind could play alarming tricks, and that your senses could become disorientated. At work, his supervisor, old Cheesman, had it in for him. Lately, he'd been putting pressure on Douglas to up his performance, stressing him out, maybe sufficiently for him to become jittery enough to imagine things.

The taxi slid to a halt outside Tracy's flat. Douglas paid the driver then hurried up the moss-strewn drive to the front door. As he pressed her buzzer, he sensed something. He spun around quickly and stared into the night. He was sure he saw a figure dart back into the shadows. When Douglas stepped into Tracy's flat, she could see something was wrong.

"What's wrong?" Tracy asked.

"It's nothing."

"For you to look like this, it must be something," she pressed him.

Douglas said he was all right. Tracy thought otherwise, let it drop, and made them tea. She hated it when her boyfriends hid things from her. Peter had always been secretive. Living with Peter had been like living with a KGB spy. He'd also been a control freak. Tracy had been surprised that he hadn't protested more when she'd left.

She was thirty-three and wanted to find a partner to stick with—a Mills and Boon romance.

Judging by his strange behavior, Peter Rivers hadn't been that guy.

She and Douglas entered the lounge and slumped on the sofa. Later, after tea, Douglas started to relax, deciding his misty escapades were all part of a furtive imagination. Tracy kissed him lightly on his rough lips.

"What's that for?" Douglas asked.

"Does there need to be a reason, Johnny?"

Douglas held Tracy and kissed her, leading her to the bedroom. They made frenzied love, Douglas pushing harder than normal when inside her. When they'd finished, and they were lying in each other's arms, Douglas opened up. "You're going to call me an idiot, but ever since I left work tonight, I've had the feeling that someone has been following me."

"You're not an idiot. You spend all day in artificial light, enclosed in the laboratory, then you go home in the creepy fog. I'm not surprised you're seeing things."

Douglas wasn't so sure. He let the matter drop, not wanting Tracy to think he was a frightened rabbit. In the morning, he was relieved to see that the sky had cleared. He got the bus to work near the stop along the street. After one change, he arrived outside the laboratory in West Dulwich just before nine.

As Douglas showed his pass to a security guard at the gate and entered the laboratory, Dexter watched from his parked car across the street.

Last night had nearly been a disaster. Douglas had been aware of Dexter's presence. The incident with the cop had unnerved Dexter, as he'd only been twenty yards away in the shadows when it happened. At Douglas's apartment, when he had lingered in the foyer staring out into the fog, Dexter had been sure Douglas was onto him.

Dexter would be more careful in the future. It was nearly time to make his move, but first, he needed to know a bit more about Douglas. However, any further surveillance would have to wait, as tomorrow he was off to Wales to work on his first movie for Regal.

Dexter drove off. He had clothes to pack, things to do. Loitering around the laboratory gates was not a good idea, as he didn't want to be noticed. In his head, he'd formulated the plan, the preparation was nearly complete.

Before he made a move, he needed to observe Douglas's movements a little longer. Dexter was as diligent in preparing for this as Regal was in their preparations for making a movie. There'd be no slip-ups. He was the consummate professional, not just in his camera work, but also in the art of murder.

CHAPTER 16

Linda and Diane both had great tits. Rome lay back on his hotel room's king-size bed, admiring their buxom curves. He now had to make a big decision—a decision the boring working man was never encumbered with—which one was it going to be first? Linda had fawned all over him from the moment in the hotel bar when she'd realized he was a big movie star. Diane was more racy. When they'd kissed in the lift, he'd found she had a teasing searching tongue, a tongue he could imagine exploring every contour of his muscled body.

At the foot of the bed, the girls started kneading their breasts. Rome took control and told them what he wanted them to do. He looked at women as numbers, so many women passed through his bed when he was on location that he could never remember their names. Rome wasn't a stupid man, unlike the "it'll never happen to me, brigade."

Rome considered it very likely, with his promiscuous behavior, that without precautions, AIDS could definitely happen to him. He always wore a condom. He had a big supply of every variety the Western world had to offer in his suitcase. Customs officers often made sarcastic quips about them when they rummaged through Rome's suitcase. In England, Customs always searched his bag. The fact that Rome was a former heavy drug user made him fair game for any customs officer looking to make a name for himself. Rome found it insulting. If he was still using drugs, did they really think that he'd be stupid enough to carry the stuff through in his suitcase?

Rome pulled down his bulging Calvin Kleins and started playing with his cock.

He was already hard, harder than he'd been in a long time. Linda was gently stroking his manliness when the phone rang, Rome ignored it. The phone wouldn't be ignored. It was insistent. Rome could feel his hardness receding rapidly. Now, there'd be no way of reawakening it until the irritation of the phone was gone.

"I'll be back in a minute, girls," he said, grabbing his dressing-gown and heading for the lounge. He answered. It was Morty Schultz. "Can't this wait, Morty?"

"Not really. I've been talking to the beer company. They're prepared to offer you two million for a ten advert beer commercial deal."

"I'm starting filming the movie next week, can't this wait until I've finished the movie?"

Schultz was irritated. "If it could wait, I wouldn't be ringing you. They want you to fly to LA and film the first one next week."

"And you think Thompson will agree to my leaving England for the States for a couple of days the first week of filming the movie?"

Dumb cunt, Morty thought, American movie stars called everywhere in Britain, England. It led to confusion. "Don't worry about, Thompson, I'll handle him."

Rome wasn't sure that Thompson would buckle under Morty's pressure like most directors did. In Thompson, Rome had detected an iron streak. He reckoned that Thompson was likely to drop him from the movie, rather than succumb to one of Morty's stunts.

"You have to put them off until I've finished the movie," Rome said.

"I can't, they're talking about going with someone else if you don't show up." Schultz couldn't believe how negative Rome was being. "They plan to show these adverts all over North America for the next two years, which would give you maximum exposure. You need this, Paul."

It would mean that even when he didn't have a movie out, Rome would still stay in the public eye. He knew, from when he'd been in rehab how quickly you were forgotten. He agreed to it.

When he put the phone down, he decided that Morty had underestimated Thompson. Rome stared at his limp dick, and it reminded him of his first sexual experience in the back of a Ford with a neighbor. Brooklyn had been swinging for a young Abe Costello. He knew he was good looking, and so did the women in his neighborhood. He'd signed with Morty Schultz after he'd played a bit part in a B movie. Schultz had made changes. He'd started with a name change, and Brooklyn Abe had suddenly become Paul Rome.

Schultz had hired a personal trainer to get Rome into shape, resulting in Rome soon having on-screen abs that women couldn't get enough of.

Rome sauntered back into the bedroom, hoping that maybe the girls were into each other, but he was disappointed to find them just sitting on the corner of the bed, talking.

Regrettably, they were straight. It took all sorts to make a world. Rome decided that he'd been hanging around with Californian fruitcakes for too long. "How would you two girls like to be in a movie?" he asked.

The girls smiled. Obviously, the thought appealed to them. Rome secretly clicked a switch under the bed that started the camera filming. When he'd arrived in his hotel room, the wardrobe camera had been the first thing he'd installed. "What kind of movie is it?" Linda asked.

"An action thriller," Rome lied, moving closer and licking her nipples.

Diane winked at Linda when Rome wasn't looking. Both girls knew this trip back to Rome's hotel room could be the ticket to greater things. Working for a no-prospects car-hire company was always something that made a girl ambitious. Linda and Diane were ambitious, something Rome noted as they tried to fulfill his every sexual fantasy in a night of unbridled passion. In the morning, he told them he'd ring them but knew he wouldn't.

When they'd gone, he turned the camera off. Nobody could say that Paul Rome wasn't a man of his word. As he removed the camera from the wardrobe, he contemplated how this movie with the Welsh tarts would look among his collection.

When he downloaded the movie, he'd title it, *The Valley of Shattered Dreams*—an apt title—because, when the girls found out he was lying about their part in a movie, shattered was what their dreams would be.

CHAPTER 17

I want you all to contribute," Thompson told everybody on the first morning on the set of filming *The Valley of Dreams*. "I mean everybody."

Thompson glanced at the technicians, cameramen, makeup girls—each of them had a part to play, no matter how small, in a Clay Thompson movie. In all his years directing, Thompson had noticed that the little people sometimes noticed things that others didn't.

Debbie listened intently, she was trembling with excitement. The warm, dewy morning air was sending tingles down her spine. They were about to film the first big scene of the movie, it was the moment when a presumed dead, John Foster, returned to the village after years of captivity in a Japanese prisoner of war camp.

Rome had grown a rough beard for the opening scenes, Debbie decided that it aided rather than depreciated his stunning looks. So far in her dealings with Rome, he'd been polite, but hadn't gone out of his way to be friendly.

Ray Jones, Thompson's assistant, got the scene ready while Thompson gave Rome a brief pep talk. Debbie viewed the scene in silent wonder. It was everything she wanted, needed.

Thompson finally decided he was ready. He made sure everybody was in position. "Okay, Scene Three, Foster arrives home from the war."

The clapperboard clicked, cameras rolled. Dexter was on the zoom lens and was tasked with catching every emotional twitch of the homecoming. Debbie stood at the gate of her flower-laden garden staring down into the misty valley at Rome's ambling figure walking toward her. Her expression slowly changed from contemplative to joyous as she realized it was her husband. Thompson loved it, Debbie hadn't gone overboard, had shown just the right degree of emotion. Most actors went over the top. It was a fine line between perfection and being pathetic, a line a lot of actors crossed.

Rome was nearly as good, grabbing her in his arms the way a man should if he truly loved his wife after such a long time apart. They kissed longer than Thompson thought necessary, Thompson filmed everything then cut the film. Everybody stopped instantly. He had a well-drilled crew who knew how to obey instructions. He would have it no other way, there could only be one boss when making a movie.

"How was it?" Debbie asked.

Thompson thought it was perfect. "Very good, but I think we need to film the kiss again."

Thompson would start filming how he meant to carry on. He didn't want his cast to get overconfident too early in the film. It was a good time to reel them in, make them think that they weren't as good as they thought they were. He could see by the disappointed expression on Rome's face that he'd thought the scene had been good. Rome didn't protest, Thompson was pleased. At least it showed that he was prepared to listen.

They filmed a few minor scenes up to lunch. At lunch, Rome sat with Debbie.

She knew of his womanizing, decided she'd have to tread carefully. She'd be working with Rome for the next couple of months, and she'd have to get on with him. Still, she was pleasantly surprised what good company he was. He laughed and joked with her, a man supremely confident in himself.

Thompson joined them for dessert, deciding to fan a few egos. "You looked superb on the set this morning, Paul," he said.

"I've always looked good under the lens. I'll invite you to my mum's next time you're in New York. She'll show you all my cute baby pictures."

Debbie smiled. Mothers were the same the world over, liked to embarrass their children with their baby photos. "What part of New York?"

"The Bronx, I loved it so much I moved to LA," Rome joked.

"I come from Bedfordshire, a quaint little town called Luton," Debbie said.

"We moved to Guildford when I was three—I don't remember it that much."

Thompson smiled. He had never heard a grubby town like Luton described as quaint before. As they ate the meal, he could see that Rome and Duncan were getting on fine together. If the two main stars of the film got on it made things easier, and he was a great believer in making life as easy as possible on set.

When they broke from filming at the end of the day, Thompson rang Jodie and confirmed that he'd be using some of Spinner's designs in the movie. Jodie was jubilant, the way she always sounded when she was on the cusp of a new venture. Next time he saw her, they'd have great sex. He made a note to go home for the weekend.

The others all went for a drink at a pub in Ebbw Vale. Thompson declined. He had too much editing work to do. Throughout filming, he constantly changed things.

A script was never ready. When the camera rolled, you noticed things that words couldn't portray. Thompson had found over the years that some writers had a knack for overwriting that no amount of editing could subdue. Tristan Deneuve, the writer of *The Valley of Dreams*, wasn't such a man. Deneuve knew how to cut things down to the bone. With Deneuve, everything was always clear and sharp. Deneuve was due to arrive the next day to help Thompson rewrite parts of the film. Thompson was looking forward to meeting him. He'd been a Deneuve fan for many years.

As the orange-red sun was setting, Thompson sat in his trailer with his on-set script editor, Willy Hand. They both drank cold beers.

"I like the general feel of the story, Clay, it's punchy and has an impact," Hand said.

"I wouldn't be filming it if it didn't have."

"Do you think that Paul Rome realizes how good Debbie Duncan is?" Hand asked.

"Probably not, but he will do when he attends the viewing."

"In the few scenes we've filmed her in, her presence on the set is mesmerizing," Hand confirmed. "She's going to be a big star, Clay."

Thompson respected Hand's opinion. Hand had been present at most of Thompson's movies, had seen all the greats come and go. "If Rome thought the same, Willy, she wouldn't be in the film."

It didn't matter how much sway that a director had, the stars always came first at Regal. It was why Thompson always sucked up to the stars so much. He worked on the premise that if he kept the stars happy, then Regal would give him the opportunity to keep making bigger and better films. He scrubbed out some deletions from the script with a red pen. "She's going to steal the movie, Clay."

Thompson couldn't agree more, deciding he wouldn't let Rome view any of the edits until the film was well under way. "By the time he understands the situation, it'll be too late to drop Debbie."

"You can never be sure how someone like Rome is going to react," Hand added.

Thompson was sure Rome would never pull out of this movie. He knew that the movie was going to be a roaring success, and, in Thompson's experience, stars only pulled out of movies they thought were going to bomb. "Rome will stay with the movie. Don't worry, Willy."

Hand was always amazed how Thompson understood film stars. He was glad that Thompson was his friend—he sure wouldn't want him as an enemy. After they'd finished making their alterations, it was late. Thompson dismissed Hand and called it a day.

When Hand had left, Thompson opened another beer. While on location Thompson slept in his trailer, it made him accessible, always available if there were problems. He'd installed all the latest mod cons, it had everything a man could desire apart from being at home. He stared out the window at the twinkling stars, the air was so fresh around here, the sky void of the congestion that it seemed to have around London. He thought of how beautiful Debbie had been on the set today.

Debbie was a special girl, a girl who didn't seem to realize how much sexual power her beauty gave her over men. He was trying to avoid temptation. There was definitely an attraction between them, even if Debbie claimed otherwise. He was thinking about what she'd be like in bed when his phone rang. It was late, it had to be Jodie. When he answered, and it wasn't, he was shocked. What the caller told him bludgeoned the life out of him. What he was told showed him how insignificant the film world really was.

CHAPTER 18

You can all go home early," Jodie told her staff. It was half an hour before finishing time, and the staff noted that after speaking to her husband Jodie had an excited gleam in her eyes. The girls all thanked her and left. Most of them realized the way Jodie was talking lately about the influx of new business, their time off in the future would be limited.

Jodie shut the shop just after five, counted the till takings, made it ready for the night safe where she was going to deposit it on the way home. She checked the shop over and then left just after half five. It was a warm, bright evening. She'd timed it badly, got stuck in the rush hour traffic. Nothing could dampen her mood since she'd spoken to Clay and he said he was going to put some of Spinner's designs in the movie. She was going to make a fortune out of the new clothing line. Each day she loved Clay more. Clay brought the best out in her, encouraged her ambition in a way that no other man she'd ever been with had.

She pulled up at the night safe just before six, put her hazard warning lights on, and rushed toward it. She was about to deposit the money in the safe when a rough hand grabbed the arm she held the money in. "Let it go, lady," a grubby tramp ordered.

Jodie struggled to free her arm. The tramp panicked, and she felt the lunge of cold steel rip into her chest. The tramp grabbed the money bag and ran. Jodie fell to the cold, cobbled pavement, bleeding and sensing the gathering ghouls around her. Everything in the street became hazy as she floated in and out of consciousness. The pain above her rib cage seemed to be boring deeper within her. She blacked out just before the screeching siren signaled the ambulance had arrived.

"A tramp stabbed her," a pensioner told the paramedics.

The paramedic shook his head as he treated Jodie where she lay. The knife had plunged fatally deep into Jodie's lung. When she was stabilized, they lifted her gently onto the stretcher, slipped it into the back of the ambulance, and departed in a rush of noise and flashing lights.

At the hospital, an Asian doctor rushed outside as the stretcher was lifted down and pushed into the emergency room. As the stretcher moved along the corridor surrounded by shouting nurses and the doctor, Jodie drifted in and out of consciousness. When she arrived on an examination table, the doctor frantically worked on her, desperation reeking from every sinew. After two hours of working on Jodie—three times bringing her back to life from the brink of death—the fourth time there were problems, insurmountable problems.

The fourth time, after desperately working on Jodie Thompson for over two hours, at nineteen-hundred-thirty-five hours, Doctor Sing officially pronounced Jodie Thompson dead.

CHAPTER 19

There was a break in filming. The director's wife had been killed in a mugging, and a distraught looking Thompson had gone home. Dexter was always a man who could be relied upon to seize on other people's misfortune. This was now Tracy's time, and he wanted it to be her time more than anything. He'd watched Douglas several times, establishing a pattern of his movements. Douglas visited Tracy every Monday evening, never missed, Monday evening was the perfect time for the kill.

"I've got to go home for something," Dexter told Sam, the makeup girl he'd been seeing. "It'll only take a couple of days. I'll be back on Tuesday."

Samantha Jacobson took it well. In the short time she'd been seeing Peter Rivers, she'd noticed how reliable he was. It was a pleasant change. The stuntman she'd dated before was all beefcake and no brains, proved it when he'd forgotten to hide the knickers of the floozy he'd cheated on her with. Sam had found them by the side of the bed in his apartment, had immediately kicked the cheating fucker out of her life. Sam had far too much pride in herself to ever let a man cheat on her. She didn't give men a second chance.

Dexter found it hard concentrating on the road as he drove home. He had too much on his mind. Tracy's murder was going to be brutal, so much so that the judge would be horrified enough to give Douglas a life sentence. It was all going to be about timing. If he was going to establish a watertight alibi, then there had to be no doubts, in the eyes of the court, that it was impossible for Dexter to have killed Tracy as he couldn't be in two places at once.

At nine in the evening, he arrived home, tired and grumpy. He had two days before he had to be back in Wales. He knew what he had to do. First, he had to hire a van and then it was time for the master-stroke. On Sunday morning he was up early studying the large sheet of paper he'd jotted everything down on. Everything had to be planned with military precision.

The hotel was a hundred miles from Tracy's flat, and he had to arrive at the hotel Monday afternoon. At the hotel, he'd park the van in a position near reception where it could be seen by the staff. He noted down times. It would take three hours to get to Tracy's and back, giving him an hour to perform the deed. The phone call to the police had to be timed just as Douglas arrived at Tracy's apartment. While the police were at Tracy's place interrogating Douglas, Dexter would be at Douglas's place planting evidence. Dexter stared at the kitchen knife he'd purchased from a superstore near Douglas's home. He'd worn a coat and hat just like the ones Douglas wore, making sure his face had always been facing away from the CCTV camera by the counter when he'd made the purchase. If the police looked back over the surveillance tapes, they'd see a man of similar height and weight as Douglas, looking like Douglas, purchasing a knife at the same time as the receipt said. Dexter was going to plant the receipt in a bin at Douglas's flat.

He regretted ever getting involved with Tracy, the whore. For all her plain looks, Tracy somehow thought she was better than everybody else. Tracy would soon find that she was no better than the others, that her complexion was just as gray-white as the others when she was dead. Death was a great leveler, stripped away a person's delusions of grandeur. Dexter parked the white van in a quiet alley at the rear of his house near his garage, loaded it with everything he needed, including a Suzuki motorbike he'd stolen and re-sprayed.

Monday lunch-time, he left home to drive to the Glendow Hotel, halfway between home and Wales. Just before he arrived, he hid his motorbike and rucksack in nearby woods.

At the hotel, he ate dinner at five, retired to his room at half past. By six o'clock, he'd left in disguise via a fire exit and was speeding toward Tracy's flat on his motorbike. His rucksack contained all that he needed. The bike, his gloves, and rucksack would all be discarded in the woods before he returned to the hotel later that night. Tracy was about to pay for not worshipping him as required. Sluts like Tracy needed to die horribly. Dexter would ensure that she did. He would make sure as he lunged the knife into her that the last image the stubborn slut saw in this world was him laughing at her.

CHAPTER 20

The wind swirled around Dexter's knees, making it hard to keep his balance. Heavy raindrops thumped against his back as he carefully edged along the slippery moss-laden roof tiles toward the bathroom window. His foot momentarily slid onto the plastic guttering. He could feel the guttering sagging under his weight, but somehow he got back on the tiles before he broke it, stumbling onto the flat roof situated just below the open bathroom window.

He stood silently in the dark for a few moments, composing himself. Down below his eyes hunted and searched, studied the flat entrance for any sound of presence or sign of movement. Dexter stared at the dirty window, studying the slut's point of vulnerability. Tracy lived in the attic apartment and had assumed that, at such a height, it was safe to leave a window open. Dexter slipped his hand inside the gap and pulled the window open wider. He knew the layout, that she placed her toiletries on the ledge, and knew what he had to avoid to make a clandestine entry. As he stood on the damp bathroom floor, he glanced at his watch, there was only half an hour until Douglas's usual arrival time. If Dexter was going to murder her, then it had to be now.

Silently, he crept along the hall clutching the sharp kitchen knife he'd taken from his coat pocket. In the living room, he could hear the sound of Bach booming out from Tracy's sound system. As he entered, he could hear Tracy humming along to the music. She was seated with her back to him on a faded leather sofa a few yards away. The smell of perfumed candles wafted the air. The bitch had a thing about sweet-smelling rooms. As he approached, her flame-red hair twitched as she was suddenly aware of his presence. She turned, a look of horror captured in a freeze frame on her face as she realized who the intruder was.

She stood and tried to run, but Dexter was too quick. She'd moved barely a yard when Dexter plunged the knife into her heart, ripping open her left ventricle. She screamed. Dexter rammed a cushion over her face to mask the poor demented cow's death throes. Her fight for life quickly ended, as he thrust the knife deeper. As her body flopped dead over the blood-strewn sofa, she looked like a discarded child's rag doll.

Dexter stared for a moment at Tracy's cold dead eyes, smiled as he remembered the horror of recognition as he'd struck. He didn't have time to savor the moment. Douglas would be here shortly, and Dexter needed to depart. He let the knife drop out of his gloved hand to the floor then backtracked slowly to the bathroom, wiping the floor with a towel to clean up his wet footprints. He shut the bathroom window then left via the front door. He didn't slam the Yale lock door shut, left it slightly ajar, in case Douglas didn't have a key to enter. As Dexter mounted his motorbike on a dark secluded street corner away from street lighting, a taxi passed him. In the front passenger seat, he could see Douglas. Dexter waited until

Douglas was in the building, then he rang the police on his mobile phone. He covered his mouth with a hanky to muffle his voice, told the police Nine-Nine-Nine receptionist that he could hear screaming coming from Tracy's, gave the address, then hung up.

He sped off on his motorbike toward Douglas's apartment. When he arrived, he opened the entrance door with his skeleton keys then crept up the stairs until he reached Douglas's landing. He kept his crash helmet on. The helmet made him unrecognizable to any potential witness. Inside Douglas's flat, Dexter rushed to the kitchen and deposited the receipt for the murder weapon in the kitchen bin.

Two hours later, after discarding the bike and rucksack back in the woods, and still wearing his disguise, he was back in his hotel room. The disguise would be ditched in the morning, he decided, as he took it off and threw it in a bin bag. After a quick shower and a change of clothing, he headed downstairs to the hotel bar. In the bar, he sat for an hour casually drinking. Then, when he was sure a few people had noted his presence, he went to the reception desk and asked the bored-looking receptionist for a seven o'clock alarm call. The more people that saw him, the more his alibi would stick, Dexter thought. He decided that he was showing his usual brilliance in anticipating flaws in his alibi before Tracy's murder investigation.

In bed, he lay for hours, thinking of that cold lifeless look in Tracy's dead eyes as she'd lain dead on the sofa. It was a look he'd encountered many times in his life—a look you only encountered in death, a look that Dexter couldn't get enough of. He had learned from an early age that he had the ability to turn his emotions on and off at will.

He felt no different when killing Tracy than he

would about squashing a fly. Everything had to die eventually—it was just a matter of perspective.

After a sleepless night, he was awake before the alarm call. By eight o'clock, he was on the road heading back to Wales. At nine o'clock, he paused in a quiet backwater to dump the motorbike—he'd loaded back on the van earlier—into a deep river. At ten o'clock, he dumped the rucksack and the bag containing his disguise into a motorway service bin.

By midday, when he was eating a burger at a Burger King, all traces of the previous night's activities and any record of his trip to Twickenham were gone.

CHAPTER 21

Douglas knocked twice on Tracy's door and was surprised that she didn't answer. The silly cow had left the door ajar when she'd come home from work. In this ever-more-violent world, Douglas decided it was a terrible lapse in her home security. He entered, hoping that maybe she'd left the door ajar on purpose moments before his arrival and was lying on the bed waiting for his imminent arrival in an alluring suspender set. As he called out her name and was greeted with silence, he decided that something was definitely wrong. They were still in the early stages of lust in their relationship, and Tracy always rushed to the door, keen to see him on his Monday night visits.

He could hear the sound of music playing loudly in the background, Classic FM, Tracy's favorite station. He shouted once more and was again met with an eerie silence. It was as he stepped into the living room, his horror heightened. He saw Tracy lying dead in a pool of thick crimson blood on the sofa. On the floor, a blood-strewn knife lay. The knife dominated his attention. With her vacant death stare, the look on Tracy's face would forever remain locked in Douglas's memory every time he thought back to this moment and the night of her murder.

On reaching the body, he desperately checked for life signs but found none.

Suddenly his senses became alive to the danger of the situation. Was the murderer still in the apartment? He grabbed the knife off the floor to use as a weapon then took out his mobile phone to call the Emergency Services. Before he had time to dial, he heard the sound of approaching sirens, wondering if Tracy had managed to call for help before she died.

When he heard the sound of footsteps thumping up the stairs, he dropped the knife and rushed to the front door. As he opened the door, he was greeted by cops, not paramedics.

A neighbor reported a disturbance, sir," a burly cop said. "He said he could hear screaming coming from this apartment."

"She's dead," a confused Douglas said.

Burly's partner, skinny and athletic, elbowed past and entered Tracy's flat. When he reached the living room and found Tracy's corpse, he shouted, "Bloody hell! Be careful, John!"

Burly removed a Taser from his belt and pointed it at Douglas. Douglas froze and leaned back against the wall.

Skinny returned with his baton drawn. "There's a woman knifed to death in the front room."

"Her name's, Tracy," a dazed Douglas offered feebly.

"Turn around and put your hands behind your back!" Burly shouted.

Dumbfounded, Douglas obeyed then stood motionless while the cops handcuffed and frisked him.

"I didn't kill her," he pleaded as the cops took him

back to the car and called in the murder squad.

"You can tell that to the detectives," Burly said, and they sat in the car waiting for the murder squad to arrive in a flurry of flashing lights.

Douglas stared out the window, watching the car headlights. He couldn't blame their suspicions for they'd discovered him as the only other occupant of the flat at a murder scene.

He was confident he could sort this mess out with the detectives. Someone must've seen or heard something and would know why some evil bastard had killed his girlfriend.

His eyes became teary as his shocked body finally released the build-up of pent-up emotion.

As the tears streamed down his face, he thought of Tracy's corpse lying upstairs. He wondered if it was a break-in that had turned ugly. Had she been raped? All these awful questions needed answering, questions that Douglas didn't know any of the answers to. Would the police believe him, realize he was just a dupe? As the cavalry arrived, Douglas realized he was certain of one thing—that he would shortly find out.

CHAPTER 22

Clay Thompson stood at his wife's graveside, staring blankly into the distance at the lead-gray clouds racing across the angry skyline. The threatening rain soon began to fall, and tears ran Debbie's makeup as she watched Jodie Thompson's coffin slowly being lowered into the dampening grave. Clay Thompson's world had collapsed around him, and Debbie reckoned that all his success probably counted for nothing in his life as he viewed his murdered wife's burial. As the burial service ended, people wandered past, commiserating with him.

Thompson said little in return and was still standing staring down at his wife's coffin when most of the people had departed.

Debbie patted Thompson on the shoulder then went back to the limo she was sharing with Paul Rome. As they drove away, Rome said, "I liked Jodie, she always had time to talk to you."

Rome had met Jodie a couple of times at parties recently. She'd told him that he should grow up when he'd tried to chat her up while her husband was busy mingling.

Rome wasn't used to women's rebukes and respected her for her fidelity. There were plenty of other film wives who'd passed through Rome's bed over the years, plenty of women who appreciated his attributes.

"I don't think we'll be filming for a while," Debbie said.

Rome shrugged. "Who knows? Maybe Thompson will want an out for his grief and will plow all his energies into his work."

Death affected people in strange ways. When he was a kid, Rome could remember when his brother had been knocked down by a car and killed. Rome went off the rails for a while shortly after. There was no way anybody could forecast how Thompson would react to this tragedy.

Debbie stared out the tinted limo windows at the depressing rain clouds dancing across the sky. All she could picture was the look of cold desolation in Thompson's lifeless bloodshot eyes as he stood at his wife's graveside. Rome was wearing shades, so it was impossible for Debbie to fathom how emotional he was. Rome was a hard guy to understand.

He could be witty company when he was in the right mood, yet, if you caught him on a bad day, you encountered a sinister streak.

The limo splashed into a lake-sized puddle as they arrived outside Thompson's mansion for the wake. As they entered the mansion's living room, Debbie sought the anonymity of the quiet corners. Such a luxury was impossible for Rome, as people he barely knew came up to talk to him, hoping that some of the superstar glitz would rub off. For the first time in the brief time that she'd known Rome, Debbie decided that his street cool had gone and that he looked uncomfortable.

"Let's get some air," Debbie said, pushing Rome out

through the elegant French doors and onto the beautifully paved patio.

When they were seated in two pine garden chairs under an awning, Rome nodded. "Thanks, Debbie. Today, I can do without the circus."

And what a circus it was, Debbie thought. Since Rome had been filming the movie, Debbie had noticed that he never seemed to get a moment to himself. They lapsed into silence, respecting each other's right to be alone with their thoughts. After a few minutes, they weren't alone, as Max Spinner wandered outside for a smoke.

Spinner looked surprised to find them out there but he obviously didn't want to appear rude by ignoring them. "The funeral went well," he said.

"It couldn't have gone much better," Debbie agreed.

"I'm Max Spinner," Spinner said, shaking Debbie's hand, "I was Jodie's partner in a clothing company."

"I'm in the movie that Clay's been filming," Debbie said.

Rome didn't say anything—he decided he didn't need to. After years of adulation, he had long ago decided that everybody knew Paul Rome, the movie star. As Rome saw Thompson's limo arrive, he lost interest in the little people and wandered back inside. Debbie and Spinner followed. Debbie stood and observed the pain on Thompson's face. It was the face of a man who just wanted to be on his own but was going through the motions as the funeral's host. After people started leaving, Thompson slipped into his study to be alone. Debbie followed shortly after and found a distraught-looking Thompson lying on a sofa with an empty bottle of whiskey beside him.

As he lay snoring in a drunken stupor, Debbie sat in one of the comfortable red-leather study chairs and observed him. Seeing a man so usually in control of everything and as full of life on set as Thompson reduced to this was unsettling to Debbie. People like Thompson were meant to laugh at adversity, always be available for their public, or so the movie magazines would have you believe. After half an hour, there was a rap on the study door, then Rome entered.

"Is he okay?" a concerned Rome asked.

"He's as good as any man who's just lost his wife is going to be."

There was an uncomfortable silence. Rome broke it. "Are you staying?"

"For a while, I want to make sure his staff put him to bed."

Rome nodded and then left. Debbie hunted out a maid and asked for a pot of strong coffee. When he awoke, Debbie would try and get some of the coffee into him. For all the opportunities that Clay had given her to break into the movie industry, the least she could do, to repay his faith in her was to try and help him here. To lose a wife was bad enough, but to lose a wife in the way that Clay Thompson had lost one was the worst way of all, Debbie thought. As the coffee arrived and she set to work with the maid at trying to make him stir, she thought about how drunk he'd been since Jodie's death, and what it all meant for his long-term wellbeing. It was at that moment, she made a promise to her dead friend, Jodie, that she wouldn't let Thompson succumb to booze. She would get him through this, because, as far as Debbie was concerned, that was what real friends did.

CHAPTER 23

Dexter stood at the back of the mumbling crowd of film people, waiting for the announcement. Everybody working on the film had been called to the meeting. Dexter was surprised, in light of recent events, that instead of some lowbrow executive, it was a sad-looking Clay Thompson who appeared. He strode to the front of the village hall then addressed them. "Thanks for coming, everybody. I expect you're all anxious to hear what's happening with the movie. Well, I'm pleased to announce that, from tomorrow morning, we carry on filming."

Jimmy Murray, shouted, "I want you all back on set at seven!"

With that, Thompson and Murray went back to Thompson's trailer. As Dexter stepped outside, he was alarmed to see a car pull in the set car park and a man and woman step from it. They were talking to Barney, a technician. When Barney pointed at Dexter, Dexter knew they were cops. He pretended not to notice and started looking over some of his camera equipment.

In an instant, the gorgeous blonde and her pudgy

male assistant's shadow stood over him.

"Mr. Peter Rivers?" Detective Inspector Sarah Machin asked.

An innocent man had nothing to fear, Dexter tried to tell himself. He looked up inquiringly from his work. "I'm Rivers."

"I'm Detective Inspector Machin, and this is Detective Sergeant Roberts," Machin confirmed and then showed Dexter her ID. "We're here to see you about a former girlfriend of yours, a Miss Tracy Sparshot of Nineteen-B, Beaufoy Gardens, Twickenham."

"So she moved back there?" Dexter asked.

"Pardon, sir?" DS Roberts said.

"She moved back to her old place. When our relationship ended, her brother moved her things out of our flat when I was at work one day. I wondered where he'd taken them—Beaufoy Gardens was where she lived before she moved in with me."

The detectives let Dexter ramble on. Machin was hoping for a slip, something that would confirm him as a suspect. Dexter told them nothing. When he had said nothing relevant, Machin realized that she'd have to confirm the reason for their visit. "I'm afraid we've got some bad news, sir. Tracy Sparshot was brutally murdered in her apartment Monday night."

Dexter looked suitably shocked. It would've been disrespectful not to. "I can hardly believe it," he mumbled.

"I know this must be a shock, sir, but we have to check out everybody who had close links with Tracy. Tracy's brother said you were going out with her for several months. You'd been living together for three."

"That's right. She moved into my flat in April. It didn't work out. I came home drunk one night, we had a row, and she left me," Dexter confirmed. If they'd spoken to Tracy's brother, they'd already know all this. To lie would be suspicious.

"She was brutally murdered, sir. In such a case we have to check out everything, especially if she was recently in a relationship and it ended acrimoniously." DI Machin let her words hang in the air. Rivers was calm and relaxed. If he was the murderer, he was a remarkably cool customer, she decided.

"I understand, Inspector. I'd expect nothing else—ask me anything you want."

Co-operative Dexter—the police detective's friend.

"We need to know what you were doing the night of the murder," Machin pressed. "Have you got an alibi for Monday night, sir?"

After talking to Tracy's brother about the hostile end to Dexter's relationship, Peter Rivers was sure to be high on the police's suspect list, Dexter surmised. With that in mind, he had to be careful. "When was she murdered on Monday night?"

"Forensics put her time of death at some time around seven," Machin stated. "We need to know what you were doing at seven, Monday, Mr. Rivers."

"Monday," Dexter thought aloud. "I was on my way back to the set after a trip home. I stayed at the Glendow Inn, just outside of Gloucester because I was tired of driving, and I didn't want to fall asleep at the wheel."

"And you arrived there at what time, sir?" Machin asked.

"I can't remember exactly. I think it was about three o'clock."

"We'll check it out," Roberts said.

"And what time did you leave the hotel?" Machin pushed.

"I asked for an alarm call at seven the next day. I was on the road just after eight."

Machin had been told by Tracy's brother that Rivers was weird.

She wasn't sure about him. If he could prove that he was at the hotel, had witnesses to corroborate the story, then he was in the clear. Douglas was still protesting his innocence, even after they'd found damning evidence against him.

His fingerprints were on the murder weapon. According to the patrolmen, they found Douglas in a stupefied state, weren't sure if it was genuine shock or if it was horror because he'd murdered Sparshot.

Machin had her doubts. She googled the hotel on her phone, and Rivers confirmed it was the hotel where he had stayed. Machin told him they'd check it out and to not go anywhere away from the set as they might want to talk to him again. Dexter said he'd stay put and watched as their car disappeared around a bend in the road up the valley.

His girlfriend, Sam, put a hand on his shoulder. "Are you okay, Peter?"

"Not really, I just had some terrible news." Dexter sat down on a nearby bench with Sam beside him. "A girl I used to live with was murdered. They asked me if I knew of any enemies she had." He could see a moment of doubt in Sam's eyes. Women always wanted to believe the worst about you, so he decided to allay her fears. "The night she was murdered, I was staying at a hotel outside of Gloucester. I can prove I didn't do it—"

"You've no need to prove anything, Peter, I know you couldn't kill anybody."

"It's not what others will think, Sam. Others will think there's no smoke without fire."

Sam didn't say anything. Film crews gossiped. Many would have noticed the police talking to Peter. Peter was known as an introvert, which was what drew Sam to him.

She was tired of movie loudmouths, full of their own importance.

She and Dexter went for some privacy into her makeup hut as people were now busy in preparation for the start of filming in the morning.

"What do you think of Thompson coming back to work so soon after his wife's death?" Sam asked.

"People fight grief in their own way," Dexter said, locking the door. "I'll show you how I come to terms with mine."

As he leaned into her, Sam could feel Peter's hard phallus pressing against her jeans. She turned and flipped the buckle free on his belt. His trousers slipped down easily, revealing his throbbing penis.

Peter Rivers was a big man in every way, Sam thought, as she guided his lusting manhood inside her.

CHAPTER 24

I didn't kill her," Douglas pleaded, for what must've been the hundredth time in his interview. "I don't know who killed her, but it wasn't me."

"You're being silly, Douglas. All the evidence says you did it," DI Machin said. "If you admit your guilt, then I'll do what I can for you."

"My client has told you he didn't do it, Inspector. He's got nothing more to add," Ravi Dev, Douglas's solicitor, said.

"What about the receipt for the murder weapon that we found in your rubbish bin, Douglas, how do you explain the receipt?" DI Machin asked.

"I didn't buy the knife. I've no idea how the receipt got there," Douglas said.

"I suppose the magic pixies put it there, Mr. Douglas," DS Roberts quipped sarcastically.

"My client is answering your questions to the best of his ability. I think we should refrain from sarcasm," Dev remonstrated, and his hard brown eyes gave DS Roberts a loathsome stare.

Machin gave Roberts a ticking off for the benefit of

the interview tape and Dev, then she turned back to Douglas. "Let's examine the facts, Mr. Douglas. You were alone at the scene of a murder, your prints were all over the murder weapon. We found a receipt for the kitchen knife used to fatally stab Tracy Sparshot in your rubbish bin. Looking at the evidence, I'm sure you and Mr. Dev can understand how bad this looks and why we might think you did it."

Dev calmly looked at his notes. "Don't you find the call from the neighbor suspicious, Inspector? Have you managed to trace the neighbor?"

They hadn't. The call had come from an untraceable mobile phone. "A lot of people report crimes but don't want to get involved, Mr. Dev," Machin said.

"It's still dubious, Inspector," Dev said. He knew from personal experience that some members of the public never got involved. He thought back to his father's corner shop, targeted by the National Front in Hounslow in the eighties. The police never arrested anybody, the community didn't want to know, the skinhead intimidation had eventually forced Dev senior to sell up and retire. Ravi had learned at an early age the need for education. Education meant you could beat the system, education meant that you didn't get trapped like his father had been.

"Your client was found in a stupefied state in his murdered girlfriend's apartment, the murder weapon had only his fingerprints on it," Machin stated.

"I've explained about the knife. I picked it up to use as a weapon because I thought the killer might still be in Tracy's flat," Douglas said.

"If it wasn't for the receipt, I might believe you, Mr. Douglas. We've studied CCTV footage from around the cash desk of the superstore at the time the knife was purchased. We can't see your face which you've deliberately kept out the camera, but the clothes you're wearing match clothes we found in your wardrobe," Machin stated. "We are quite certain that we can prove that you're the man who bought the knife, Mr. Douglas."

"I didn't buy the knife! I'd never seen that knife until I entered Tracy's living room on Monday night," an irritated Douglas pleaded. "As I told you, I was home alone when the knife was purchased. Whoever bought it wasn't me."

"Being at home alone isn't an alibi, Mr. Douglas," Roberts said. "All that proves is that you could've bought the knife."

Douglas rounded angrily. "I didn't kill Tracy, I don't know how the receipt got in my bin."

"As far as we're concerned, we have the right man, Mr. Douglas," Machin said and then concluded the interview.

Douglas and Dev were left alone in the interview room to discuss the interview.

Bail hadn't been requested, as Dev quickly decided that Douglas wouldn't be able to afford it, even if it was granted.

Outside, in the corridor, an irritated Roberts said, "Can you believe the nerve of the guy? We've proved he bought the weapon, his fingerprints are all over the knife, yet, still, he denies it."

"He's never going to admit it, Sergeant, nobody is going to admit to brutal murder. There were no signs of a break-in, but there wouldn't be if the killer already had a front door key," Machin concluded.

It was hard to see the killer being anybody other than Douglas, and yet…

"I didn't like Sparshot's ex, Rivers," she continued. "There was something creepy about the guy."

"Rivers's alibi is watertight, ma'am. Witnesses saw

him in the hotel bar in the evening, reception says that his van never left the hotel car park. On the way to bed, he asked reception for an early morning alarm call. Rivers isn't the murderer, ma'am," Roberts concluded.

"According to the brother, Sparshot and Rivers had a volatile relationship. The brother said that Sparshot left Rivers because of his weird behavior," Machin said.

"His alibi is tight, ma'am."

Roberts was right, Rivers had an alibi. There were no reports of Rivers pestering Sparshot since the split. If it wasn't for Rivers's alibi, Machin might have quizzed him further. With the alibi and with Douglas's fingerprints on the murder weapon, there seemed to be little point.

Machin believed in checking everything out. They'd check the fine points of Rivers's alibi one more time and, if it proved watertight, then Rivers was out of the equation.

With the weight of evidence against Douglas, this investigation, Machin decided, would soon be over.

CHAPTER 25

The morning's filming hadn't gone well. Debbie looked at the harsh lines of Thompson's taut face while she was off set. He hadn't smiled since they started shooting, the un-Thompson-like way he was rattling through the scenes without his usual care and attention showed everybody how badly he was suffering. If he carried on like this, the quality of the film was sure to be affected. At lunch, she would talk to him, try to get him to analyze his behavior.

In a bedroom scene where Rome had to strip to his underwear, a couple of female extras giggled playfully in the background, Thompson erupted and dismissed the girls from the film. After they'd gone, he then ranted at the rest of the crew about nothing, upsetting the flow of the movie. As Debbie entered the bedroom and Rome slightly mumbled his lines Thompson shouted through his megaphone, "sharp and concise, Paul! Sharp and concise!"

Rome nodded, wanting to say something to Thompson about not being allowed enough time to deliver his lines properly, but Debbie persuaded him to ignore

Thompson's behavior until she'd spoken to him at lunch. In the bedroom scene, Rome gave what he thought was an excellent performance. Thompson thought otherwise and made him film the scene several more times until Thompson was finally happy.

"This is impossible," an angry Rome said to Debbie as they were being attended by makeup. "I can't work like this. We all know the strain he's under. If this is how he intends to plow through the rest of the film, then the movie is going to be a disaster."

He was right, Debbie thought. Rome was an experienced pro. If he thought the film wasn't working, then you had to listen. Debbie had noticed flaws in a couple of the scenes they'd filmed this morning, flaws that Thompson, in his current state, hadn't noticed. If they continued like this, the movie would be a flop, and some of Thompson's aura as a director would be lost. The big box-office success that would ensure plenty of future work for the cast, therefore, wouldn't happen. There was a lot riding on this movie, enough for Debbie to realize that her reasons for talking to Thompson were probably selfish.

At lunch, she followed him to his trailer. He didn't look happy to see her. "Can I have a word?" she asked.

"I'd rather be alone," Thompson said.

"It's important," Debbie insisted.

Thompson thought the half bottle of Scotch he was going to consume during the lunch break was more so. Booze would help him get through the day's filming, had helped him keep going through the desolate days since the murder. As they sat, Debbie noticed how disheveled the normally immaculate trailer was. It was obvious that Thompson hadn't cleaned up since he'd heard about Jodie's murder. Debbie could see that at the moment Clay Thompson was a mental train wreck.

"You said it was important," Thompson pressed.

"This morning you directed like a bumbling amateur, Clay. Paul was excellent in his scenes, yet you continually made him re-film them. What I saw this morning wasn't you—"

"I don't need this!" Thompson rounded. "Who the fuck do you think you are, Debbie Duncan? You've only been in films for five minutes, you don't know anything."

"I know enough to know that if friends who care about you can't be straight with you, nobody can," Debbie persisted.

Thompson poured himself a glass of Scotch, drank some and relented. "Just leave my trailer and let's forget you ever came in here."

"Drinking yourself to death isn't the answer," Debbie preached.

Thompson laughed. "If it wasn't for me, you'd still be in Christmas panto."

Thompson knew how to wound, Debbie thought, Christmas panto was the star's graveyard. She ignored Thompson's alcohol-fueled comments. "I know I owe you, Clay, I also like to think I've got talent."

"Just go to lunch and leave me be," Thompson said.

Debbie started toward the door, just before she stepped through it, she said, "I want you, while you sit and booze, to consider one question, Clay. Do you think the work you did this morning was up to your usual high standards?"

As Thompson watched Debbie's lovely arse walk away, he knew she was right.

The morning's filming, particularly his directing, had been crap. Not many people in the industry would've had the courage to confront him about it. He poured himself another drink, was about to drink it, then stopped. He angrily threw the glass against the wall and then watched the whiskey and shattered glass fall, like his life, to the floor. He thought about his recent history, of what a bummer life could be. And then, in the quiet of his own company, he wept loudly.

Debbie headed to the mobile cafeteria for lunch. She sat next to Rome, picking at her lasagna. Rome's dinner companion, Chantelle, a young starlet, wasn't impressed. Rome didn't help Chantelle's black mood by sending her to get him a coke while he spoke with Debbie alone.

"What happened?" Rome asked.

"I told him his work this morning was crap. Whether he came up long enough from the bottle of Scotch he was drinking to listen, God knows."

"He likes you, Debbie. He may have listened." Rome respected Thompson. In the short time he'd worked with him before Jodie's murder, he'd seen how good he was.

"Promise me you'll give him a chance to work through this, Paul," Debbie said.

"The guy deserves a break, I won't make a fuss," Rome said, lightly patting Debbie's arm as leggy Chantelle returned with his drink.

A jealous Chantelle smiled falsely at Debbie as she gave Rome his drink.

Debbie made an excuse and left.

"What did she want?" Chantelle asked, not liking the way that Rome was leering at Duncan's rear.

"Just talking about the script, baby."

Chantelle didn't believe him. Rome was an outrageous womanizer, Chantelle decided she'd have to watch Duncan around him. There was a danger that Duncan, through her association with Rome, might get the drop on Chantelle in the publicity stakes surrounding the movie. Alas, this was something publicity-hungry vixen, Chantelle Carey, could never allow. Her agent, Tania Stenson, had told her to get herself seen with Rome by the media. He was hot in the tabloids. Anything that rubbed off on

Chantelle could do nothing but further her career.

Tania had invested a lot of time in Chantelle and had frequently told her she had what it took to push herself to the top. Tania had gotten Chantelle a small part in *The Valley of Dreams* and told her it was up to her to make the most of it. Chantelle would milk it. A television crew was coming to interview Rome later today about his role in the movie. She would stick to him like a limpet mine. Rome was Hollywood royalty so she'd probably have to sleep with him, though sleeping with him was a small price to pay for moving her career along.

Her sisters worked in a supermarket. Her mother was a siren, her father an unemployed drunk. Chantelle was tired of her family's lack of ambition. She was going to be different. Her first inkling she was a stunner was when her mother was out at bingo one night, and her father had tried to rape her. She'd got tired of his attention, her friends' fathers' stares. She ran away. When the social services caught up with her, she was living in a squat in Manchester. Because of her father, she'd refused to go home. They'd taken her into care. She hadn't spoken to her family since. At eighteen, she'd changed her name to Chantelle Carey and invented a new identity.

It was on her twentieth birthday that a friend suggested modeling. Stenson noticed her on the catwalk, liked what she saw, and signed her to the Stenson agency. In under a year, Tania had got Chantelle a small part in a Clay Thompson movie. Now, she figured that stardom almost beckoned.

As she left the cafeteria with Rome, she walked as close to him as physically possible. To an outsider, they looked an item, to the paparazzi, an ideal photo opportunity.

Rome knew what she was doing but didn't care. Morty encouraged him to surround himself with beautiful women, and, looking at Chantelle's stunning legs, Rome decided that she came well within that category. When the TV crew arrived, he didn't shoo her away.

Chantelle had been well trained by her mentor, Stenson. She knew all the right moves.

Rome would let her bask in the shadow of his glory—who was he to take away a young starlet's brief moment in the Paul Rome sun?

CHAPTER 26

The Hotel Glendow was an isolated country hotel. On first glance, it looked more like a businessmen's retreat than a traveler's stop off. It was off the beaten track. Machin couldn't fathom it. Why would Rivers stop here, rather than a Travelodge just off the motorway? The room Rivers had stayed in cost eighty-five pounds a night, which seemed rather excessive for a stopover. This hotel was the main thing about Rivers that Machin didn't like—that, and his general smugness. If you wanted to create an alibi to prove you didn't kill someone, then staying the night at Hotel Glendow in the middle of nowhere would be perfect.

Machin always looked for flaws in every statement a suspect gave her. She flashed her ID at a world-weary desk clerk. "I want to talk to any of the staff who were on duty last Monday night."

"I was on duty," the clerk said.

"I want to know about a guest, a Mr. Peter Rivers—"

"The sergeant already asked about him. I confirmed that he stayed the night." The clerk looked at the check-in book in front of him. "He arrived at three-fifteen, Monday afternoon, left eight o'clock Tuesday morning."

That confirmed to Machin what Roberts had told her, but Machin wanted more. She walked around talking to people. The barman remembered seeing him, the desk clerk remembered him asking for an alarm call—his alibi was flawless. Machin took a look around, there were fire exits and toilet windows, plenty of places that a man could slip out undetected. It was possible, but Twickenham was over a hundred miles from the hotel, to go there and kill Sparshot and also be seen around the hotel as Rivers had been seemed impossible.

At least two members of staff had remembered seeing Rivers's van parked by reception all evening. Nobody gave Machin anything to contradict Rivers's alibi.

After a couple of hours' inquiries, Machin was satisfied that Rivers's alibi was sound. She decided she'd gone far enough. It was a cut-and-dried case as far as Chief Inspector Ray Cowley, her boss, was concerned. To try and take this dead end any further would only lead to her boss's unnecessary wrath.

As she drove home on the motorway, her mind mulled everything over. The evidence said that Douglas killed Sparshot. Nothing Machin had seen at the Hotel Glendow contradicted that fact. Machin could see no other options. Everybody who'd known Tracy Sparshot had loved her. The only person who didn't, Peter Rivers, had an iron-clad alibi for the night of the murder.

Machin came to a decision. Her doubts were unfounded. Peter Rivers, as far as she could see, couldn't have murdered Sparshot—which left the cold hard facts. Douglas had murdered his lover.

CHAPTER 27

Dexter found it hard to concentrate on his work. The police hadn't been back about Tracy's murder. He had read in one of the dailies that Mr. John Douglas of Twickenham was being charged with the brutal murder of his girlfriend, Miss Tracy Sparshot, also of Twickenham. Dexter wasn't happy. The police had ruined all his plans. Now, there'd been so much police fuss around him his plans to wed Sam were in tatters. The police had ruined his mood, subdued his ardor. He didn't feel the same about Sam as he had before the police's interest in him.

Did he change his identity again? That was probably not a wise move with all the police attention. Douglas's trial would have to be long over before Dexter contemplated any kind of change. Change wasn't possible without the heightening in police interest that it would bring. DI Machin had been suspicious. Dexter had sensed that she didn't believe his story.

He didn't care whether she believed it or not. If she couldn't find a flaw in his alibi for the night of the murder, then it didn't matter what she thought.

He thought of Douglas. Douglas, the poor sucker. He would soon be convicted of a murder he didn't commit. For some reason, it gave Dexter a thrill to know that fact.

When Dexter arrived at Sam's hotel room, he was cold and indifferent. Sam sensed his mood swing and asked as he sat on a sofa, "What's wrong?"

Everything was wrong, he wanted to say. He thought of all the mental games that he'd have been able to play with this woman if the police hadn't arrived on the scene. The police's inevitable questions had ruined everything. He told her there was nothing wrong. She could see there was and pushed for an answer.

"There was a report in the paper about Tracy's murder trial—it's hard not to think about her at a time like this. I often think that, if I'd stayed with her, she'd never have met Douglas, and if she'd never met that guy, then she'd still be alive today."

Sam held Dexter lovingly, in an attempt to take away the pain. He reckoned that Sam was a woman who cared. "I'll help you over this," she promised.

No, she wouldn't, Dexter thought. He wanted a fresh start with a new woman. He'd decided he was tired of the small worlds of Sam and Tracy. Dexter wanted more. When he married this time, he wanted a depth of challenge he'd never encountered before. Sam wasn't that challenge—something he would make plain to her when he dumped her tonight. This time, Dexter was after love—a true love that would lead to the ultimate life experience with that love's murder. If only he could get a woman who depended on his every breath, every motion of hers in tune with his. Such a woman would lead to endless possibilities.

Sam could've been such a study, if only she had proved herself worthy.

Dexter decided now was as good a time as any to

break her illusions. "I think we should stop seeing each other for a while."

She looked completely shocked.

He decided things were going better than he had expected. "Tracy's murder has affected me more than I thought. A break of a few weeks might turn us around."

"Turn us around? What are you talking about, Peter?"

Dexter wandered over to the window, staring outside at the bland tarmac car park with military lined flowerbeds surrounding it. "I've made my decision, Sam. Please understand that, at this moment in my life, I need space."

Sam was annoyed. Perhaps this guy thought he was an astronaut or something. "If you don't want to see me, don't use Tracy's death as an excuse," she protested.

"It's not an excuse. It's how I feel." Dexter walked to the door and opened it.

"Where are you going? Please, stay and talk," she pleaded.

Dexter thought she was pathetic. *Talk?* In his experience, all women ever wanted to do was talk. No amount of talk was going to make him change his mind. "It's for the best," he said, staring into Sam's gray-green eyes.

Sam loved his smoldering hazel eyes, but she didn't know what else she could say.

One moment, Peter could be as romantic as a Latin lover, next as cold as Icelandic cod.

Peter Rivers was a mass of contradictions. She sadly concluded he was a man she could never hope to understand. Rivers left. Sam thought about running after him. The way he'd treated her tonight, dropping her without warning, she knew he wasn't worth it. None of the men who'd crossed over into her life in recent years were. Sam went to the bedroom and lay on the bed, trying to figure out what she'd done wrong. She didn't understand.

It was impossible to make him out. As she cried into her pillow, she decided there was one thing she did understand, and that was that Peter Rivers was a bastard. That, she knew for certain.

CHAPTER 28

The faded orange glow from the dimmed restaurant lights and the effect of drinking too much wine had made Debbie feel dizzy. Her head was spinning. She could see Rome's lips moving but couldn't understand what he was saying. All she could think about was getting back to her hotel room and crashing on her bed. She normally didn't drink. She didn't like the lack of control that being drunk brought with it. When she got this bad, sleep was the only answer.

"I need to go," she said, bashing her knee painfully on the table as she stood.

Rome didn't argue. He could see from Debbie's lack of coherency that she was drunk.

They'd drunk a couple of bottles of strong wine with the meal. Looking at Debbie, he could see that it was obviously one bottle too many. Rome found it cute. Back in LA, he was used to dating Hollywood sirens with hollow legs, so it made a change to go out with someone who couldn't hold their drink.

"I'll ring my driver." Rome did, and the car arrived a few minutes later. As they stepped out of the restaurant into the chilly night, a blinding white flash caused Debbie to shield her eyes.

How did the press always know where Rome was? she wondered. Rome drew them toward him like a cannonball to a magnet. He laughed as they stepped into the Limo, and they were quickly on their way.

"What's so funny?" Debbie asked.

"That'll be on the front page tomorrow: 'Star and co-star arm in arm, are there wedding bells?' You could write the headline yourself, Debbie."

Marriage to Paul Rome, what a prospect, Debbie thought. It was a prospect that most girls would jump at. Rome was fantastic looking, probably a great lay. With all the paparazzi complications and his constant womanizing, being married to him would turn into a nightmare. Women flocked to him, and he enjoyed it. He was easily tempted. The Paul Romes of this world weren't put on this planet to be faithful.

The car slid to a halt on the gravel outside the hotel's brilliant, well-lit reception. Debbie hurried from the car to the toilets where she was violently sick. She wiped her mouth with toilet tissue and flushed the toilet. As she washed her face at a sink, she wondered if her toilet escapade would've been glitzy enough for Hollywood.

A receptionist appeared. "Are you okay, Miss Duncan? Mr. Rome was worried about you."

"Tell him not to worry, that I'm going to be here a while. Please thank him for the lovely evening and tell him I'll see him tomorrow."

The receptionist left to relay the message and Debbie leaned against the sink with the room swaying, trying to get her balance.

This wasn't good. Maybe she should have asked Rome to wait so he could make sure she got to her room safely.

Much later, she stumbled out the toilet and somehow managed to make it to the lift.

Her blurred vision made it difficult. She pressed the button for her floor, and the lift jolted to life, almost causing her to be sick again. As the lift opened on her floor, she fell out of it into the corridor and banged her head on a nearby fire extinguisher. For a moment, while she lay on the floor, she was dazed and confused. As she tried to get up from her fall, strong hands grabbed her, lifted, and then carried her. Her Good Samaritan took her room key from her purse and opened her door. The Samaritan then gently laid her on the couch and wrapped her in a blanket. She'd seen the guy somewhere on the set. In the blurred confusion of her drunken state, she couldn't think where.

He asked about a doctor. Debbie was too tired to answer. She was fast asleep as Dexter stepped out the door and locked it by pulling it shut behind him. As usual, everything Dexter did was pre-planned, including slipping a Mickey into Duncan's drink at the restaurant. Dexter had followed them back to the hotel, lingered in the bar until a drunken Duncan had exited the toilet. Situations were easy to manipulate. Any woman, no matter how strong-willed, could be maneuvered into a position. Rome and Duncan had just been completely taken in, and they hadn't even realized it. Dexter, the Good Samaritan, the man who'd saved Debbie Duncan from coming to harm. In the morning, she'd have faint memories, memories enough to realize Dexter had come to her rescue. He smiled now as he lay on his bed, thinking of how well it had gone. Dexter smirked as he realized that today a new game had just begun.

CHAPTER 29

Debbie decided the dark sunglasses she was wearing weren't dark enough. She needed at least triple their current thickness. At the moment, she didn't care if she ever saw the harsh glare of the sun again.

"Are you ready, Debbie?" Thompson asked, striding around the cottage's kitchen, checking everything was set up right. He had long ago realized that a movie set was all about details. You got the details right, and everything else fell into place.

"I'm ready," Debbie said, removing her sunglasses. Even in the glare, she could still see that Rome was smiling mischievously.

"Are you feeling precious this morning, baby?" Rome joked.

"Not funny, Paul," Debbie said, sitting on a kitchen stool while Sam from makeup attended her.

Thompson waited patiently. Everything had to be right. Debbie's little talk in his trailer had made him stop drinking and funnel his attention back to the movie. She was a great actress, a fantastic person. He was sure that she'd get a nomination for best-supporting actress at the Oscars for this movie. After a half an hour and a couple of takes, the scene was successfully over.

"Great work," Thompson said, adjourning the morning's work for lunch. Debbie walked over. He knew what she was going to say and preempted it. "Don't worry, it'll be food, not booze."

Debbie left it at that. As she was leaving the cottage, she noticed the cameraman packing away his equipment. She hovered near him, and Dexter started. "I'm sorry," she said. "I thought you'd seen me." She studied his features and quickly came to a conclusion. "It was you who picked me up when I collapsed in the corridor last night, wasn't it? I'd like to thank you—"

"There's no need, Miss Duncan," Dexter interrupted. "Any decent bloke would've done the same."

"There is a need," Debbie insisted. "You saved me from no end of trouble."

"Like I said, there's really no need. We all get like that sometimes. You had a few too many drinks and fell over. We've all done it. Please don't worry about it."

She noted Dexter's stunning hazel eyes. His fuzzy hair was in a bit of a state, but it was nothing a hairdresser couldn't deal with. "What's your name?"

Debbie Duncan was asking his name, and Dexter joyously noted that Sam was looking on. "Peter Rivers."

Debbie patted him on the shoulder. "Well, don't be a stranger, Peter."

And with that, she was gone. Dexter watched her buttocks moving gracefully beneath her dress as she headed for the set canteen. She was stunning, not that ugly fake tan look that seemed to be a horrific modern fad with women. Duncan had grace, poise, and smooth porcelain skin that accentuated her looks. Sam walked past and gave Dexter an evil stare. There was plenty of spirit in Sam's eyes, immense promise at that moment—what a shame that she hadn't shown such a spirit of defiance before he'd dumped her.

He needed time to think. He grabbed a sandwich and sat alone at the edge of the set, watching meandering cows chewing dewy grass in a field. Things were getting confusing. Sam was still around, but now she was showing the spirit that he liked in his women. Debbie Duncan seemed to like him. Maybe it was enough for her to become his next specimen. He thought about Douglas's murder trial. The sooner Douglas was convicted, the better for everyone. As Dexter stood up to go back to work, he saw Duncan and Rome ambling back to the set together. He'd followed them when they went out for dinner yesterday.

Rome was worryingly close to Duncan—something Dexter needed to change, and the sooner, the better—if Debbie was to become his new specimen.

He wondered if they were an item. He'd seen the newspapers. There was a photo in the press of the two of them leaving the restaurant the night before, worrying rumors about them being a couple. Dexter tried not to think about it. Instead, he grabbed his camera and went back to work. This afternoon, they were filming an action scene. Rome was going to rescue a child from a burning building—Thompson knew how to grab the filmgoers' attention, though never in an over-the-top fashion like some of the other directors.

As Debbie ambled past Dexter, she smiled at him. He smiled back, staring into her cornflower-blue eyes with a look that he hoped said he was available. He noted Debbie didn't avert her gaze.

He went back to his hotel room at the end of the day, happier than he'd been in a long time. Tonight when he masturbated, he wouldn't see Tracy or Sam or Carol. Tonight the image locked in his mind would be Debbie Duncan, the movie star.

In a few days, he'd make a play for her, regardless of any risk involved. The chance of getting a specimen to work on like Debbie Duncan only happened once in a lifetime, and Dexter had no intention of letting all his maneuvering go to waste.

CHAPTER 30

Johnny Douglas stared at the prosecuting barrister, trying to remain calm and controlled as he answered from the witness box in the gleaming mahogany courtroom. "I don't care what the evidence says, I didn't kill Tracy Sparshot."

There were loud murmurs from the public gallery from where the Sparshot family viewed proceedings. An angry uncle shouted, "Murdering bastard!"

"Silence in court!" Judge Wilfred Holmes, presiding over the murder trial, shouted. "I want that gentleman removed from my courtroom."

A policeman moved in and escorted the uncle out. As he was led away, he shouted a few obscenities directed at Douglas.

Douglas tried to remain impassive. It was a hard mindset to achieve when all the world seemed to hate him. Judge Holmes told the jury to ignore the uncle's tirade. Douglas studied the jurors' faces and could tell, by the abhorrence lingering there, that they hadn't. As Douglas was led from the witness box at the end of his cross-examination, the Sparshot family stared at him evilly.

When he sat back with Dev, Dev tried reassuring him that no damage had been done. Douglas wasn't reassured. The jury looked inflexible, like people who'd already made their minds up. Douglas sat silent and brooding as he listened intently to the evidence against him. Nothing sounded good. Everything pointed to him being the murderer.

DI Machin took the stand. Her statements were clear, concise, and condemning.

She told the jury about Douglas's fingerprints all over the murder weapon then casually dismissed Dev's protests that Douglas picked up the knife to defend himself. The crown prosecutor was Veronica Vickers. Vickers was an extremely competent barrister. One look at her battle-hardened, age-lined face told you she was there to win and nothing else. Machin was confident that, with her in charge of the prosecution, Douglas would be found guilty.

"Why didn't Mr. Douglas run when the police arrived?" Dev asked Machin. "He must've heard the siren, seen the police approaching. If he was the murderer, don't you think he would've fled the scene before the police arrived?"

"I'm just a policewoman. I don't understand the mind of a murderer," Machin said calmly.

"I have to admit, Inspector, nor do I. However, if Mr. Douglas was the murderer, then surely he would have had time to flee the scene long before the police arrived." Dev paused to let the jury take in his remarks. "The fact that he didn't run was because he was an innocent man who had stumbled upon a murder, and because he was innocent, he saw the police as friends come to help him find his girlfriend's murderer."

Dev took a moment to look at the notes on the table in front of him. "Mr. Douglas always stayed at Tracy

Sparshot's flat on Monday nights," he stated. "The night in question, he arrived at the flat in a taxi at eight p.m. and discovered the body just as the police arrived. After just finding a girl you love brutally murdered in her living room, I'm not surprised that, when the police found Mr. Douglas, he was dazed and confused."

"I only deal in facts," DI Machin said. "When we examined the body, we found no signs of a struggle. Miss Sparshot was slumped over the sofa, the knife had pierced her lung through the front of her body. The fact that there wasn't a struggle makes us think that Miss Sparshot knew her attacker."

"Just because Miss Sparshot might've known her attacker doesn't mean her murderer was my client. You must surely have investigated others for the murder?" Dev asked, in desperation.

"With a murder, we always investigate everybody who's had recent contact with the victim."

Dev waited. He knew all the tricks. Just as Machin was starting to relax, thinking the question had passed, he said, "Which means, you think that there are other suspects in the Sparshot murder?"

"Any other suspects have been investigated and eliminated," Machin confirmed irritably.

Dev didn't say anymore. He'd planted a seed, created doubt. He picked up some notes and looked at them. "Let's move on to the phone call from a neighbor to the police. The call was from a mobile phone at just after eight o'clock. According to your records, the call lasted for about a minute. The caller said he was a neighbor, and that he could hear a woman screaming in Sparshot's flat. Did you find out who made that call, Inspector?"

Machin shifted uncomfortably on the stand. "No, we didn't. Regrettably, some members of the public don't want to get involved in criminal cases and refuse to leave their name."

"Isn't it more likely that the killer of Tracy Sparshot, someone the police already admit must have been someone she knew, rang the police in a bid to set up my client?"

Vickers bristled. "I object, your honor. We're here to deal in facts, not guesses from the defense."

"Prosecution has a point," Holmes said. "I want facts, not your personal supposition, Mr. Dev."

Dev apologized and moved on. "If the neighbor had nothing to hide, why didn't they just give their name and address?"

"Like I said, sometimes people don't want to get involved," Machin said.

Dev continued grilling Machin for a few more minutes, and then Vickers tried to repair some of the damage, pointing out facts. At the end of the session, when Vickers and Machin were seated outside the court on a bench, Machin asked, "How did I do?"

"He tore a few holes in the evidence, nothing too damaging."

"How good are our chances of conviction?"

"I'd say sixty-forty in our favor. You know how juries work, Inspector. Nothing is certain." Vickers looked at her watch, informed Machin she had to be somewhere else, and departed.

Machin sat and reflected. They were four days into the trial. By now most of the jury would've formed their opinion. She was still confident about their case, but slightly less than yesterday. She took her notebook out and stared at what she'd written down.

A witness had come forward—said they had seen a man rush out of Sparshot's flat and jump on a motorbike up the street close to the time of Sparshot's murder. The witness was an old guy walking his dog. He'd only come forward after seeing news about the trial on TV.

Machin now had some doubts about Douglas's guilt. With a motorbike, Rivers could've gone to Twickenham, killed Tracy Sparshot, and then returned to the hotel in time to be seen around the hotel bar late in the evening. Since she'd met Rivers, she'd sensed something about him. It was nothing tangible. Sometimes, a detective just had a feel for such things. One thing Machin knew for certain, Peter Rivers was going to get a more thorough investigation into his life. The hotel had convinced her. It was as if the smug git had gone out of his way by choosing that hotel to create an unbreakable alibi. Machin decided nothing in this world was unbreakable—something Peter Rivers was soon going to find out.

CHAPTER 31

"Thank you," a smiling Clay Thompson said, handing Debbie Duncan one of the largest bunches of flame red roses she'd ever seen. He'd arrived unexpectedly at her hotel room an hour after filming had ended for the day.

"What are they for?" a puzzled Debbie asked.

"You know what they're for," Thompson said, looking embarrassed. "Without you, I'd be an alcoholic."

Debbie put him out of his misery. "They're lovely, Clay, but you shouldn't have."

"Of course, I should."

Debbie didn't know what to say. Before Jodie's death, Thompson had flirted with her. She'd kept her distance because of Jodie. Now that Jodie was dead, did he think he could try again? "It's nice of you, Clay, but I don't want—"

"Don't say what you're going to," Thompson begged. "I didn't give you the flowers for romantic reasons. I gave you those flowers to thank a friend for pulling me through a difficult period of my life."

Debbie kissed him lightly on the cheek. "If that's the case, then it's a wonderful gesture."

Thompson had been on the brink of a breakdown, and Debbie had snapped him out of it. She was so good at getting inside you emotionally, he was already jealous of the guy who'd win Debbie's heart. There was so much in her for a man to admire. She was a woman who no man could ever dominate, Thompson reflected, and he then started to leave.

"Have a cup of coffee with me," Debbie said.

Thompson shook his head. He was outside, heading toward the lift, and Debbie followed. "Let's just leave it like this," he said then stepped into the pinging lift before Debbie had a chance to say anything else. As the lift went down, Debbie stared at the orange numbers signifying its downward path to the lobby.

When it was there, she went back to her room. She smelled the sweet, pungent aroma of roses and thought of the wonderful gesture of Thompson bringing them there.

Tonight had been the first time she'd seen Thompson off set since he'd returned after the funeral. It meant he was starting to wrestle back control of his life, get a grip on things. How far forward he'd gone tonight was impossible to tell. There was one positive about his visit. At least it seemed to enable him to understand what she felt for him, that they were never going to be lovers, just good friends.

She put the flowers in an oriental flower vase she found in one of the cupboards, displayed them on the window-ledge so they could bask in the sun's glory.

She thought about Jodie. There'd been so much to admire about her. Debbie wondered why all the good ones seemed to die young, while evil bitches went on to spit venom into their twilight years. Debbie sat by the window and tried to read over some of her lines. It was difficult, Thompson's visit had emotionally unnerved her.

She decided she couldn't concentrate, so she gave up, went down to the hotel bar, and ordered a machine-gun. As she sipped it, she thought the Cointreau was nice, but the white wine wasn't as chilled as she'd like it. It was as she drank her drink that she noticed Rivers sitting in a booth sipping beer nearby. She hadn't seen him much around the set since the night he saved her.

She boldly picked up her drink and joined him. "Hello, stranger."

Dexter looked up from the magazine he was studying. All his hours of patience had, at last, paid off. It had to look casual, never pre-planned.

"I didn't notice you," he said.

"I'm easy to miss," Debbie said.

"I wouldn't say that."

Debbie looked hard into his eyes. "Because you're a nice guy, you wouldn't," she decided.

They drank and talked. Debbie found him interesting. He was good-looking, but his mop of unkempt fuzzy hair spoiled it. "Why do you have your hair like that?" she asked. "It would look much better slicked back."

"My mum always said that hair and looks are irrelevant. It's what's inside a man that matters."

"Yes, of course, that, and his cock size."

Dexter nearly choked on his drink. A walrus-moustached barman clearing a nearby table suddenly became attentive until Debbie gave him a hostile stare. She laughed. Men were easy to shock. They liked to think they were the dominant sex. Debbie knew otherwise. She knew how to make them squirm. Dexter was becoming more intrigued. Debbie Duncan knew how to titillate. It made him realize how dull Tracy Sparshot had been. She'd been unworthy of Dexter's talents, needed to be killed so he could make a clean start. Death was the only way he could find release. Was he ready to start a new relationship? He'd had to give Samantha Jacobson up because of the worrying police presence. It didn't feel right starting again without having killed her.

Sometimes, you had to make exceptions. Dexter stared at the vibrant woman sitting next to him and quickly came to the conclusion that Debbie Duncan was a woman worth making an exception for. It had taken him nearly a week to arrange this supposed chance meeting. He'd watched and waited in this bar every night for her to make an appearance, like a spider waiting for a fly.

"If I get my hair cut would you let me take you out for a meal one night?" Dexter asked.

She playfully ruffled his hair. "Get it cut, and I'll think about it."

Debbie didn't commit but liked to leave men hanging.

"I'll get it cut tomorrow," Dexter promised. And he would. He'd do anything necessary to increase his chances of possessing her.

She gave him a sassy smile as she went back to her room. He watched her stunning body until the lift doors had shut and she'd disappeared from view.

This wasn't going to be easy, he concluded, though any woman worth possessing in life never was. The rewards for his patience of sitting in the bar night after night waiting were plainly there to see. He was certain this woman could be his. Debbie Duncan was the perfect specimen for a long-term project. Tonight showed that her resistance to his charms was wavering and he was almost ready to buy another ring, bring Miss Debbie Duncan into the family.

CHAPTER 32

J ust follow my instructions to the letter, Constable," Machin ordered a dithering Headley as he stepped through the stairwell door by the fire exit.

Constable Wayne Headley exited via the fire exit. DI Machin and DS Roberts followed him outside. Roberts had a stopwatch running, but he wasn't sure what they were doing. Machin had explained it, but what she wanted sounded more plausible on paper than it probably was in practice. Headley jogged over the hard gravel to the end of the drive, where a Yamaha motorbike was hidden behind a crumbling Beachwood gatepost. He mounted the Yamaha and then sped off up the road in the direction of the London road.

Roberts thought they were wasting their time. This was all just theory. They were working on a hunch of DI Machin's, a woman's intuition. They went back into the hotel to have dinner as there was nothing more they could do but wait until Headley returned in a few hours. In the dining room, they ate and talked.

"Why have you suddenly got doubts, ma'am?" Roberts asked.

"The witness said he saw a man get on a motorbike near Sparshot's flat at the time of the murder. A motorbike would fit nicely into the back of Rivers's van—a motorbike would explain why the van never left the car park all evening."

"People saw him around the hotel in the evening. Unless he's got a twin brother he couldn't be at Twickenham and here at the same time," Roberts said.

Machin finished a mouthful of salmon. "If you look at our notes, you'll see that nobody remembers seeing Rivers in the bar until after ten p.m. He finished his dinner at four-thirty p.m. There's a gap of over five hours between him finishing dinner and being seen in the bar."

"And you think he could've gone to Twickenham, committed the murder, and ridden back in that time."

"We'll find out when Headley returns," Machin suggested. "I told him to spend an hour at Sparshot's apartment before returning."

"I can't seem to find anything about Peter Rivers in any records dating back over three years," Roberts stated. "There's a lot of inconsistencies in the man."

"It's his alibi that bothers me. His alibi is almost faultless. It's as if the man has prepared an alibi for that particular night, as if he knows that the murder is going to happen."

For Roberts to be unable to find any past records for Rivers meant he must've changed names, she decided.

They finished their dinner and went and watched TV in the bar. When it got to nine-thirty p.m., Machin began to get twitchy. Then at nine-forty-two p.m., when they heard the sound of Headley's bike skid to a halt outside reception, she found that all her twitchiness had suddenly gone.

CHAPTER 33

It was a decent German white. Debbie sipped her wine slowly. She was attentively listening to Rivers talking about his life. "I don't know what got me into the movies," Dexter confessed. "When I left school, I had no idea what I wanted to do, stumbling from one disastrous job to another. I took a job with MTV as a messenger boy. A friend told me that cameramen made good money, so I studied to become one," he lied.

Dexter always exaggerated the truth and left out the part about Lomax and the trainee cameraman job he'd been sent to by the agency. He was creating the history that he thought his latest catch wanted to hear. Debbie was about working your way up on the ladder of life through hard work and ingenuity, something Dexter had shown he was capable of through his phony rise at MTV.

"I always knew what I wanted to be," Debbie said. "I wanted to be a pop star. When I was a teenager, my bedroom room wall was plastered with pictures of 'Take That.'"

Dexter laughed. Debbie was good company. She was such good company that he decided that today wasn't the day for starting his games. The games could wait until later. Today was charm day, a day to sit in this busy elegant restaurant among happy people wining and dining his latest girl.

They ate apple strudel and a moist gateau for dessert. Dexter ate his gateau slowly, savoring every minute of this wonderful evening. "When I found out I couldn't sing a note, I turned to acting. Any school play, you'd always find me in it. After school, I got involved in amateur dramatics. It was while playing in a production of Macbeth, I was lucky to have Clay Thompson discover me."

"The film's going to be big at the box office, Thompson's a great director."

Dexter knew how to press all the right buttons, knew that by praising Debbie's friend, Thompson, it would give him nothing but brownie points with her. He didn't say any more. He knew it was easy to sound nauseating if you overdid the praise. They finished their meal around eleven, and, in the taxi on the way back to the hotel, Dexter asked, "Could I see you another night?"

Debbie liked him but wasn't sure. He was good company and looked like a gorgeous hunk, now that he'd cut his hair. She stared into his dazzling eyes, which were his best attribute—model's eyes, so convincing that they made her agree to go out with him next week.

At the hotel, Dexter made no move to seduce her. Debbie was a woman who needed to be nurtured with constant reassurance. After raiding the mini bar in his room, he sat on a sagging armchair thinking about Debbie. In her room, she'd now be slipping off the figure-hugging catsuit she'd worn on their date. Firm breasts and a magnificent body—a body that, in the movie world, would lead to her becoming a legendary sex symbol. Thinking about her naked made sleep impossible.

Next date, he'd be more adventurous, show her a little more of what he was about.

Debbie Duncan was a new kind of specimen, the type of woman he had no experience of.

Filming had been suspended for a couple of days while Regal sorted out some technical problems, which meant that tomorrow Dexter had a day off. He opened a newspaper to take his mind off Debbie's body. On the fourth page was a report of the Douglas murder trial.

It said the jury was out trying to reach a verdict. Dexter angrily thumped his fist against the wall. Surely, it was just a case of rubber-stamping the guilty verdict.

He decided not to wait around the hotel like some lovesick puppy. He wanted to be in court when the verdict was read out, see the look of horror on Douglas's face when he realized he was going to prison for life for a murder he hadn't committed. The look was what Dexter lived for—the look when they realized what a fiend you were. It was a look that stripped away all the pretense in their life, a look that told you that they really did hate you. The look, in Douglas's case, would be one of fear and trepidation as he realized that his story wasn't going to have a happy ending.

CHAPTER 34

Dexter was relieved when he arrived for the afternoon court session to find that the jury was still out and hadn't returned a verdict. He was huddled at the back row of the public gallery, keeping well away from the Sparshot family. He also wanted to avoid the attention of DI Machin, who sat behind the Crown Prosecutor far below. If he'd known that Machin was going to be there, he wouldn't have come. There was something about Machin he didn't like. When he'd spoken to the woman, he could tell in her mannerisms and tone of voice that she had doubts about him regarding Sparshot's murder.

Dexter had tried to fight it, but the urge to see Douglas suffer was too strong, and he had to be in court today. The need to see Douglas's face when he was pronounced guilty outweighed everything. Dexter glanced at his watch. How much longer would they be out? How long did it take to convict a man with such a weight of evidence against him? He left the gallery. He didn't want to linger too long, in case Machin or the Sparshot family saw him. He'd check back intermittently. It couldn't go beyond today—he was sure the verdict would be today.

As he walked toward the exit, he saw Machin ahead of him. Dexter stepped behind a Romanesque pillar out of sight, and, when she stepped outside, he slipped into a nearby toilet. In a cubicle, he sat and waited, deciding it was safer to stay there for a while.

The courtroom was dangerous, intoxicating, and he loved it. Without this buzz, life would be nothing. He sat there for half an hour then cautiously returned to court. He couldn't see Machin and decided that busy police detectives with a heavy caseload didn't have the luxury of sitting around in court all day. At two o'clock, the judge returned and announced that the jury had come to a verdict. Dexter was relieved, relaxed, so much so that he sat admiring the court's architecture. Everything about the court was solemn, intimidating, exactly how a theater of justice should be.

Tension filled the air as the jury filed back into court. In front of him, he could see the Sparshot clan bristling with anticipation, as this was the moment that Douglas was going to get what was coming to him. The judge called for silence. "Would the jury's foreman stand and give the verdict."

The fat-faced foreman stood. Dexter could see beads of sweat running down his cheekbones.

"Have you reached a verdict?" the judge asked.

"Yes, your honor," the foreman said, his lined face etched with tension.

"Do you find the defendant guilty or not guilty of the charge of murder?"

"Not guilty, your honor."

Dexter's mind was filled with horror, as his brain was unable to register in his head the foreman's words. The way he had set Douglas up had left no room for doubt about his guilt. Dexter gripped the chair rest tightly when he saw the joyous smile on Douglas's face, as he embraced his barrister. This couldn't be happening, Dexter thought. There was no look of self-loathing, hopeless desolation, or fear on Douglas's face. The Sparshot family erupted in a rage of fury at the decision. When the shouting and swearing was at its worst, Dexter slipped out the courtroom and headed toward the exit. He thought about the setup, tried to figure out what he'd done wrong. He stood in the shadows as Douglas was bustled past the press by his family and friends into a waiting taxi. Press cameras flashed as cameramen bustled and jostled to get a better picture of the free man.

As the taxi departed, Dexter hurried away. At a zebra crossing, he glanced back at the court steps where he saw Machin and Vickers standing arguing. Machin was too engulfed in her argument to notice him. The police had come to court with an open-and-shut case, and now it was open again. Dexter knew the police now had no choice but to visit him again.

He caught a black cab back to his van he'd parked in the quiet leafy suburbs. He wanted no record of his visit to the capital, no record of a congestion charge or CCTV image of his van near the courtroom. He had now gone into stealth mode, his senses heightened by the sudden realization that once again he was the police's prey.

As he drove back to Wales, the lead-gray sky deposited large spools of water on his windscreen. The sky matched his somber mood. He didn't know where the verdict would leave him. Would he be the main suspect in the new police investigation that was now sure to follow? Dexter went back over his actions in the set-up and could see nothing that could lead the police to him. Any one of his murdered lovers could've led to this predicament he now found himself in. Up until now, he'd always been able to stay one step ahead. Was staying ahead of the police now still possible? If it wasn't for Debbie Duncan, he'd change his identity and move on. He had a problem—Debbie now made moving on impossible because she was special and worth the risk of staying around for. Dexter was confident the police had nothing. Whether they thought he'd killed Tracy or not didn't matter. If they couldn't prove it, none of it mattered. He would show them who the daddy was. Hadn't he always?

CHAPTER 35

The atmosphere in DI Machin's office was tense and electric. They'd been back from the court for an hour, and already she was getting flak from her superiors, who could not understand how she had bungled it.

"It has to be Rivers," she said, seated behind her desk opposite Roberts.

"I don't know, ma'am—"

"What's there to know? The court says that Douglas is innocent, and DCI Cowley says we need to come up with other suspects. What other suspects have we got apart from Rivers?" She didn't want to look any further than Rivers. He had had a volatile relationship with Sparshot, and, from what she could see, he was the only suspect worth a second look.

Roberts had checked into Rivers's past, Rivers was a mystery man. Roberts could find barely anything about him. He had a birth certificate, passport, driver's license—all the usual spiel. There was no record of a family. According to the social service records, he was an orphan and spent the first sixteen years of his life in an orphanage. The orphanage he spent his early life in had closed down seventeen years ago after a fire, so there was little chance of verifying whether any of that history was fake or true.

"I still think Douglas did it, ma'am."

Roberts thought they'd had enough evidence for a conviction. Nobody could understand the mind of a jury—totally unpredictable and plainly unreliable, considering today's verdict. It must've been the neighbor, the mysterious neighbor who had reported hearing screaming coming from Sparshot's flat. Because the neighbor hadn't identified himself, there was always a doubt in the jury's mind that the neighbor might've been the killer.

"You're not the only one, Sergeant. There are plenty of others who think that Douglas did it." But Machin wasn't one of them. Since Headley had made it to Twickenham and back on the motorbike before ten o'clock, and nobody at the hotel remembered seeing Rivers until then, she reckoned that Rivers was definitely in the frame.

She thought that Rivers's past was the key. If they could unlock the mysteries of his identity, learn what he'd been doing in the missing years they couldn't account for, then they might be closer to understanding the man.

"What do you want to do, ma'am?" Roberts asked. He genuinely didn't know where to go with this.

Machin knew. "I want you to search deeper into his past, there must be something." She would also get someone to tail Rivers for a few days, keep an eye on his movements.

Roberts left to carry out his task. She did some paperwork and made sure that everything was up to scratch in all her cases. Mistakes came back to haunt you. Bureaucracy killed police investigations. All the time that Machin wasted in the office was valuable time lost on the street. When she was in the middle of reading through a report on a spate of rapes in the capital, Roberts knocked and entered. He was holding an open newspaper which he laid down on the desk in front of Machin.

"Look at the story on Douglas's trial, ma'am." She looked, started to read.

Roberts stopped her. "Not the story, look at the picture."

Machin looked at the picture. It was a picture of a triumphant Douglas leaving court with Dev after the not guilty verdict. She didn't understand. "What's wrong with the picture, Roberts?"

"Look at the people in the background."

Machin looked and suddenly saw. In the distance watching Douglas's departure, she could see the face of Peter Rivers. Rivers had been at Douglas's murder trial. It could be curiosity, a chance to see the face of Sparshot's killer. She didn't think so. She suspected a more sinister motive. She thought it was the action of a killer making sure that the man, he'd set up for a murder he'd committed was found guilty.

Roberts went back to his work. Machin sat back in her high-backed leather chair and shut her eyes a moment, lost in thought. Where did Rivers going to the trial leave them? No closer to finding evidence against him than before. Again she reflected that Rivers's past was the key. People who had no secrets were easy to follow on their life's path.

Until they discovered what he had been doing in those missing years, they had no hope of uncovering Rivers's personality. He was unusual. According to Sparshot's brother, he was weird. Weird enough for brutal murder? Machin didn't know, but one thing was certain, she intended to find out.

CHAPTER 36

"Who's that cameraman over there?" Rome asked Thompson, pointing at Rivers as they sat and talked in a quiet moment off set during filming.

Thompson wasn't sure whether Rome meant Eddie or Rivers.

"The good-looking guy with the short, gelled hair," Rome pressed.

"That's Peter Rivers—he's good—he used to work for MTV."

Rome already knew he was good. He had seen how good he was by the way Rivers had wormed his way into Debbie's life and was now dating her. Rome noted that Rivers had already taken Debbie out a couple of times, and Rome was jealous. He wanted Rivers off the movie.

"There's something about him. I don't like him, and I want him replaced."

Thompson knew all about the Hollywood stars' power games. Some directors catered to their whims. Thompson wasn't one of them.

"Sorry, Paul, he's good at his job and understands

what I'm trying to do—you'll have to live with him."

Rome thought about arguing. He quickly decided that arguing with a man like Thompson, so respected in the business, would be pointless. He strode back to his trailer, giving Rivers an angry glare in passing. When Rome was gone, Dexter smiled. This whole situation was getting better—Paul Rome, superstar, jealous of little old Dexter. It meant that the time he'd been dating Debbie was fast becoming the most precious moments of his life.

He was feeling cocky and reassured. A couple more dates with Debbie and then he'd be ready to move on to stage two. Stage two was the attempt to control her. It couldn't be done quickly. Controlling a woman meant saying a few devious remarks at a chosen moment or dropping hints of a deep mental scar, never to be revealed to anybody other than a true love. Dexter knew all the mental levers to pull, and, with Debbie Duncan, he was about to pull them. Within a month, he'd have her worshipping at the temple of Peter Rivers, and, in the process, he'd soon remove her stubborn streak. Dexter was unraveling some cable near Thompson's trailer when Thompson asked him to step inside his trailer for a minute.

"Is something wrong, Mr. Thompson?" Dexter asked.

"I'm not sure. Have you had a run-in with Paul Rome?"

"Of course not," Dexter said, his face registering surprise, "I've barely spoken to him since filming began."

Thompson didn't understand Rome's request. There had to be a reason why Rome wanted Rivers removed, but if there was, Thompson couldn't see it. He told Rivers to forget their conversation and dismissed him. Dexter left the trailer, happier than he'd been in a long time. He knew the reason why Rome had spoken out against him.

Macho man, Rome, had a soft spot for Debbie, and he looked at Dexter as opposition. If he couldn't have Debbie, then no cameraman was going to, was obviously Rome's reasoning.

It was time for Dexter to turn his attention to Paul Rome. Upsetting a star like him was the ultimate turn-on. In the future, whenever he kissed Debbie, he'd make sure that Rome was around to see it. The mental torture he could subject the superstar to was exquisite.

When they started filming again, Dexter moved his camera forward a few inches closer to Rome. He could see him perspiring and smiled. Sweat, little piggy, sweat, you'll be doing a lot more sweating before I've finished with you, Dexter thought.

Rome mucked up his lines several times, Dexter smirked to himself, his face hidden behind the camera lens. After several takes, the scene finally ended, and Debbie came over to speak to him. Dexter laughed and joked with her, making sure that Rome took it in.

Thompson saw it all. He pretended to be reading the script in his chair, but he was really watching Rome's reaction to Rivers' and Debbie's interplay. Rome's reaction was like that of a jealous, spoiled child. Rome shouted at a makeup girl as she accidentally caught his eye with her powder brush. Thompson could see he was going to have to do something. The way Rome was acting meant that the calm, steady performance that Thompson was striving for from Rome in the film wouldn't happen.

When filming finished for the day, Thompson was going to order Rome to his trailer for a frank talk. As far as Thompson was concerned, there was no room for personal problems on a Regal film set. Everything else paled into insignificance when the welfare of the film was at stake.

All that mattered to Thompson during filming was the movie.

Dexter asked Debbie out, and she gleefully accepted. Rome's face went a hideous shade of scarlet, Dexter noted cheerfully. He looked hard into Debbie's playful eyes and could almost see her used up and on the brink a few months from now. Dexter knew how to wipe out a woman's soul. When their mind had gone, and you were left with a blithering wreck, then Dexter got tired of them, and it was time to kill. Death would be either slow or quick, the manner of it depending on how much pleasure the specimen had given him. In Debbie's case, he saw endless hours of pleasure in front of him as his mental torture made her steadily unwind. Because of the joy she'd give him, he wouldn't make her suffer at the end. A knife to the jugular, a gunshot to the heart, the choices for a quick kill were endless.

He ignored such thoughts and decided to spend the rest of the afternoon trying to wind Rome up. Rome had no idea what he was dealing with. He would never have had anybody play with his mind like Dexter could. Dexter was the best. The problem was nobody on this movie set knew it yet. Paul Rome and Debbie Duncan were about to find out how fucked up they could become at the hands of an expert. Dexter was the ultimate drug, alas, Debbie Duncan was soon to find out it was a drug of the lethal variety.

CHAPTER 37

Huis schooling doesn't exist," Roberts stated coldly.
"All records of it were lost in the orphanage
fire." He sipped his coffee, rustling through the
papers strewn across his desk looking for further info.

"So we know absolutely nothing about his life in the
nineties," Machin said, seated next to him.

"The first thing we definitely know about him is his
application for a passport two years ago," Roberts read
off one of his sheets.

"What about dental records?" Machin asked.

"There's a dentist he's recently started to go to for
check-ups. I've been on to the dentist. He'll send over
what he's got on him later today."

Bureaucracy, everything was later, Machin thought.
First, you had to get legal proceedings in motion to force
the dentist to turn over private, confidential patient information.

The tempo of an investigation usually ground to a
halt, locked in some complex bureaucratic web. Every
morsel of information they'd gleaned from Rivers's past
had been hard won. All the facts about him seemed to be

strategically placed to create maximum confusion.

It was the orphanage that had done it for her—the orphanage with a fire that wiped out all its records was the perfect past for someone who wanted to change their identity. She was in no doubt that Rivers had changed his name. What he'd changed it from was the big question—a question that needed answering if they were ever going to make progress in unmasking his identity.

Roberts couldn't see the need for any of this. As far as he was concerned, Douglas was the murderer. They just hadn't been able to prove it sufficiently enough to leave the jury with no doubts about his guilt. Machin was driving the investigation in this new direction. Both of them knew that, if they didn't find anything soon on Rivers, then the case would be history. There were other cases to be investigated, others that didn't seem to end in a dead end like this murder now seemed to.

Machin wondered what to do. Did she bring in Rivers for questioning? Did she alert Rivers to the fact that she was onto him? Once he knew she was still pursuing him, he'd clam up, produce a lawyer who'd show how little evidence Machin really had. Defense lawyers were the backbone of a democracy's justice system but, to Machin, they would always be an interfering pain in the arse.

Roberts went back to his computer. Machin sat drumming her thin fingers on the hard desk. What was she going to do? She'd never felt as irritated about a case. *'If you care, you have to feel,'* her old boss had once told her in one of his frequent dissertations on police life before he'd retired. She had already interviewed some of the MTV staff that had worked with Rivers before he'd switched to Regal, they all said he was a loner, none of them seemed to know much about him, nobody knew about his past.

She was called to DSI Cowley's office for a progress report. Cowley was a stickler for details, wanted to know everything as soon as Machin knew it. Being regularly called to his office got in the way of an investigation, something a bureaucrat like Cowley never seemed to understand. He was the force's golden boy who never put a foot wrong in the promotional stakes that had moved him smoothly and swiftly up the career ladder. His political know-how and the damage that knowledge could do to Machin's career made it necessary for her to keep on the right side of him. The problems with the Sparshot murder trial, and the bad press the force had received because of it, had meant that Cowley had been forced to get involved.

As Machin entered the boss's office, she noticed a rough-bearded man in a blue pinstripe suit sitting near Cowley's desk. "This is Trevor Higgins, Customs and Excise," Cowley said, "He needs our help."

He went on to explain in his usual banal manner about a DVD smuggling racket and the murder of a local tradesman, suspected of handling the illegal DVDs. She was relieved that he wasn't asking about the Sparshot murder investigation. She listened to Cowley's baritone voice drone on. She noticed Higgins fidgeting, his deep-set eyes trying to look attentive. Machin dutifully hung on Cowley's every word. This distraction was going to buy her time, divert her boss's attention from this new murder while she went after Rivers—or that was what she hoped.

CHAPTER 38

Dexter, standing at the dark oak bar, finished his cold lager then went to the toilet. It was early evening, and the hotel was quiet and tranquil on a weeknight. Dexter found the hotel's deep pastel blue décor and the soft classical music piped through the lobby's sound system extremely relaxing. He urinated as music gently serenaded him through the toilet's speakers. As Dexter washed his hands, Paul Rome entered. He smiled at Rome, but instead of going to the toilet, Rome just stood and stared at Dexter.

"I want a word with you," Rome said.

Dexter acted indifferently. "I'm listening," he said, wiping his hands on a scented towel.

"I'm giving you a warning, keep away from Debbie!" Rome ordered.

Dexter gave Rome his best infuriating smile. "Why should I? We get on well, she likes me. What I'm trying to say, Mr. Rome, is, fuck off!"

Dexter started to leave, Rome swung a punch at him. It was uncontrolled and angry. Dexter knocked it aside then butted Rome on the bridge of his nose, Rome stumbled, banged his head on the bleach smelling sink as he crumpled to the damp tiled floor. Rome was dazed but conscious. Dexter left him lying there and went back to the bar. Five minutes later a disheveled looking Rome exited the toilets, Dexter found it hard to suppress his mirth.

"You'll pay for this, Rivers," Rome threatened in a passing shot as he headed to the lift to go back to his room.

Dexter smiled, sat there, and waited until Debbie arrived. He ordered her a drink, and then they sat in a quiet booth. He brought up the subject of Rome. "I met Paul Rome in the toilet a short while ago—he wanted a word with me."

"Peter, you've hardly spoken to him since we started filming. What would Paul want with you?"

Dexter paused. He didn't want to sound too willing. The secret to having a damning impact was to be reluctant and not seem to want to tell tales. "I'd rather not say. I'm not one to tell tales, Debbie. You'd better ask him about it."

Debbie was irritated. She didn't want a boyfriend who hid things from her. "Tell me what happened."

Dexter told her. Debbie couldn't mask her anger as the story unfolded. "I didn't want to tell you I'd got into a fight with him. I thought it'd be wiser to let the matter drop.

Rome is a big star, I'm just the little guy, and nobody will believe me when I tell them that he started it."

"I believe you." She stood up. "Wait here, I'm going to have a word with Paul Rome."

Debbie stormed off to the lift. Dexter watched the floor lights flicker on the lift panel until the lift reached Rome's floor. It was safer this way. After Debbie chewed Rome out, Dexter was certain he wouldn't try and get him fired. If they sacked him, Dexter would make sure the media got hold of the story. He smiled. There was no danger of them sacking him. With co-star Debbie Duncan in his corner, Dexter was safe.

Ten minutes later, Debbie returned. "Paul Rome won't bother you again."

Dexter hoped not. The last thing he needed at the moment was Rome drawing attention to him. They left for dinner, and Debbie became more relaxed when they arrived at a classy French restaurant. The anger she had shown when Rome had interfered in her life showed astronomical potential. This was a woman who wouldn't be broken easily, a challenge. They picked at their meals as neither of them was really hungry. Dexter could sense that Debbie was still seething after her confrontation. He slipped his hand gently into hers across the table. "I love being with you, Debbie. Can I date you when the filming is over?"

"Let me think about it," Debbie said.

Dexter was stunned. The bitch should've been honored that he'd asked.

Instead of ecstasy, he'd been met with indifference. He felt stupid. He'd asked too early. He should've anticipated the situation and asked her at a more appropriate moment.

He went to the toilet, smashed his knuckles against the flower-patterned wall tiles.

He broke a couple of tiles and a trickle of blood appeared along his knuckle line. He washed his hand and then dabbed it with a towel. How could the bitch not be enthusiastic about him wanting to make their relationship more permanent? She'd shown all the signs of acquiescence, the way she'd fought in his corner with Rome. His misjudgment was his own fault. He should've realized how strong-willed she was, how much harder it was going to be to manipulate her than the others.

After he'd stemmed the flow of blood from his knuckles, he returned to his seat, slipping his bloodied hand out of sight beneath the table. He listened to her conversation, barely took in any of it. The only thoughts he had for her now were evil. The bitch had to pay for her affront. Of that, he was certain. He hadn't decided how to achieve his goal, but the only way to achieve it was to first control her.

Before the police turned their attention to him for the Sparshot murder, the wisest move would be to change identity and flit. At the moment, they had nothing, a fact that could quickly change if they looked in the right direction. As he and Debbie stood to leave at the end of the meal, she saw his cut knuckle.

"Peter, your hand's bleeding."

"I banged it on the toilet door when it swung back on me. I thought I'd just bruised it."

"When we get back to the hotel, I'll bandage it," Debbie insisted.

As they drove back to the hotel in the taxi, Dexter stared out of the window at the dark, uncompromising night. Now was the time to control his fury. The last time he'd felt this black, he'd ended up killing Carol. After Debbie bandaged his hand and left, he took the knife he had hidden in his underwear drawer out. He stared at it, imagined plunging it deep into Debbie's heart, tearing open ventricles. He put the knife away. It was far too easy, he decided. After tonight's affront, the bitch had to suffer mentally before he killed her. Dexter had the worrying feeling that the clock was ticking at an alarming rate concerning the time he had left with Debbie. Machin was closing in, he was sure. The hatred of him he'd sensed from the inspector would ensure she'd maximize her efforts to prove he was a murderer.

Would he be allowed one last hurrah? Dexter didn't know. He just knew that Debbie Duncan wasn't a woman he could easily walk away from.

CHAPTER 39

Machin and Roberts sat in police pathologist, Ryan Stewart's office. Stewart had been checking Peter Rivers's dental records for the last week. He said he'd found something.

"I didn't think you'd find anything," Machin said.

"Everybody has different teeth, Detective. They're like a person's fingerprints—you just have to find the right match." Stewart studied the folders he'd brought with him, his age-lined face a picture of concentration. "The records you gave me for Peter Rivers are the same as for this man, Trevor Slater."

"We have to be certain," Roberts said.

Stewart looked slightly perturbed that Roberts doubted him. He rubbed his salt-and-pepper beard, locked in a moment's consideration. "I'm certain, Sergeant, that Peter Rivers and Trevor Slater are one and the same guy."

That was good enough for Machin. Stewart was superb at his job and wouldn't confirm this unless he was certain. "How did you make the match?" she asked.

"It was in the institution's files. Slater had a couple

of fillings while he was incarcerated there. Slater spent six years at the Park Manor Institute in Hertfordshire. It's not an institution for the criminally insane. This institution is more a soft option for the mentally disturbed."

Slater, alias Rivers, had made a mistake. He'd had work done on his teeth while on location for MTV in Oslo and, to claim the money back, he'd had to submit the dental records as proof of treatment. The Norwegian records were excellent, and there was no doubt that Slater and Rivers were the same man. It wasn't evidence. All the dental records did was show that Rivers had changed his name.

The reason for the name change on paper looked obvious. Former mental institution inmates weren't the first pick for employers. Machin sent Roberts off to get everything he could on Slater. It was a new angle, and at least it gave Roberts something to make his investigational juices salivate.

"What's this all about?" Stewart asked.

Machin explained, adding, "I think Rivers killed Tracy Sparshot. The problem is I can't prove it."

Thinking and proving were two different things. The fact that Rivers had spent time in an institution was at least evidence that he wasn't playing with a full deck. It made it possible that he was a brutal killer, and the possibility that Rivers was the murderer was all Machin could ask at this stage of the investigation.

At last, she had something to confront Rivers with. It was a revelation that might achieve something, and it might at least wipe the smug look from the seemingly untouchable man's face. There were many questions that needed answering, the first one being what had Slater been doing since leaving the institution? The new name meant they, at last, had something to work with. Roberts at least had a name that might open a few more doors.

Machin shook Stewart's hand and left. As they drove back to her office in her car, she felt they were at last within touching distance of unlocking the mystery that was Peter Rivers.

CHAPTER 40

Rome was seething. He paced up and down the room angrily, ruminating about the night's events. He wasn't used to being treated like this, assaulted by the hired help. Who did the frigging guy think he was? In Rome's mind, he was a street fighter and thought that Rivers had got lucky with a sucker head-butt. It wouldn't happen again, he would make sure of it.

Rome slumped in an armchair and pressed an ice-pack hard onto his nose. The physical pain would soon subside, but it was the mental humiliation that would take much longer. When Debbie had marched to his room and chewed him out, his humiliation had well and truly been complete.

He sipped a glass of whiskey trying to deaden the pain. It wasn't going to be a good morning on set tomorrow. Makeup would have their work cut out trying to cover the break. He thought about how to explain it—he'd have to say that he'd had a fall. Rivers seemed to be taking some kind of vindictive pleasure in the mental anguish he was causing Rome. When he filmed Rome, he seemed to thrust the camera closer than necessary. It was subtle, so much so that if Rome complained to Thompson about it, Rome was sure that he would say that he was imagining it.

Debbie was a wonderful woman, far too good for a rat like Rivers. Rome had never felt this way about a woman before. There'd been his teenage engagement to Molly Campbell back in the Bronx—puppy love, more teenage infatuation than love. It hadn't lasted. Over the years, none of Rome's relationships had ever lasted. The thing that had caused the easy-going Molly to blow and throw his engagement ring in the Hudson was when she'd come home early from her mum's and found Rome in bed with her best friend. He often wondered what happened to Molly. Could any man ever forget their first love? In his leap to the stratosphere, he had never forgotten Molly. Even for superstars it was an undeniable fact that no man ever forgot their first love.

He sipped the last of his whiskey, snatched up the phone, and dialed long distance.

The phone rang for a couple of minutes until it was finally answered by a tired-sounding Morty Schultz. When Schultz realized it was Rome, his star client, he was suddenly awake and interested. "How's the movie going?"

"I've got a problem." Rome cut straight to the point. "I need your help."

Rome explained, didn't leave anything out. Schultz was a fantastic agent, providing you were straight with him. "The fight in the toilet was the limit," he grumbled.

Schultz laughed. "You're only upset about it because you lost, Paul."

"The guy is causing me trouble, Morty."

"Have you told Thompson you want him removed?"

"I told him. Thompson says he's good behind the lens and won't get rid of him."

Schultz knew about Thompson's reputation, about him not pandering to the wishes of movie stars. They wouldn't get anywhere with Thompson—his refusal to let Rome fly back to America to film the beer commercial during the filming of *The Valley of Dreams* had proved this. Schultz knew there was only one way of getting rid of Rivers and that was the Morty Schultz way. He would somehow do it. Rome was his meal ticket. Schultz's percentage for getting Rome the best deals averaged out at about five million dollars a year.

Rome was one meal ticket he couldn't afford to let go.

"If you want him gone, he'll go, Paul."

Rome didn't like it when Schultz talked in this dark, menacing tone. Schultz had some dodgy connections in and out of the movie business. "I don't want him dead, Morty," Rome emphasized.

Schultz laughed. "You've been watching too many De Niro movies. You don't want to believe all those stories that you hear about me. Those connections of mine in Little Italy existed a long time ago. If this guy is a hassle and you want him removed, I'll find a way of doing it."

Rome's childhood had been riddled with Mafioso. If they weren't from the organized mob that hung around his former neighborhood, they were streetwise punks out to make a fast buck. "Just do it, Morty."

Schultz said he would and then hung up. Rome hadn't a clue how he was going to do it. He didn't want to know. The less he knew about Schultz's shenanigans the better. Whatever needed to be done had to be done quickly. Rome couldn't take Rivers's presence on the set much longer. He thought about Debbie in that bastard's arms. Debbie, a wonderful English rose, a woman Rome would be proud to marry. This was an experience Rome wasn't used to.

He respected Debbie because she wasn't interested in sucking up to him to further her career. On the other hand, how could she be interested in a lowlife like Peter Rivers when Paul Rome, the movie star, was interested in her? Debbie was a complete contradiction, unlike any other woman he'd met. What made her so appealing was that she always seemed tantalizingly just out of his reach. He knew he could never fully hope to own Debbie Duncan like he could other women. All he knew for certain was that he was in love with her and that love was the rawest of all human emotions—a feeling he'd never encountered before.

CHAPTER 41

It was their fourth date, and after returning to the hotel from the pub, they stopped outside of Debbie's room in the lush, carpeted corridor.

After his fight with Rome a few days ago, Dexter sensed that Debbie was still rattled by the confrontation. He offered yet another apology. "I'm sorry about the other day. I should've walked out before it came to blows."

Debbie kissed him lightly on the cheek. "It wasn't your fault, Peter."

Debbie thought Rivers was a lovely man. She'd thought about this moment all day.

They'd been seeing each other for a couple of weeks. He was easy to get along with, and she decided that now was definitely the right time. Dexter looked surprised when she said, "You can come in if you want."

Dexter wanted. They entered her room. He noticed Debbie's clothes scattered about the place, but masked his irritation—her untidiness was going to be the first thing he changed.

There was a picture of a golden-haired brat perched on a table, did Debbie have a daughter? A single woman with a child was the sum of all men's fears. "Who's she?" he asked, lifting the picture for closer inspection.

Debbie smiled. "That's my niece, Emma. She's a lovely girl. I take her picture with me everywhere I go."

"She's beautiful," Dexter said. He thought what a wonderful specimen Emma would be when she was older. Only when she was older. Dexter wasn't one of those monsters who preyed on kids.

"We think so," Debbie said, then moved closer so Dexter had no illusions as to why he was in here. Debbie was tired of playing games.

Dexter pulled her toward him. He kissed her hard on her soft lips, and he could feel his manliness thrusting forward. Debbie laughed as her long slender fingers undid his trousers and released his erect phallus from its prison. Her lively hands worked his penis. It had been a while, and Debbie didn't believe in the endless monotony of one-night stands. She fumbled in the bedside drawer, handed him a condom. Dexter slipped it over his penis and penetrated deep inside her. Debbie was a willing demanding lover. Her body moved in an easy, gentle rhythm. She knew what she wanted, and she wasn't scared to show it.

As they lay in bed afterward, Dexter concluded sex with Debbie had been the best sex of his life. He went to the bathroom, studied his naked reflection in the full-length mirror. He didn't like what he saw. His skin looked pasty, his muscles flabby, no longer could he forgo the luxury of avoiding the gym. On a nearby stool, he saw her patterned Chinese dressing gown lying across it. He removed the gown's cord and wound it tightly around his hands. It was strong and pliable, he pulled it tight—it was the perfect weapon for strangulation and murder.

He thought about choking the life out of her, seeing that look of horror and desolation on her face as she suddenly realized that he was as far from being the one as he could get. He waited until his calmness returned and put the dressing gown cord back. When he returned to the bedroom, Debbie's smile was full of luster and promise. At dawn, when she lay sleeping, Dexter slipped back to his room. Things had gone better than he'd expected.

He lay on his bed, listening to birds summoning the dawn with a chorus from a chestnut tree outside his window. Last night was the turning point when Dexter and the specimen had at last become lovers. He'd sleep with her a few more times before he moved on to the next phase. Until he completely controlled her, he could never be happy. Debbie wasn't a woman who would surrender her soul without a fight. It was going to take time, careful manipulation. He could feel he was within touching distance, ever closer to her subservience.

His phallus was rock hard again as he thought about the pleasure of domination that awaited. He went to the bathroom, had to relieve the agony. When he masturbated, he'd think of Debbie's eyes pleading for mercy, at the moment he thought about the mental kill, he'd ejaculate, as that was the way it had always been.

CHAPTER 42

The British Airways 747 landed at three in the morning. Milkman time, the ideal time whereby a tired-looking businessman could slip through unnoticed. Keefer casually strolled through customs. With his short haircut and brown pinstripe suit, he was just another businessman clutching a travel bag. Today Keefer was in London. He was paid ten grand a week by the client for his services. Today that client, Morty Schultz, had told him to fly to England. Schultz had paid for first class, Schultz had class, unlike some of Keefer's other penny-pinching employers.

Keefer took a cab to a Travelodge. In England, he found that the Travelodge gave you a level of anonymity that most other hotels couldn't muster. He'd get what he wanted in England. Schultz had deposited Keefer's working fund into his bank account. He'd purchase the cocaine from Russel later in the day. No risk, all the jobs he did these days were jobs without risk. His big-money-mercenary days were gone. These days he had to rely on recommendations from colleagues and friends.

He didn't have a family, had too many secrets to get

emotionally involved in a relationship. Kids weren't an option, women had never interested him. He'd learned quickly in his youth in Nam and the opportunities in Saigon with male prostitutes, that he was gay. He'd make time while in England to try the Brighton gay scene. Life was full of surprises, Keefer tried to make each day vibrant and alive. Surprise was the key. The Viet Cong sniper had been surprised when Keefer had ambushed him in the tunnels of Cu Chi. It was Keefer's first kill in the tunnels. Even now, he still pictured the look of hate and horror as the sniper realized that, as far as he was concerned, his revolution was over. Only brave men died in those tunnels, dying with only fear, a handgun, and a torch as company. A grenade had ripped Keefer's leg tendons to pieces in a battle, and he'd been pensioned out the army soon after. His brief escapades as a mercenary hadn't been successful, which meant that he'd needed a new avenue for his talents.

Fear was what drove America. There were a lot of frightened people in the country, people willing to pay vast sums to allow the security that would enable them to sleep safely at night. Keefer had learned about security, weapons, industrial espionage, financial fraud—if you wanted to work for clients who paid good money, you had to be the best.

At eleven, he left his hotel and went into London. In Oxford Street, the air was choking, the streets claustrophobic. He went from shop to shop, gathering supplies and equipment. Only the best would suffice, a fact he proved by buying an overpriced glossy map book of South Wales. In his room, he laid all the equipment out on his bed before carefully packing it into the sports holdall. He rang Russel on his mobile and arranged to pick up the coke just before he set off for Wales. The rest of the day he'd spend in his room, fine-tuning his plans.

The Schultz job was a big job for him. Success in setting up Rivers would lead to recommendations from Schultz to his friends and mean plenty of jobs in the future. The secrecy and discretion that Keefer guaranteed was a vital commodity to wealthy clients in this ever-more-ruthless world. Keefer would meet Russel after dark then drive to Wales and be there before the morning. Sometimes Keefer's existence was bland and soulless. To live it, you had to be mentally strong. Strength was a commodity he had in great abundance.

He could look after himself, he had to. If he didn't, then who else would?

CHAPTER 43

There were five more important scenes to film, which Thompson had saved until the end, as he wanted to make sure every detail was perfect. These were what movie making was all about—the moments he lived for. He examined the set from every camera angle, Camera Two was too close, was almost on top of Rome. Thompson told Rivers to move it back.

It hadn't been the first time he'd noticed Rivers crowding Rome, and Thompson was starting to wonder if there was any credence to Rome's moaning about Rivers.

Thompson waited until Rivers was in position then walked over to him.

When everybody else was out of earshot, he said, "Leave him alone, Peter. If you mess this scene up for me because of your rift with Rome, you'll never work on any of my pictures again."

"I've done nothing wrong. It's Rome who needs to control his jealousy," Dexter replied.

"Do I look stupid, Peter? I can see what you're doing. You are trying to wind Rome up because he likes Debbie."

Dexter didn't argue. He could see Thompson was too aware of the situation. "If Rome leaves me and Debbie alone, I'll leave him alone."

Thompson left it there. As far as he could see, it was obvious a jealous Rome wasn't going to leave them alone. If it didn't affect the filming, then it wasn't Thompson's problem. It was only if their feud interfered with filming, that he'd come down hard on both of them. The result of moving Rivers's camera back meant the next scene was much better.

At an afternoon tea break, Thompson noted the atmosphere among the film crew was more relaxed. He didn't lecture Rome and Rivers further, didn't want to act like an ogre.

Filming ended at six without any further drama. In two weeks, the filming would be over. With Jodie's murder in the middle of it, this film had been the hardest film that he had ever made. With the constant demands of filming, he'd had no time to grieve—time that, if he didn't get eventually, would end with him having a nervous breakdown.

After he'd edited the movie, he was going to go away somewhere quiet on his own. Since Jodie's death, everything seemed to be closing in on him.

He sat in his trailer sipping a beer. Rome knocked and entered. "Can I see you a moment, Clay?" he asked.

"If you're here to moan about Rivers—"

"No, Clay, I've come to apologize. My behavior in the last couple of weeks has been appalling, particularly in light of your recent loss. You'll get no more trouble from me on this movie."

Thompson was surprised. This wasn't the Paul Rome he'd read about in the papers. "I don't know what's gone on with you and Debbie. I don't want to know. All I know is that you're a great actor, Paul, and it would be a shame to taint our time on this film with only memories of your feud with Rivers."

"I promise you, Clay, I won't argue with Rivers again in this movie. In fact, I'll go out of my way to avoid him."

Rome smiled and then left. In the interests of the film, Thompson wanted to believe him. He watched Rome walk slowly back to his limo then locked the trailer door. He could understand a man losing himself over Debbie. She was special, a woman worth fighting over. Rivers was a lucky man. Debbie had chosen him over a host of guys who'd tried it on with her. Rivers was bland and normal, compared to Paul Rome and himself.

Perhaps that was what she saw in him. Maybe she was fed up with the movie egotists and wanted something normal.

Thompson picked up a bottle of Scotch and fingered the gold top. He'd been drinking a lot lately, and Debbie had lectured him recently about it. When Debbie spoke, he tended to listen. She was a good friend—she'd proved that by looking out for him after Jodie died. He put the bottle down and went to lie down. He had a feeling that Debbie had crossed his path in life for a reason, and that reason was his salvation from booze and to stop him from spiraling into the depths of despair.

CHAPTER 44

Keefer sat reading a newspaper in the hotel lobby. When you were over sixty, nobody noticed you. From his position seated just to the side of the entrance, he could see anybody who exited or entered. Just before seven, a group of film people arrived back from the end of the day's filming. Keefer looked at Rivers's photo wedged inside the newspaper and was pleased when Rivers finally walked into the lobby, laughing and joking with Debbie Duncan.

He watched them step into the lift then go up to their rooms. Keefer had gotten a computer-hacker friend to hack into the hotel computer, so Keefer already knew that Rivers was in room twenty-nine.

Keefer limped to the hotel cafeteria. His bad leg was giving him gip in the damp climate. He sat drinking coffee. Tomorrow he'd make his move and would plant the coke soon after Rivers left for the day's filming. After it was planted, he'd call the police, tell them he was staying at the hotel and that he'd seen Rivers exchange money for drugs with a drug dealer in the hotel's toilets. It wasn't foolproof, but it would be enough to remove Rivers from the film set. At breakfast, he'd follow Rivers to the cafeteria, replace the sugar bowl on Rivers's breakfast table with one laced with coke. Keefer was thorough in his work and had found out that Rivers took sugar with his morning coffee. Once the cocaine was in Rivers's bloodstream, then they had him. He'd deny it, the police would search his room, and they'd find the coke. Rivers, thinking he had nothing to hide, would agree to a blood test. It was then they'd find the coke in his bloodstream, compelling evidence that recently he'd taken cocaine.

Keefer hated himself sometimes. He finished his coffee and headed back to his room. His mind was on the job, so much so that he ignored the smile of a nice-looking porter.

Keefer's days of rough trade ended in the brothels of Saigon. In his hotel room, he lay on the fresh-smelling bed, thinking of tomorrow. He taped the drugs underneath a drawer in his dresser, no point in taking chances. He'd plant the coke the moment Rivers had left for the film set. As he drifted off to sleep, he wanted to dream of beautiful boys and warm sun-kissed memories. Alas, such dreams were a rare luxury for Nam veterans. He knew that, once again, his mind would drift back to the infernal tunnels. Part of his teenage soul, along with most of his friends, had been lost in the dark, unforgiving world of the tunnels of Cu Chi.

CHAPTER 45

octor Duggan's office was cold and sterile. There were no pictures of family or trophies from sporting success, Duggan was obviously a man that believed a psychiatrist's office should be bland but functional, Machin concluded.

"What sort of a patient was he?" Machin asked him as she sat down.

Duggan adjusted his large-framed spectacles, which she decided made his face look like an owl. "It was a long time ago, Inspector, I'm the only member of staff at the institution left from back then, and I can barely remember anything."

"Whatever you can tell me about him will be helpful," she prodded.

Duggan opened up some computer files. He showed her a picture of Trevor Slater on his console screen. The picture was that of a younger version of Peter Rivers.

"What I remember about Slater is limited. There are some things that stand out. We did some intelligence tests—I remember that he scored highly. Also, when I did my patient interviews, I never seemed to be able to get inside his head. There always seemed to be a barrier blocking me from breaking in."

"Do you think his psychiatric condition could make him capable of murder?" Machin pressed.

"Has he murdered someone?" a ruffled-looking Duggan asked.

"That's what I'm here to find out."

"Everybody is capable of murder in the right circumstances," Duggan suggested.

"I'm not talking about lashing out after finding a man in bed with your wife. I'm talking about clinical, calculated, murder. What I think Slater has done wasn't a random act, I think he murdered a former lover and tried to set her current boyfriend up for the murder. Is he capable of that, Doctor Duggan?"

She didn't want to divulge too much—in her experience the less you said and the more you listened, the more you found out.

Duggan thought of the young man that he'd encountered all those years ago, and the memories flooded back. He remembered how uncomfortable he felt in Slater's presence. There was something definitely not right about the boy. He tried to give an honest assessment from memory. "Yes, Inspector, I think Slater could be capable of that."

Duggan told Machin and Roberts everything he could remember. It wasn't much, but it was enough. They had a name for Rivers, and they'd uncovered his institution history.

Now that they had a name, they could check into what Slater had done when he left the institution. At last, they had something to investigate, a name to confront Rivers with when they interviewed him. That interview would be soon. Machin's team would find out everything they could on Slater first. The more you had at an interview, the better to surprise the suspect, and she was sure the first time that she addressed him as Trevor Slater, Rivers was going to be very surprised.

CHAPTER 46

Johnny Douglas sat in his favorite armchair in his flat, staring out the open window at the fading brown leaves on a rustling willow tree. He'd been housebound for days. He wasn't eating, was finding sleep difficult. He was worried that the Sparshot family might still think he murdered Tracy and be looking for retribution. He'd already decided that he needed to make a clean start, would have to move. His flat was in a slummy area of Twickenham. It was too small for a family, barely big enough for a single person. He'd already concluded that it was going to be hard to get rid of. He'd thought about renting it to his sister, the talking had ended when Kirsty found one of the many threatening letters in a drawer that Douglas had received since his acquittal.

He'd told the police. They hadn't done much other than pay the Sparshot family a visit and warn them off. It hadn't been reassuring. Douglas was living in terror. In all his thirty-four years, he had never felt so vulnerable and alone. Once the press interest died, so would the police's interest in keeping an eye on him and making sure the Sparshots stayed away.

The phone rang for the fifth time that morning, Douglas didn't answer—it was either the Sparshots ringing up to threaten more mayhem or the busybodies of the press asking for yet another comment.

Douglas was exhausted with it all. Tracy had been murdered, he'd been wrongly accused of that murder, and, still, after the court had pronounced his innocence, he was being hounded by Tracy's family and the press. His solicitor had advised him not to say anything—he was off work with stress and on medication. The last thing he needed after his ordeal was to be back at work facing accusing colleagues' stares. His damnation was evident when a news report just after the trial had a police spokesman stating that the police had no further leads. It was tantamount to saying that the police thought that Douglas did it, but couldn't prove it.

Douglas knew he hadn't killed her. He hadn't killed her, but she was dead. That led him to Peter Rivers. Tracy had spoken about Rivers's weirdness. It was Douglas who'd persuaded Tracy to leave him. From what he knew, he concluded that Rivers was the murderer.

Who else but Rivers would know enough about Tracy to easily gain access to her apartment? Who else but Rivers would want to set up Douglas? Rivers probably blamed Douglas for the breakup. It was a motive for this madness. Rivers's ironclad alibi for the night of the murder had persuaded the police otherwise. Douglas didn't have to work within the police's constrictions. Tracy had told him that Rivers was a film cameraman and that he was always away on location. During his internment before the trial, Douglas had racked his brain, searching for answers.

Tracy had no enemies. The only oddness in her life had been Rivers. Douglas flung a handful of clean clothes and toiletries into a sports holdall. He needed to get away.

He made some inquiries. The girl on the switchboard at Regal Films had told him that the camera crew was on location in South Wales, filming a movie. As he checked everything over one last time, he wondered if one of Tracy's relatives was waiting outside. At midnight, he moved. He left via the back door and by climbing over a high garden wall. He went to an all-night café down by the river to wait for his train. As he sat with his tepid coffee and stale tasting doughnut, he reflected on what lay ahead.

If Rivers was the murderer, he'd been clever in setting Douglas up and was not a man to be underestimated. What Douglas was going to do or say when he confronted Rivers he had no idea. The one thing he knew for certain was that it was going to be messy. Whatever happened, it was necessary to act. Tracy's ghost cried out for revenge. Ever since the trial, Douglas had learned one thing. He'd learned that the stigma of suspected guilt hung all around him and that the only way he could ever lead a normal life again was to prove his innocence.

CHAPTER 47

The lock was easy. Keefer had been taught by the best. Any skill was accessible in America, the land of the brave and the free. All you needed was to know where to look and have the right amount of greenbacks to pay for it. As he gently shut the door behind him, he wedged a chair under the door handle. He didn't want some snooping chambermaid disturbing him while he looked for a place to plant the drugs. The room was unusually tidy for a single man. The white tiled bathroom was small and compact, and, in the air, Keefer could smell the whiff of flowery aftershave. The bathroom cabinet was too obvious, he gave up the bathroom and entered the bedroom—the bedroom looked more promising. There wasn't much furniture, he decided upon a bedside cabinet, taped the drugs to the underside of a drawer. Keefer retraced his steps. When planting something, you had to think how a detective would think. Nothing could be too obvious. If it was too neat, the police immediately became suspicious.

When he arrived back in his room, he sat down to think. The sting had to be right. If he rang the police before Rivers came back off the set, it would reek of a set-up. He'd ring the police in the evening after the film crew returned. This was the part he hated, the waiting was always frustrating. He didn't close his eyes and try and sleep as sleep meant the torture of awful Nam memories. Could you ever forget lost comrades? Could you ever put past nightmares behind you? Keefer suspected not. Keefer knew he'd never find answers within himself without the aid of a psychiatrist's couch. Although seeing a psychiatrist could be his salvation, it could also be his death knell. All those secrets he had to tell, waiting to be unwound if he let a shrink inside his head. It meant that a shrink was never going to be the answer, because all those secrets, along with all his demons, were best left undisturbed.

CHAPTER 48

Douglas had traced the Regal film location to a small village called Rockall, North East of Ebbw Vale. He'd tried a few local hotels to find where the film crew was staying.

On his fourth call of the morning, he spoke to a receptionist at the 'Winchelsea Hotel,' and told her he was Peter Rivers, one of the film crew, and wanted to know if a package had arrived for him. When the receptionist said it hadn't, but promised to keep an eye out for it, he thanked her and hung up.

Douglas smiled. The receptionist hadn't said that the film crew wasn't staying there. At last, he had a starting point. Douglas got a taxi to the hotel and checked-in under the name Mark Hamlyn. Because of the film crew's demands, it was one of only three rooms left.

In his room, he laid out his bag of goodies: handcuffs, mace spray, a gag, some hair curling-tongs—they were a special surprise for the bastard.

The replica gun was an ace up his sleeve he was relying on to intimidate Rivers into a confession. He'd started his preparations, had now reached the point where he either went back to Twickenham or followed this through to its messy conclusion. As he lay on the bed in his room, he thought of the last time that Tracy had lain beside him. He couldn't chase away her ghost, as every conscious moment he was racked by guilt. He hadn't been there when Tracy needed him. He thought back to the weeks before when he'd been twitchy, thinking someone was following him. Could that someone have been Rivers?

He'd told DI Machin all about this when she'd questioned him. Machin had seemed doubtful of his guilt, and yet she'd still persisted with the trial. Douglas saw no reason to trust the police. It was better if he took matters into his own hands. He stared at the alarm clock on the dresser—it read, two-oh-seven. It was early—the film crew was out for the day.

Tonight was the night for retribution. He had to know the truth, regardless of the consequences. There was no time to wait. Tracy's ghost wouldn't let him. Her image was omnipresent, and each time she pointed an accusing finger in Douglas's dreams she moaned about inactivity in the pursuit of her killer. She was pointing it in his direction.

CHAPTER 49

Machin and Roberts studied the computer console screen. There were big gaps, anomalies, breaks in time that neither detective could explain. Slater/Rivers's National Insurance records were erratic. For a few years they were non-existent. When he explained the gaps on official forms, he always put the same explanation, and that was that he'd been traveling. Machin was starting to wonder where Rivers had traveled to? Judging by the few vague records Roberts had procured, she decided it must've been the dark side of the moon, looking at how sketchy and indecipherable they were.

Machin sighed. "It's easy to see how people defraud the DHSS, Roberts."

Roberts didn't disagree. He'd been involved in a couple of DHSS fraud cases and couldn't believe the levels of deceit the fraudsters would stoop to. "He's an elusive bastard, ma'am."

So elusive, Machin concluded, that their check back on his past was getting them nowhere. "He seems to disappear at random—there's no structure to his identity."

"A man trying to hide something," Roberts said.

"I agree, but what?" she asked. She was certain that Rivers had killed Sparshot. After their talk with Doctor Duggan at the institute, in her eyes, there was no room for doubt.

"We've got no evidence, ma'am. All we proved was that Rivers could've got to Twickenham and then ridden back to his hotel before ten p.m. on the night of the murder, but we can't prove that he actually made that trip."

Machin leaned back in her high-backed chair. "The problem with all that I'm seeing here, Roberts, is that it shows a man who doesn't stay around anywhere for long, which makes me think that maybe he's not going to be around in his current identity for much longer either. Any inkling that we're onto him or the slightest whiff that we're closing in, and he'll be gone."

"At the moment, he's still filming the Thompson movie in Wales."

Machin laughed. "I wouldn't go much on that, looking at the gaps in his past, I doubt if he's the type of man who worries about abandoning everything."

"He's been working for MTV and Regal for three years. He seems to like his current vocation," Roberts added.

Three years was a blip in time in most people's working lives. But looking at Rivers's erratic employment record, in his case, it seemed a substantial investment. Machin had already checked with Regal, filming in Wales would be over by the end of the week.

She made a decision. "We need to bring Rivers in to talk about his past. Maybe the mention of Slater might unnerve him and open some doors."

Roberts wasn't convinced. In their previous interviews with Rivers, he'd seemed a cool customer who didn't scare easily. But they had no choice. Machin was being pressured by DSI Cowley, who, in turn, was being criticized by the Press. He wanted an arrest for Sparshot's murder fast. Machin rang Cowley and asked to see him. After arranging an immediate meeting, she stood up to leave.

"Do you want the locals to interview him?" Roberts asked.

"Of course not, I need to be with him in the interview room every minute of the time we're allowed to hold him."

Roberts didn't argue. When she made her mind up about something, nothing moved her. It meant another drive to Wales, another evening not at home with his wife.

They'd be leaving immediately as Machin wanted to move fast. She liked to move an investigation along. Roberts tried to watch and learn. Over the years, he'd noted how fantastic an investigator she was—the master of ringing a confession out of a suspect in the interview room.

Roberts got their things together for the trip while Machin went to see Cowley.

He seemed on edge when she sat opposite him. "Sorry to bother you, sir, I wanted to give you an update."

"Don't be sorry," Cowley said. He liked to be kept up-to-date with developments in a case and also hated nasty surprises.

"I'm going to Wales to talk to Rivers again."

Cowley leaned forward in his chair with heightened interest. "Why?"

Machin explained what they'd discovered. Cowley's expression remained unmoved as she talked. "I need to talk to him, sir. His behavior is odd."

"I've taken a lot of flak with the press on our failure to convict Douglas, Sarah. If you go after Rivers, I need something positive to come out of it." His gray-green eyes stared hard at her. "You need to be certain he's the murderer, Sarah."

Machin was certain, or as certain as her intuition could be. When she left Cowley, she didn't feel reassured. He was the perfect politician—he gave her his support, but only supported her so far. As she drove to Wales with Roberts, she thought about her conversation with Cowley. He'd emphasized the importance of her being right and had hinted at the implications to her career if she was wrong.

She was under no illusions. If she failed to convict Rivers of Sparshot's murder, hopes of any future promotions were over.

CHAPTER 50

Can we go for dinner straight after filming?" Rivers asked Debbie during a break.

As Rome walked past, Rivers kissed Debbie on the lips.

"Let's see how I feel later," Debbie said as she pulled away after the kiss.

Rome's face flushed as he stomped off toward the canteen. Rivers smiled, thinking about the discomfort he'd caused. "There's something I need to talk about—"

"Let's talk at dinner," Debbie said, kissing him on the cheek, and then headed over to see Thompson.

Rivers was irritated. The filming was coming to a conclusion at the end of the week, so he needed to force the issue. If he was going to make Debbie suffer, he had to get a toe-hold in her life. Rivers went back to his work. The time to talk to Debbie wasn't around the set. He needed her alone—alone in a situation he knew he could control. Debbie sat on a bench talking to Thompson.

"I know what he wants to talk about, Clay. He wants to talk about our relationship. I am sure he wants it to continue after the film."

"And you don't."

"I've just started in movies. I need time to discover myself, find my way. I don't need a relationship." Debbie didn't want to become the little wife at home. She wanted to forge a career, a career that would dazzle the world.

"You need to tell him it's over, and quickly."

Thompson was right. Debbie did need to tell Peter quickly. There was something about Peter. He was lovely most of the time, then there were moments, brief moments when you glimpsed a dark side to his character. It was only briefly. As quickly as it arrived, it was gone.

Debbie couldn't get close to him. He'd never tell her stories of his past or the odd childhood reminiscing that would help break through his intensity. Debbie was a woman of depth and emotion, it helped her with her acting, she didn't want to be with a man who couldn't reciprocate and be open with their feelings.

Dexter stared at her through his camera lens the rest of the afternoon. He knew he still had so much to learn about women. Debbie was a new kind of woman for him, a great leap forward in that learning curve. If he could tame her before he killed her, what a wonder that would be. Possession and power were all that mattered. The Apache Indians knew of the benefits for mind and body of torturing a man to death to possess their power. Dexter had studied the Apache rituals in great detail. He found that every woman he killed increased his own mental power. The killing of strong-willed Debbie would lift his personal power into the stratosphere.

He'd realized that without the power surge he achieved through taking a woman's life his life would be meaningless. His sister Becky had slipped, the police post-mortem had said. She'd been playing too near the cliff edge.

He didn't regret Becky, the look on her face when

he'd pushed her, a delectable mix of surprise and shock.

As Dexter adjusted his camera lens for a close-up shot, he focused on Debbie's face.

The makeup girls had made her face look porcelain white perfection. Dexter watched every line and contour awestruck, realizing that killing her would be the greatest moment of his life.

All the men wanted her, but none could have her because she was Dexter's. Rome looked awkward and cumbersome in her presence, stumbling on his lines. It took five takes for a scene that should've taken one. Dexter focused on Rome's face with his camera, feeling the ecstasy of the moment as he had the privilege, with Rome's bumbling performance, of seeing the moment when Rome's threat to Dexter's opposition crumbled before him.

Tonight was going to be Dexter's coronation. She was the one, the one woman that would eclipse everything that had gone before. Dexter, the trailblazer, was going to go to places in the mind with Debbie that he'd never gone before. He needed her commitment. He had to have it. Her commitment would be the culmination of everything he'd strived for over the years. The depth of her commitment would determine how long she lived or died.

CHAPTER 51

Douglas awoke to the shrieking sound of the radio alarm clock. He switched it off.

Stunned from his deep sleep, it took a moment for his mind to adjust. The flower-patterned wallpaper baffled him, the lumpy bed so unlike his Tempo mattress at home wasn't helping his back problems. The banality of the decor quickly reminded him that he was in a hotel room.

He focused his tired blurry eyes on the bold luminous digits of the radio alarm clock, the clock read four-thirty-three. He stumbled out of bed, showered, and changed, wanting to be fresh and alert for what awaited him tonight. He didn't know when Regal would finish filming for the day, but he had a feeling it would be soon. There was no time to waste. He zipped up his holdall, and everything was ready. The only vital component missing from his preparations was Rivers. Douglas sat by his window, overlooking the car park, and watched and waited. An hour later when the film crew returned from the set, he was alarmed to see that Rivers was not amongst them.

As the evening wore on, Douglas realized that Rivers had gone out somewhere. This wasn't how he'd visualized events unfolding. In his dreams, by now, he would have already tortured a confession out of Rivers and be on his way to the police. He looked at his shaking hand and wondered if he had the nerve to do what he had to. He decided he couldn't just sit here waiting. He went down to the bar, which was empty apart from an old couple sitting at a table and a baggy-eyed barman. Douglas got a beer and then sat in a position where he could see the lobby entrance. Harry Connick Junior tinkled over the sound system as Douglas noted that the film crew was having dinner in the hotel restaurant. All Douglas could do was to wait and watch until Rivers returned. He had the feeling that this was going to be the longest wait of his life.

CHAPTER 52

Keefer was bored waiting. He'd been sitting in the restaurant when the film crew descended for their evening meal. Rivers wasn't amongst them. He was sure Rivers would've been back by now, and didn't like it when one of his plans hit a snag. He couldn't ring the police until Rivers had been back at the hotel for a while. It was getting complicated, not going to plan, but Keefer, as usual, was ready to adapt to each new twist and turn.

He left the restaurant and went to the bar. The bar was empty apart from an old couple and a young guy nursing a beer in the corner. He ordered a Jack Daniels and sat on a bar stool watching the entrance door to reception. He had to know the moment Rivers entered the hotel. Keefer needed Rivers to be seen around the hotel a while before he called the police.

The planted drugs would be suspect as evidence, if Rivers hadn't been to his room all day.

Rivers's defense would rightfully claim the drugs were planted. The coke from the laced sugar earlier in the day would say otherwise, a police blood test would confirm coke in Rivers's bloodstream and show he was a drug user.

As time ticked on, Keefer found himself getting more irritated, there were only a few days left of filming. Schultz would want Rivers thrown off the set today. He went outside for a walk in the hotel grounds, a cold east wind whipped a chill through his thin summer jacket as the watery sun was setting and thick mist began to descend. Britain was a cold, damp land that played havoc with Keefer's rheumatism. He didn't like where this was going. Rivers was a hard man to corner, dangerously unpredictable when setting up a sting.

Keefer now regretted the fact that the speed of the operation meant that he hadn't had enough time for checking on Rivers's movements beforehand.

When he went back to the hotel bar the film crew had descended after dinner and the quiet banality of earlier was now replaced by noise and bustle. It felt much better, more of a cloak to his activities. He had to keep his wits about him. He'd now revised his plan, too.

Once Rivers arrived, he'd make the call to the police shortly after. Keefer wouldn't panic, panicking got you nowhere in his sordid profession. He bided his time by going over and over the set up in his mind, checking for loopholes. Keefer knew there weren't any as he was a man who prided himself on his professionalism. It was why he was the best, it was why he intended remaining so by satisfying Schultz, his client over here.

CHAPTER 53

Debbie's warm smile and sparkling eyes lit up the dark dimly lit romantic corner of the aromatic Italian restaurant. The pencil-moustached waiter poured the wine and departed.

It left Dexter and Debbie alone, alone to talk and discuss their future. Dexter tried to rest his hand on Debbie's across the table, but noted she quickly pulled her hand away. It was only a little thing, barely noticeable to the average Joe. To Dexter, who'd spent a lifetime studying every nuance of women, it was something major.

As they ate parmesan topped tomato soup for a starter Debbie said, "This is nice, Peter."

Nice! It was more than fucking nice! Dexter thought. He'd studied the inflated prices on the menu when he'd ordered. Fish and chips from a bag were nice, for the prices these guys were charging this meal would have to be magnificent.

"I wanted it to be nice. It's probably the last meal we'll have down here before the filming ends."

Debbie was finding it hard to hold his gaze. She liked the guy—the sex was good, but not good enough to drop her film career for. "Where do you go after this?" she asked.

"There's talk of a documentary, somewhere in South Africa."

"Thompson says he might use me in a movie next year," Debbie mentioned.

"He'll use you, believe me. When *The Valley of Dreams* comes out, your awesome performance will mean you're inundated with job offers." Dexter wasn't lying. From behind the camera, you saw everything good or bad on a movie, and Debbie fit squarely into the category of good.

Debbie could see this wasn't going to be easy. Peter really liked her, supporting her in her work. It was becoming more and more obvious to Debbie that he regarded them as a couple. They talked and ate, slowly beginning to unwind from the stresses of the day's filming. It was as they were starting their dessert that he said it. He told her he wanted to see more of her after the movie, wanted them to become an item. Debbie rested her elbows on the tablecloth, looking softly into his penetrating hazel eyes. "This is what I was worried about, Peter, I knew you wanted more."

Dexter wanted much more than more. Dexter needed to possess her, claim his trophy in front of Paul Rome. "Why would you be worried when we get on so well together?"

Dexter was finding it hard to mask the irritation in his voice.

"It's no reflection on you, Peter. You're a smashing guy, good fun." She paused and could see his face was suddenly full of loathing. "At this moment in time, with my career about to take off, I don't want to get involved with anybody in a permanent relationship."

Dexter sat stunned and silent. Rejection wasn't an

option. He held himself together. "I won't get in the way of your career. I'm adaptable, I can be what you want me to be."

What had the bitch made him say? He'd lost control, needed to reassert himself. Before he had a chance, Debbie said, "We both know that isn't fair, and it wouldn't work. You're looking for someone permanent in your life, Peter, and I'm not, it's as simple as that."

Simple! This was far from bloody simple. Dexter could feel his flesh crawl. The bitch had been using him, had seen him as a bit of fun while on location. This wasn't how things happened to Dexter in life. She'd given him few options. Her actions meant that he had no choice now but to kill her quickly. It would be disappointing, to forego her soul's possession for a quick kill. Alas, regrettably, this now seemed his only option. His head was swirling, she was talking, but he wasn't really listening. He stared at the veins on her smooth white neck while she waffled on about all the usual spiel about staying friends and not losing touch. He wondered how quickly those veins could be severed with an Italian dinner knife?

He slipped on her shiny leather coat by the cloakroom as the taxi arrived. He stared at her swanlike neck looking for the perfect angle of incision for a quick kill. It was her own fault that she was soon going to die badly. He admired her perfect legs for one last time as she stepped into the taxi. Debbie had magnificent legs, legs that any woman would die for.

She was soon going to die for them—them and a lot more. She would die of her own choice, for it was she who'd signed her own death warrant the moment she had chosen to leave him. As Dexter sat in the seat next to her, inside his coat pocket he could feel the razor-sharp Italian dining knife prodding against his side. As Debbie lapsed into silence on the drive back to the hotel, Dexter wasn't bothered. Tonight all the talking had been done. He knew exactly where he stood. He contemplated how, when he slit her throat with the knife, Debbie was going to suffer the longest silence of them all.

CHAPTER 54

It would've been difficult even in daylight with the sat nav playing up. But in the swirling mist and darkness, finding their way to the hotel around the rambling county roads was proving almost impossible. Machin was losing her cool. "Where the hell are we, Roberts?"

Roberts nervously rapped his fingers on the dashboard. She could become a diva when angered. "We should be there in under an hour, ma'am. I think that sign back there said Rockall was five miles away."

Machin glared at the sign. She could barely make out its outline let alone what was written on it. "Just get us there, Roberts," she snapped.

Roberts drove as quickly as the visibility allowed. When they reached Rockall, they stopped by an orange-yellow street light to get their bearings. Machin was irritated by the delay. When they got to the hotel, they'd immediately take Rivers in for questioning at a local police station. They'd try and unnerve him. Rivers had tried to remain anonymous, portray himself as a good citizen trying to earn an honest living, but she could see through it.

The conversation she'd had with Doctor Duggan had made her see through it. She couldn't wait to see the expression on the creep's face when she confronted him with what they knew.

She would push Rivers hard and go to the limits of what was permissible in a taped interview.

When they finally arrived at the hotel's reception desk, Machin took the lead. She discreetly showed her badge to Gary, the young sandy-haired receptionist. They stepped into a back office, and, after an explanation, Machin got Rivers's room number. Gary gave her a pass key to enter Rivers's room with. As they rode up in the lift to what could soon end in a violent confrontation, Roberts could feel the tension.

"Do you think he'll get violent?" Roberts asked.

"You heard Duggan, he reckoned he was capable of murder. Who knows how a desperate murderer is going to react when cornered by the police."

Badly, Roberts reckoned. He knew as the junior detective it was going to be him who had to tackle Rivers if there was trouble. When they arrived at Rivers's room they knocked a couple of times. When there was no answer they let themselves in. Machin was relieved when she saw that all Rivers's belongings were still there, at least it showed he hadn't done a runner. Now that she had established that Rivers was coming back they went back to the lobby and waited for him. She smiled as she nursed a coffee and sat waiting for Rivers's imminent return, whatever happened tonight she decided one thing was certain, he had an infinitesimal amount of questions to answer, and that his days were numbered.

CHAPTER 55

Douglas had noted Machin and Roberts's arrival, had grabbed a newspaper off a nearby table, and pretended to read it, his face now sheltered from their view. When they went into the reception office with the young receptionist, Douglas seized the opportunity to rush to the stairwell. With the detectives hanging around the hotel, sitting in the bar waiting for Rivers where they might see him was no longer an option. In the stairwell he hurried up the stairs to the third floor, the floor of Rivers's room. He opened the landing door slightly and peered through the crack, looking along the landing at the door to Rivers's room.

The detectives had been the last people that Douglas had expected to see. It couldn't be coincidence. The only reason for them to be here was to see Rivers. It put all his plans in turmoil. When they stepped out of the lift a few minutes later and used a pass key to enter Rivers's room, there could be no further doubts as to why they were here.

Douglas had no other option but to abandon his plan. As he quietly shut the door and was about to leave, he felt the cold steel barrel of a handgun pressing firmly at the nape of his neck.

"Keep quiet and do as you're told, buster," Keefer said. Douglas was told to carry on up the stairwell to the top of the building where a door led onto the roof.

"If you're robbing me, I haven't got any money," Douglas said. His statement was met with silence. "Really, I haven't."

As they stood on the roof, Keefer quickly frisked Douglas. When he found nothing, he then opened the bag that Douglas had been carrying and found the replica gun, handcuffs, gag and tongs. "Going to a bondage convention, buddy?" Keefer asked sarcastically. When his comment was met with silence, he said, "You're standing in a stairwell spying on the police carrying all this shit in a bag, I think you've got some explaining to do."

Douglas remained silent. Keefer slapped Douglas across the face with his pistol butt, Douglas stumbled and fell, smacking his shoulder as he crashed into a rusting air vent.

"Just tell me why you were spying on Rivers's room?" Keefer pressed, the damp cold air seeping into his aching joints.

The Yank had said Rivers. None of this made sense, Douglas didn't know what was going on here. Keefer kicked Douglas hard in the ribs. For an old boy, he was alarmingly strong and worryingly intimidating. Douglas was terrified, this guy wasn't going to take no for an answer. Douglas told him everything as he didn't want to die a meaningless death on a hotel roof in Wales.

Keefer was stunned by what he was told. The situation was weird, complicated. If he'd known it was going to be like this, he'd have charged a lot more for his services. He didn't like complications, especially complications involving the police. He had so much to think about, but firstly, what to do with Douglas. He was like a frightened rabbit. Keefer had no intention of murdering a pathetic innocent.

He grabbed the bag and sneaked Douglas out at gunpoint through a rear door to his car parked in a shadowy corner of the car park. At his car, he handcuffed and gagged Douglas, then threw him in the boot. He'd threatened him with death if he made any noise and could see, by the nervous sweat running down Douglas's frightened face, that he wouldn't be any trouble.

Keefer went back to the hotel with no idea what to do. Rivers still hadn't returned to the hotel, the police detectives were sitting in an alcove by the door waiting. He went back to the bar and sat with a coffee. The whole situation was starting to get as confusing as a Viet Cong offensive. He'd been paid by Schultz to find a way to get Rivers off the set. It looked like the police were obviously still interested in him for the Sparshot woman's murder. As he pondered the problem, Rivers and a woman stepped through the front door of the hotel reception. Keefer made the call to the police on his mobile, claiming he'd seen Rivers involved in a drug deal in the hotel toilets, adding yet another layer of confusion to the night's events.

He went back to his car. Now he had to lose Douglas for a day. One day would be all that was required. The police were about to arrest Rivers and Douglas's thirst for revenge had been crushed by Keefer's arrival. Douglas had quickly realized that he was playing out of his league and that he didn't have the bottle for Keefer's world. Keefer would threaten him further then abandon him in a quiet back wood. By the end of the week, Keefer would be back in the States and, hopefully, have left this debacle behind him.

CHAPTER 56

"Come to my room for a nightcap," Dexter asked Debbie as they stepped into the lift.

"I think it's better if we let things drift, Peter."

Dexter was fuming as he thought what a death knell to a relationship the phrase, "let things drift," seemed to promise. She was talking as if she could just discard him like a piece of rough trade she'd picked up in a bar. It was time Miss Debbie Duncan realized how things were. Dexter now recognized that he was never going to have her the way he wanted.

It looked like he'd have to go for the consolation prize.

"If that's how you want it," Dexter said as they stepped out the lift into the dimly lit corridor. He followed her across the landing to her room, pleading, "Can't I just come in and talk—"

"It's not a good idea, Peter. Filming ends in two days so let's end our relationship on friendly terms." She opened the door, expecting a sulky Rivers to stomp off to his room.

Instead, he pushed her into the room and locked the

door behind them. "I want you to leave right now!" a nervous-sounding Debbie demanded.

Dexter edged toward her. She didn't like the glazed look that had suddenly come over his eyes. He pushed her slowly to the wall. When she was wedged between him and the wall, he said, "You can't discard me that easily, my love, there are things we need to discuss before we cement our union."

He'd trapped her, she couldn't move. "If you don't leave now, Peter, I'll scream!"

Rivers stooped forward, leaning into her, fumbling in his pocket. She thought he'd finally seen sense, but then she saw the can of mace spray in his hands and felt the burning liquid squirting into her eyes. Blinded, she fell to her knees, tried to fight back with flailing arms.

Rivers punched her hard in the face. Stunned, she felt him dragging her toward the bedroom. In the bedroom, he threw her on the bed, tying her hands roughly to the bedstead with a dressing-gown cord.

"Don't worry, darling, I'll relieve the pain in a minute," he promised.

Debbie could feel her jeans being tugged off and heard the sound of ripped sheets. Dexter then used strands of sheets to tie Debbie's legs to the bedposts. She tried to plead, but he gagged her with some pantyhose fumbled from a drawer. Debbie's mind regaled in horror, Peter was a caring considerate lover—

As he ripped her panties away, her panic-stricken face was a mask of horror. He went to the bathroom, and Debbie frantically struggled with her bonds. He'd tied them too tight and well for her to move them. As he returned carrying a flannel, she froze. The monster washed her eyes with the wet flannel. Her stinging eyes started to clear, and she could see him standing over her smiling. She tried to say something through the gag, but it came out as an indecipherable mumble. Dexter laughed and punched her on the jaw.

The room spun round as the effect of his punch made her dizzy. She heard the sound of him fumbling with his belt buckle. His jeans brushed against her sweat-soaked leg as he threw them aside. When his penis brushed against her pubic hair, it was solid. Her legs struggled frantically. The ropes didn't move. He'd tied them with expert knots, too expert for a novice. He thrust on top of her like an animal. He pumped brutally inside her, mumbling incoherent nonsense about possession and dominance. As he thrust harder, Debbie felt his demon seed ejaculate inside her. When he had finished, he flopped down beside her, lying next to her, staring at the ceiling. She tried to turn away his exploring hands, but their cruel pokes and prods were beyond her previous life experience. When he finally finished and sauntered off to the bathroom, she lay there, unable to comprehend how the gentle lover she'd known had suddenly turned into a monster. She concluded that no man could suddenly become so and that the monster had always been lying dormant within him.

Now he'd raped her, she dreaded what was coming. The film crew knew that Debbie was seeing Rivers. Rivers knew that there was no way he could hide what he'd done.

Horrific images of death and destruction danced before her. After what he'd done to her, he couldn't let her go. What could he do with her? Debbie didn't like the answer—there was only one. When he got tired of raping and abusing her, then he had to kill her. She wrestled frantically with her bonds like a tethered animal before its slaughter. They didn't move. Tears streamed down Debbie's face as she realized all that was left for her was to lay there helplessly and wait to die.

CHAPTER 57

Thompson lay in his trailer tossing and turning unable to sleep. He was having a bad night. He dozed momentarily, in his mind Jodie was lying next to him. He awoke with a start and felt the empty space next to him on the bed. It was just another nightmare, she was gone, and would always be gone no matter how many times he wished it otherwise. Now the film was coming to an end he was struggling again. All the while they'd been filming, he'd managed to remain focused. The film had been everything, a reason to press on with his life.

As the film came to an end the sense of purpose was slowly being replaced by a dark cold void.

He wandered to the fridge, was about to get a bottle of Highland Spring water from within when he saw the bottle of Scotch discarded a few weeks ago on top of it.

He lifted the golden-brown bottle down, placing it on the Formica kitchen table. His suddenly nervous fingers slowly caressed the smooth metal top. After Debbie's lecture when he'd returned to the set after the funeral, she'd convinced him what he already knew, and that was that he had a drinking problem. He'd been to see his doctor.

Doctor Toh had been brutal, told him to go to Alcoholics Anonymous.

His angel, Debbie, had stood by him, had told him she would be his stop drinking buddy, and to contact her every time he felt like he was wavering. Thompson let go of the bottle moments from disaster. He'd come so far. With Debbie's and AA's help, he'd managed to control his drinking without the necessity of visiting a clinic. As everybody in the business knew, a clinic created image problems and could lead to the death of a career. Thompson needed to see Debbie. It was late, but this wasn't something you could do over the phone. His nerves were on edge, a window banging in the wind jolting him. It broke his reverie, and he replaced the bottle of Scotch back on top of the fridge then grabbed his coat and left. The only woman that could stop him from taking another awful step along the path of alcoholism was Debbie, and right now he needed to see her.

CHAPTER 58

Machin and Roberts saw Rivers and Duncan enter the hotel and go up to their rooms in the lift. She smiled, the noose was closing, she couldn't wait to see the look on Rivers's face the first time she addressed him as Trevor Slater. They waited a few minutes, they'd lull him into a false sense of security and then pounce. In the lift, Roberts looked tense and nervous. On Rivers's floor everything was quiet. There was a chance Rivers and his date would be in bed together. Machin would soon break that happy union, she thought, as she thumped on twenty-nine's door. "We know you're in there, Mr. Rivers, open the door!" she shouted aggressively.

Her gesticulations were met with silence. She knocked again, and when it was obvious that Rivers wasn't there, Roberts said, "The woman, ma'am, maybe he's gone to the woman's room."

Shit! Machin thought. She'd seen the woman around the film set when they'd come to Wales to ask Rivers about Sparshot. She was an actress. "Stay here and keep watch," she commanded Roberts. She then returned to reception where the receptionist told her that the woman that had come back to the hotel with Rivers was Debbie Duncan, the co-star of the Thompson movie. He looked up her room number and told her she was staying in Room Twenty-Six, along the corridor from Rivers's room. As Machin turned back to the lift, she saw Clay Thompson enter the lift and the doors shut behind him.

Suddenly, a detective and two uniforms walked through the main door to the reception desk. She didn't understand as she hadn't asked for backup. When the detective asked the receptionist which room a Mr. Rivers was staying in, Machin became interested. She showed the detective her badge, "We've come to interview Peter Rivers about a murder," she told him.

"Strange," Detective Evans said, "we had a phone call a little while ago from a guest here, saying that they'd seen Mr. Rivers making a drug deal in the hotel toilets earlier today."

A drug deal! What the fuck was going on? Machin wondered. Could it be coincidence or something else? There was only one way to find out, as she followed Evans's bulk into the lift, flanked by the two uniforms. She decided it was high time they talked to Rivers.

CHAPTER 59

When Thompson stepped from the lift, he noted a suspicious looking guy in an overcoat standing nearby. He ignored him and went to Debbie's room. In all his years of making movies, he'd noted that hotels were full of weirdoes. He knocked loudly on her door.

When she didn't answer, he shouted through the door, "I need to talk to you, Debbie!"

The weirdo in the coat stared at him, Thompson ignored him. His thirst for booze was strong, too strong to worry about hotel weirdoes. He knocked and shouted again, at last the door opened, and he stepped inside. The door had opened, but Debbie wasn't standing by the door—it didn't make any sense. He edged along the corridor and, as he passed the bathroom, he sensed movement behind him. He turned, something cracked hard against the back of his head and his legs buckled underneath him. Pain was searing through his head, but just before he blacked out he saw Peter Rivers standing over him holding a heavy stool.

Dexter watched Thompson's unconscious body flop

to the floor. Everything was caving in around him. He needed to regain control. In his room, he had some masking tape and a dressing-gown cord that he could use to bind Thompson and regain control. He made sure that Thompson was out cold, then he stepped out of Debbie's room into the corridor.

"Rivers!" Roberts shouted. The lift door pinged open near Roberts, revealing the other cops.

Dexter sprinted through the stairwell door and hurtled down the stairs. In the echoing stairwell, he could hear his pursuers thumping down the stairs after him. At the foot of the stairs, Dexter crashed through the door and into the empty foyer, ran through the reception doors and out into the night. When Machin and the others rushed out into the damp cold night, they were greeted by the sound of a van engine revving, and the sight of it skidding off on the gravel out the car park gate. They jumped in the Welsh cops' patrol car and, with the siren shrieking, hurtled after him. In the dank mist, they could barely see yards in front of them. Rivers was driving like a lunatic and took a couple of sharp bends at ridiculous speeds. The patrolman driving made an error on the tightest of the bends. They lost a few seconds, a few seconds too many. When they recovered and arrived at a sharp fork in the road. Rivers had gone either right or left. They had a stark choice—the driver chose left, but it was the wrong one.

CHAPTER 60

Thompson awoke with a thumping head. He was in a strange room that wasn't his trailer. As his head slightly cleared, he remembered seeing Rivers standing over him holding the stool. He was in Debbie's room—he'd come to Debbie's room. He gingerly leaned on the bland painted wall and used it as a prop to slowly clamber to his feet. He could hear a muffled scream emanating from the bedroom. His numbed body stumbled forward, and as he entered the bedroom, he saw a naked terror-stricken Debbie lying tied to the bed. It was at that moment that a stunned Thompson finally realized the horror of Peter Rivers.

Fumbling, he untied the knots and removed Debbie's gag. "He's going to kill me—get me out of here!" Debbie pleaded.

Thompson wrapped her in her dressing-gown and led her down to the lounge.

She was hysterical. Thompson didn't want to contemplate the horrors that Rivers had subjected her to.

He was surprised to find he didn't have to ring the police as they were already there.

Machin and Roberts led Thompson to a quiet corner away from the distraught Debbie, now being comforted by a female Police Constable. Machin flashed her ID at Thompson. "I'm Detective Inspector Machin, this is Detective Sergeant Roberts. We came here to take Peter Rivers back to London to be interviewed in connection with his former girlfriend, Tracy Sparshot's murder. Could you tell me what went on here, sir?"

Thompson told Machin what he'd found after he awoke from Rivers' assault.

Machin was suitably horrified, thought back to the moment that Rivers had come back to the hotel, realizing that if they'd not delayed and had arrested Rivers the moment he stepped into the hotel's foyer, then none of this would've happened. She was trying not to blame herself.

Although technically she was beyond reproach, one look at the distraught figure of Debbie Duncan, crying and being comforted, told Machin that, in her eyes, she'd always be to blame, and nothing the manual said about the correctness of her actions here today would convince her otherwise.

CHAPTER 61

Keefer's car slid to a halt on the black slag next to the hut that was once used as a restroom for the workers. What had once been a busy dumping ground for the nearby disused pit was now the Welsh equivalent of a Wild West ghost town. It wasn't ideal, but on short notice, it would have to do, under the circumstances. A few minutes away from the hotel, it enabled him to get back there quickly. The air was freezing now the mist had cleared, and the frosty night sky was alive with twinkling stars and a half-moon. When he lifted a terrified Douglas out the boot, the man was gasping for air. Keefer removed his gag. Douglas desperately sucked in air.

"Don't kill me!" Douglas pleaded as he was kicked to the ground.

"If you do exactly as I tell you, you'll live," Keefer promised.

He broke open the padlock on the hut door and dragged Douglas inside. After he'd bound Douglas's legs and arms with a washing line he'd purchased at a garage shop, and before he gagged him again, he gave him a lecture. "I'm going to leave you here for twelve hours then come back and release you. If you keep quiet and don't try and escape, then I'll release you unharmed. If I come back and find you've tried to escape, I'll kill you. Is that simple enough for you, buddy?"

Douglas nodded, his hands were handcuffed, and his legs and arms were bound expertly. He quickly decided that escape wasn't an option. He wondered if the Yank would return. In this deserted slag heap, one thing was certain. If he didn't return, then nobody else was likely to find him. Keefer gave Douglas some biscuits to eat and let him have a few swigs of water. It wasn't much, but it was enough to keep a man in reasonable shape for a day.

Until Rivers was arrested by the police after they found the drugs in his room, Keefer needed Douglas out of the way. He didn't like the threat of bungling amateurs such as Douglas ruining his plan. When Douglas finished his improvised meal, Keefer gagged him and left.

After wedging the hut door shut, he drove slowly out the pit with his lights off.

When he arrived back at the hotel, he saw the police patrol car parked near reception.

He got a coffee from a nearby vending machine and lingered, hoping to see Rivers led away in handcuffs. As he sat watching the lift Rivers hurtled out of a nearby stairwell and sprinted out through the main doors. Moments later, the police followed close behind. He heard a revving engine and saw a van launch out of the car park entrance onto the road closely followed by a speeding patrol car. They'd found the drugs, and it looked like Rivers wasn't going quietly.

It was more than he could've hoped for, better than he'd planned. By running, Rivers, in the eyes of the police, would've cemented his guilt.

Keefer didn't linger to see the result of his interference but went to his room. When he checked out at seven the next morning, the police were surprisingly still at the hotel. There was talk of a rape. Now Keefer was thoroughly confused, though the way Rivers had fled the night before, Keefer must have achieved his goal and Rivers would now be permanently off the set.

Douglas was shaken but compliant when he released him from his prison.

Keefer left a broken-looking Douglas to walk back to the hotel, the thinking being the more he made Douglas suffer, the less likely he was to cause any trouble. The look of defeat in Douglas's eyes told Keefer everything. Douglas had found he was out of his league. Whatever he'd been planning for Rivers, now that Rivers had fled, was never going to happen. Keefer arrived at Cardiff airport an hour later ready for his one o'clock flight. He prided himself on getting older and wiser. He'd learned two things in his brief stint in Britain—one was, don't take any jobs in Limey land, and, secondly, never take it for granted that anything was going to be easy.

CHAPTER 62

Debbie went through all the medical tests prior to a rape case coming to trial. She couldn't work out what was worse—her fear of the probing doctor in the cubicle or the fear of the trial that would eventually follow. It wasn't just the horror of the attack that was killing her. In all her dating life, she'd never misjudged anybody as badly as she had here.

How could Peter Rivers turn from a loving, caring man into this monster? None of his actions during the time when he'd raped her made any sense at all. He'd charmed his way into her life. She'd thought he was lovely, a man who would be a pleasant diversion from the harsh realities of filming. She thought back to the previous evening and had no doubts he would've killed her if Thompson hadn't appeared.

Thompson sat outside the cubicle, waiting. He had been her rock throughout this horror. When the doctor left, the woman police constable, Wendy Antrim, appeared. Antrim was the rape counselor, the questioner, the woman that the police assigned to get close to the victim. She was taking things slowly, trying to be gentle. It didn't matter how gentle she was, Debbie's mind found it impossible not to recoil from the horror.

"How long have you known Peter Rivers, Debbie?" Antrim prodded.

"Not for long, up to last night, he'd always shown me nothing but respect." This was the part that Debbie feared. If she told them how long she'd been seeing Rivers, and that she'd slept with him several times, would the fact that she'd slept with him prejudice how they viewed the rape?

"So last night was the first time he'd ever been violent toward you?" Antrim probed. She preferred to keep quiet in an interview and let the victim talk. This rape was the classic rape scenario, where the victim unfairly felt like she needed to apologize for allowing herself to be attacked.

"Up until last night, he'd never been violent." Debbie told Antrim everything that occurred, that she'd told Rivers their affair was over. He'd appeared to accept it until they arrived back at her room. It was at her room that he'd suddenly become psychotic and raped her. Debbie kept telling her how normal he had seemed. In other rape interviews, Antrim had noted that a lot of rapists seemed quite normal, their victims being lulled into a false sense of security before they struck. Antrim made sure that Debbie's statement didn't miss anything.

Rivers's defense counsel would latch onto any errors made now during any future rape trial. When Antrim was finished, a nervous Thompson entered. He was distraught and didn't know what to say.

"It all happened so quickly, Debbie. If I'd been more alert, he might not have got the drop on me," he said.

"You couldn't have known what he was going to do, please don't blame yourself for this, Clay."

They both lapsed into an uncomfortable silence.

Debbie knew that Thompson had been first on the scene and had seen at close quarters what the beast had done to her. Those thoughts made it hard to talk to him. He finally asked, "Is there anything I can do for you?"

Debbie decided there were a million things. He could take her back to the first time that Rivers asked her on a date so she could say no. Thompson could also have not allowed Debbie to be so foolish as to let Rivers so much into her life. She settled for saying, "Just your being here is enough, Clay," and then weakly held his hand.

Thompson smiled and gently stroked her hand. Even after the attack, she was trying to be brave. She lapsed into another uncomfortable silence. He pretended not to notice the terrible transformation Rivers had caused in Debbie. He wanted to pound Rivers's face into a pulp, make him suffer for his evil. The last he'd heard from the police, they still hadn't found Rivers, which was why a police guard had been posted outside the room.

Until Rivers was captured, Thompson intended keeping watch over Debbie.

He'd canceled filming indefinitely, wouldn't dream of continuing with the movie without Debbie. When Antrim returned to continue with Debbie's interview, he left.

He made sure that the police guard was on duty before he went back to his trailer.

When he stepped from his Datsun Jeep early afternoon on the set, he was greeted by a taut-faced Jimmy Murray, anxious to know what was happening. Thompson explained things.

"Poor, Debbie," an angry Murray said.

"She's still in shock, Jimmy—she's going to need a lot of counseling."

Thompson told Murray to discreetly inform the crew, then he went into his trailer to make some calls. He was on the second call when Paul Rome knocked and entered his trailer. "What's happened to Debbie?" he asked.

"She's in hospital—there was an incident at the hotel." Thompson was doing his best to tell Rome as little as possible because of the way Rome felt about Debbie. It was better that way.

With what had happened to Debbie, the last thing she needed was a hassle from Rome.

"If you want my advice, Paul, don't visit her. She needs time on her own."

Rome was furious. Who the hell did Thompson think he was? He wasn't a doctor. How did he know what was best for Debbie? In the time he'd known Thompson, Rome had noted that he always thought he knew best. This time, Rome would ignore him. He'd heard that Debbie had been attacked by Rivers and decided he had to see her. Rome was feeling guilty—he couldn't help but wonder if his confrontation with Rivers had caused this. Filming was canceled indefinitely, and nobody knew what was happening because the scenes they needed to film involved Debbie. He needed to see her, find out how badly she was hurt. Then there was Rivers. There'd always been something that Rome hadn't liked about Rivers. Debbie had thought it was jealousy, he knew it wasn't. Rome had seen how Rivers tried to goad him on the set by putting the camera close in his face. This wasn't the act of an innocent man—this was the act of someone with a genuine degree of psychosis.

Rome decided, when he saw Debbie, he'd stay calm, be kind and sympathetic.

Ranting about Rivers wouldn't help anybody. If only he'd acted earlier with Schultz—he should have had Schultz arrange to remove Rivers a week before. Alas, he hadn't, and this is where they were. For now, he would try and comfort Debbie, show her how much he cared for her by how gentle and delicate he was now going to be.

He wouldn't forget Rivers. Schultz knew people who could fix the Rivers of this world. Rome would be there for Debbie for as long as she needed. When she was ready, he'd be waiting. The problem was that the time when she would be ready seemed to be a long time in the future—because of Rivers.

CHAPTER 63

After filling up with petrol, Dexter had parked in a quiet corner of a service station away from the CCTV while he used the toilet. As he left the toilet he immediately saw the police patrol car parked near his van. Quickly he ducked behind a paint-flecked builder's van and surveyed his options. If he tried to walk across the forecourt and escape via the nearby fields, the police were sure to see him. He breathed slowly and deeply, the secret was not to panic—only calmness under duress would keep him ahead of the game. He decided that he wouldn't attempt an escape cross country. It would be much easier for the police to track him on open ground with tracker dogs, and helicopter cameras could pick up body-heat making even the night no sanctuary.

A coach party that had stopped at a nearby McDonald's were leaving the restaurant and stepping back on board the coach. Dexter mingled amongst them, following a group of Asians onto the bus. He walked to the back of the bus and sat on the back seat in the corner. A family sitting there stared at him warily, unhappy at the intrusion. "I was feeling travel sick, I thought if I sat at the back it might help a bit," Dexter explained to them.

They seemed satisfied, and the wife even offered him a travel sweet. Rivers thanked her and sucked on it as he looked out the window. The police were looking at the van and talking on their radios, Dexter was in no doubt that they knew the van was his. The coach door finally hissed shut after some stragglers boarded, and soon the coach was trundling out the service station behind a scruffy-looking TIR lorry. When they were a couple of miles down the road, a police car whizzed past the coach with its lights flashing, heading toward the garage.

The net was tightening, but Dexter had already slipped through it. He had no idea where the coach was going, but he'd already decided he would alight at wherever the next toilet stop was. This time he'd need a drastic change of identity. He had to find a hideaway to make the change. Changing identity was something that took patience and time. He looked out the back window at the trail of snaking yellow-white headlights and was relieved not to see a flashing blue light parting the traffic waves. All he could do was stay alert. The rest, for the moment, was out of his hands.

CHAPTER 64

How could he have escaped?" an angry DI Machin asked Roberts.

"I don't know, ma'am. They had him cornered at a service station just outside Bristol, and he somehow slipped through the net." Roberts waited while Machin's irritation subsided. "They've brought everybody they can in for the search, the hunt's in full swing."

She wasn't impressed. They'd moved too slowly, and the back-up for the manhunt had arrived too late. With the van, they'd had something, but because the locals had moved too slowly, they now had nothing. Rivers could now be anywhere. There was no point in staying in Wales, she decided, and they'd to go back to London. Cowley wouldn't be pleased—he would've expected a straightforward arrest and that Rivers would be brought back to London.

Machin would wait a few more hours as there was still a slight chance that Rivers might be captured. They booked into a motel for a couple of hours' sleep. They'd been up all night, and Machin's senses were starting to deaden. She needed to be fully awake and alert when she spoke to Cowley later in the day. After a couple of hours' sleep, they ate lunch in the motel's adjoining nautical-themed restaurant. Roberts rang the locals for a progress report and was told that they still hadn't found Rivers. Roberts related the grim news to his boss.

She was surprisingly pragmatic. "If they haven't found him by now, then he's escaped."

"What are we going to do?" Roberts asked.

"You liaise with the locals for the rest of the day, and I'll go and talk to Thompson."

Machin arrived at Thompson's trailer around noon. He was still in shock and subdued over the previous night's events. "I don't know what I can tell you, Inspector, everything happened so quickly."

"Let's start with why you were knocking on Debbie Duncan's hotel room door that time of the night." Machin noticed that Thompson shifted uneasily. "Were you having an affair with Debbie Duncan?"

"No, of course not!" an irritated Thompson snapped. He needed a drink badly but was fighting it. He decided on straight talk. "After my wife was murdered, I started to hit the bottle, Inspector. At one point, I was in a really bad way, on the verge of alcoholism. It was at that low point that Debbie intervened. It was through her intervention I stopped drinking. She told me that if I ever felt like I was going to lapse again, then I was to contact her any time of the day or night. Yesterday, I was thinking a lot about Jodie, was tempted to hit the Scotch. I decided I needed to talk to Debbie, talking to her about my booze problem was the reason I was at the hotel last night."

Machin believed him. A leading Hollywood light like Thompson was never going to admit that he had a drinking problem unless it was true. "And after you entered her hotel room, you were knocked unconscious by Rivers."

He nodded. "It was when I woke that I found her tied to the bed after the attack. You know the rest, Inspector."

Machin knew the rest all right, the rest was mayhem. She decided to show Thompson a similar amount of honesty. "We came to Wales to arrest Peter Rivers in connection with the brutal murder of a woman, called Tracy Sparshot."

"I read about it in the papers," Thompson said, and what he'd read showed that the police had botched the case against the man they'd taken to trial.

"Last night at the hotel we were waiting to arrest him when he came back from a night out with Debbie Duncan. We missed him at the door, went up to his room, and he wasn't there. I went down to reception to find what room Debbie Duncan was in. It was during that time that he must've attacked her."

"So you could've arrested Rivers before he attacked Debbie."

"It wasn't that simple. We went up to his room shortly after he returned to the hotel. There were no signs he was going to do anything."

"But he did, Inspector!" Thompson snapped. "He did, and you could've prevented it."

There was an uncomfortable silence. Machin knew Thompson was right, but she'd never admitted it. "There were no signs that Rivers was going to attack Debbie Duncan that night—she herself said that Rivers had cted normally until they arrived at her hotel room. It was at her room that he turned into a psycho."

Machin walked to the window for a moment to let things cool down.

"You knew he was a violent murder suspect," Thompson said. "You should've acted more quickly."

She agreed with Thompson's appraisal, but it was too late now. "There's nothing I can do about last night,

Mr. Thompson. You've been close to Rivers in his work for you—you must've noticed some things about the guy."

"He had a run in with Paul Rome. Apparently, there was an incident between him and Rome. Debbie cooled the situation. She was the only person that Rivers ever really spoke to out of the film crew." Thompson couldn't say much more, only Rivers and Rome knew what really went on.

Machin was desperate for anything and decided to be honest with Thompson. She told him about Rivers's name change, the spell in the mental home, the missing years unaccounted for. "His life is weird, doesn't make sense. It's like he comes from nowhere and then disappears at random." Thompson didn't like what he was hearing—all of this sounded bad for Debbie. Rivers, the rapist, was out there, and the police seemed incapable of capturing him.

Thompson wondered how much danger Debbie was in. His knuckles whitened as he angrily gripped his chair arm. "So what you're, in effect, saying is that the lunatic who attacked Debbie will soon have a new identity and disappear."

"We'll find him, Mr. Thompson."

He wasn't convinced. "So what's Debbie supposed to do while all this is going on, sit back and wait for him to attack her again?"

"He's unlikely to return. In the meantime, until he's captured, the police will keep a guard on Miss Duncan."

Thompson laughed sarcastically. "I don't think Debbie will be reassured."

Machin didn't know what to say. Rape victims always felt vulnerable, even more so the way Debbie Duncan was attacked. Machin would've liked to have interviewed Debbie before she went back to London, but knew she couldn't. Bulldozing through an interview with her wasn't an option with the attack still so raw. The rape specialists would be talking to her for the next few days.

"You're right, none of this helps Debbie face her demons," Machin said and sat down on a chair. "Please tell me anything you know about Rivers. Even if it seems trivial, it could be important, Mr. Thompson."

Thompson sighed and told the detective everything he could think of. After half an hour, Machin had three pages of notes. She gave Thompson her card in case he thought of anything later. As she went to her car, she could feel her dander rising. She wanted this bastard Rivers more than anything. If they hadn't caught Rivers by the time she got back to London, she'd keep looking for him. She needed to interview Paul Rome, but just then she saw Rome's Ferrari speeding out of the car park. She sat in her car and realized today that wasn't going to happen.

Cowley wouldn't be happy. He was known for his volatility—something which made him unapproachable to junior officers. In all her years as a detective, she had learned that failure was part of the job. The CID didn't like losers—the work ethos in the detective division was built around success. If you cared, you couldn't afford to lose when evil people like Rivers were on the loose out there. Machin cared, she wasn't an automaton. You only needed to talk to her lover, Nick, to realize how warm she could be. As she stepped into her car for the drive back to London, she made herself a vow that she wouldn't rest until Trevor Slater, alias Peter Rivers, was captured.

CHAPTER 65

Dexter was sitting on a bench in Trafalgar Square, watching a dementia-ridden old man feeding pigeons. As far as Dexter was concerned, pigeons were rats with wings. A pigeon had once crapped on his best suit on a first youthful date with a girl called Amy. Arriving at the restaurant smelling of bird poo had ruined any chances he'd had of a sexual assignation with her. Dexter never forgot anybody or anything that wronged him. It was his inability as a child ever to forgive or forget that frequently led to trouble and confirmed to him at an early age what he'd always suspected, and that was that he was a nutcase.

It was getting cold as the sun set. The shrill east wind was scattering a mass of swirling paper around the square. It would be dark shortly, and he needed to find a room for the night, lose himself in dingy apartment land. He'd choose carefully. After Wales, everybody was watching. The police would've circulated his photo, and Dexter never underestimated the police, who were not stupid.

The detective who'd interviewed him about Sparshot

hadn't been stupid, as all her probing questions had proved.

Penetrating cold ripped through his thin jacket. He'd had to leave all his belongings behind him in his sudden flight from the hotel. Traffic roared past around Leicester Square, his chest tightening in the suffocating fumes. It was all down to tension. His body cried out for rest as he hadn't slept for nearly two days. He'd disembarked from the coach when it had stopped at a service station south of Birmingham. He'd caught an early morning train to London then spent all day milling around the bars of Soho, trying to make decisions. All his usual immaculate planning was in tatters. He had a few hundred quid on him, barely enough to get a bedsit room for a couple of days. He needed time to think in the anonymity of a private room.

He ambled into a nearby Boots to escape the cold. At the hair products counter, he bought himself hair dye and scissors—anything that he felt would aid his disguise. He had no time to change his identity properly. For the moment, all he was looking for was a quick-fix solution. When he stepped back outside, yellow street lights flickered as purple-gray twilight soon became coal-black night. It was time he found an indoor haven. He had hidden money in a secret account. He could survive for a couple of months without a job on that. At the moment, he needed time to change everything—time the present manhunt wasn't going to allow him.

After looking at two cesspits, he chose the third. It was grim, the type of rundown joint where nobody spoke to one another. His bedsit room was dusty, and the wallpaper was riddled with damp. The baggy-eyed Greek who'd shown him to his room hadn't bothered with flowery rhetoric—this was one sow's ear that couldn't be made into a silk purse. Dexter had signed for the room under the alias, Giles Perkins. He had paid the Greek for three days in advance, so he wouldn't have to speak to the creature again.

Dexter settled into his pig pen. He sat on the faded sofa and thought about his new alias Giles Perkins, another name chosen at random, another name that meant nothing to him.

Names had never meant anything to him. Dexter knew who he was, where he was trying to get to. Debbie could have helped him a long way along the road to enlightenment. Alas, like most of the specimens that had inhabited his life, Debbie had let him down, just like the others. He'd offered her everything, a chance to climb to untold heights in their relationship. Debbie had been the one, the chance to learn how far you could crush a high-spirited woman's soul. He'd needed more from the woman, much more than she'd given him. Thompson had ruined everything, depriving Dexter of the time needed to salvage a brief few hours of something from his specimen.

Dexter looked at his smartphone, checking all the news links for information. The police weren't saying anything, were keeping information concerning what they knew close to their chests. There was so little he could find out about the manhunt, it made him feel helpless and angry.

All his problems had been caused because Debbie had been unwilling to succumb.

Next time, she wouldn't fool him with her tricks. As he thought about the pleasure of their next encounter, he looked up at the ceiling and stared at the brown-black cockroach waddling toward the dusty lampshade. Dexter stood on the sofa and grabbed it. It tried to wriggle free.

Dexter smiled as he slowly pulled all its legs off. The pain that the cockroach was suffering was nothing compared to the pain that Debbie would endure when he caught up with her again.

It wasn't the screams that he needed to hear. Mental torture was what drove him, nurtured his artistic side. The Nazis knew what it was all about. Pol Pot, Stalin, Amin, Dexter, had all the despots' logic behind their torture. Making Dexter's dreams reality was what it was all about. While others dreamed, Dexter acted. It was nearly time to begin again. City women had potential. Most of them were go-getters who always thought they were in control. When Dexter finished with his next specimen, they'd soon realize they were in control of nothing.

First, he needed a subject, someone to work on. Finding someone couldn't happen, wouldn't happen until the change. He let the cockroach fall to the floor, stomped on it with his boot. He slipped into the grimy bathroom along the corridor from his room, ran the hot tap while he read the dye's instructions. His new life would begin with his change of hair color—his new life had to begin there.

CHAPTER 66

It bothers me, Nick. I can't get it out of my head. If we'd arrested Rivers the moment he stepped into the hotel foyer, nothing would've happened," Machin told her lover as they lay in bed at his flat after making love. The headboard bolt was loose. Nick was always threatening to tighten it, but, as usual, it was always put on the backburner because Nick hated anything to do with DIY. It was barely noticeable to the uninitiated, but, to Machin, it was very noticeable as she loved holding the metal rails of the headboard when Nick was on top of her during sex. She didn't say anything as she knew, no matter how much she complained, her lover was never going to fix it.

"You couldn't have known he was going to attack her. You said they came back to the hotel together, nothing untoward. You can't blame yourself for every crackpot out there," Nick reassured her.

Machin knew he was right, but she still couldn't get the chain of events out of her head. She lay on Nick's hairy chest, gently running her fingers through his curls, thinking. Rivers had slipped through the police's net, nobody knew where he was. They also couldn't find any-thing to account for the gaps in Rivers's past. The institution years accounted for some, but nowhere near all of it. Rivers had raped Debbie Duncan and murdered Tracy Sparshot—a murder, after Duncan's rape, that the police were now convinced Rivers had committed. There was nothing of note they could find to connect Rivers's past with. Machin had quickly decided that, with his level of secrecy, Rivers would've made the perfect spy.

Nick gently brushed his tongue across her nipples, but Machin pushed him aside. She had too much on her mind for any further lovemaking. "No woman's safe while he's on the loose, Nick."

"If he's lost himself from the system for all those years, then he'll be able to lose himself again," an irritated Nick said.

He was right. Loners were a problem. Loners could lose themselves much better than people with friends and family. Friends and family were a weakness for the criminal. Friends and family made you vulnerable. Loners didn't crave company, never gave a damn about spending hours in solitary. Machin looked on her mobile phone for messages, but, apart from a couple of updates on the failure of the Rivers's manhunt, there was nothing. They were relying on the public. Rivers's picture had been circulated in the media. There was still a slim chance of a sighting.

"He's probably gone abroad, that's what I'd do," Nick stated.

If he'd gone to a ferry port or airport and hopped straight on a boat or plane, they wouldn't have been quick enough to stop him, Machin thought.

There were so many questions and not enough an-swers—the coke found in Rivers's room, the mysterious call to the police informing them of the alleged drug deal between Rivers and an unknown in the hotel toilets.

None of it made any sense. The person who'd been closest to Rivers in recent years, Tracy Sparshot, had been brutally murdered. There was nobody else—

Suddenly, she thought about Douglas. He had been close to Sparshot and must have had numerous conversations with her.

When everybody had been convinced he was the murderer, nobody had listened to his protestations of innocence. Now that she knew Douglas was innocent, she was prepared to listen. There was the chance that Sparshot had inadvertently revealed something—a link to Rivers's past that he might've mentioned in his time with her. It wasn't much. There never seemed much, as far as Rivers was concerned. As Nick gently kissed her neck, she could feel herself starting to feel aroused, and, when he teasingly slipped his manhood inside her, she was gone—but not gone enough to forget that the first thing she would do tomorrow would be to speak to Douglas.

CHAPTER 67

The interview room wasn't filled with a party atmosphere. DI Machin and DS Roberts sat across from what could best be described as a tetchy Douglas. She had offered him a coffee, an offer he'd irritably refused. She had no time for Douglas's tantrums.

"We now know that you didn't kill your girlfriend, Mr. Douglas," Machin said.

"That's what I told you from day one," Douglas snapped.

"The evidence looked like you were guilty," DS Roberts said.

Douglas laughed briefly. "And why do you think that was? Do you think it could've had anything to do with the fact that Rivers set me up?"

Sarcasm was the last refuge of the wrongly accused, Machin thought. She decided not to react. Instead, she said, "You can take this defiant stance, Mr. Douglas, you can shout at us, vent your spleen, and blame us for our incompetence. Whatever you choose to do, no matter how justified, one fact will remain, the man you knew as Peter Rivers will still be out there waiting to kill again."

After a moment's silent reflection, Douglas said, "When you came for me again, I was filled with dread. After what I've been through you can understand why I'll never trust the police again."

Machin couldn't blame Douglas. She would've felt exactly the same toward the police if she was in his position. "Surely you must want to bring to justice the man who killed Tracy, surely you must want revenge on this man who coldly set you up to take the fall for his evil." She noted that Douglas shifted uneasily in his seat. To the untrained eye, it was nothing. To her who'd spent most of her working life in a police interview room, it was a tangible shift in Douglas's position. "We're all batting for the same team here, Mr. Douglas," she pressed.

"We need to find him," Roberts said. "Until we find him, no woman is safe."

Roberts liked to lay on the drama, Machin thought. In her time working with Roberts, she'd noted that his concern for victims was genuine, a concern that drove him on to always give an exemplary performance in carrying out his duties.

"And what can I possibly do to help you?" a slightly baffled Douglas asked.

Machin explained what they knew. When she told Douglas about Rivers's change of identity, she could see Douglas's interest suddenly heighten. "Anything you can tell me about what Tracy told you about him could be helpful," she said.

Douglas talked. He told them about how Rivers hated smoking, would have no compunction about letting a nearby smoker know that their smoking was irritating him. He told them about places Sparshot and Rivers had gone to and things they had done together. "He was always obsessive, needed to be the dominant party in their relationship. The fact that he was a control freak who had to control every aspect of her life was the reason that Tracy left him."

Machin knew what would've happened if Sparshot hadn't left Rivers. He would've still murdered her, but the murder would've been of the slow, tortuous variety over many months and years. "During the attack, Debbie Duncan said Rivers kept shouting that she would always be his," Machin said. "What you're telling us seems to fit with what she says."

Douglas wondered if he should mention anything about the incident with the Yank? The police hadn't mentioned it, so he was fairly sure they didn't know anything about it. The last thing Douglas needed to do was put doubts in their eyes about his credibility now that Rivers was on the run. As a result of his worries, he said nothing about it. "Sometimes, when he got irritated and spoke quickly, there was an accent."

Machin's ears pricked up. "What kind of accent?"

"Tracy had cousins that came from Lancashire. She said it sounded slightly Mancunian."

Roberts was frantically making notes. Machin was already focused. It meant that Rivers must've spent some time in the northwest. It felt like a door was fractionally ajar—one that gave the hint of a past and a chance to fill in some of the jigsaw puzzle.

Douglas told them everything he could think of. There was nothing concrete that would lead anywhere in anything he told them. The accent was interesting, he thought, but it didn't mean it would help them find anything. When Douglas left, he looked less disturbed than on arrival. His trust in the police was gone, but Machin hoped that—from what Douglas had told them, and from his point of view—maybe, they'd have a chance to redeem themselves.

CHAPTER 68

Dexter looked in the bedsit bathroom mirror. It had been a week since he'd dyed his hair, two weeks since he'd shaved. He'd dyed his beard, it was no good having dark where everything about his hair was light. His look was now decidedly Swedish—he could easily pass as a member of ABBA. It wasn't ideal. Dexter preferred his disguises to be much more detailed than this. He took the cheap glasses he'd bought out of his pocket and put them on.

The transformation was astonishing. The glasses now leaned his image toward the college professor. The disguise would fool most people.

It wouldn't fool DI Machin. She didn't seem as gullible to Dexter's games as others were. He'd looked up all the details he could glean about her on the internet. She was a clever detective, had been involved in solving a couple of gangland murders that had led to major convictions. Dexter had seen her stepping from the hotel lift the night of Debbie's rape. After the failure of Douglas's conviction, she'd correctly concluded that all paths led back to him. Dexter could recognize obsession, he understood it better than most. The obsession that inflicted him in pursuit of specimens worthy of his attention was the same obsession inflicting Machin in her manhunt for Dexter.

He blamed Debbie. If Debbie had done what she was meant to, worshipped at the altar of Dexter like she ought to have, Machin's attention would have been irrelevant, and he was sure that she would have been unable to prove that Dexter had murdered Tracy.

Debbie changed everything. She would have to be destroyed for the way she'd ruined his life. Leaving such a vile specimen alive was something that Dexter could never let happen.

Today he would go to his safety-deposit box and get the documents that would make it easier for him to set up a new identity. He stared at the dirt and grime around the shower tray and decided that he had to rent a flat and soon. Dexter had money, all the money that he'd hidden from Carol before he'd killed her was relatively intact. Carol had thought she'd been clever, covered all the bases by cleaning out their joint account when she'd been about to leave him.

What Carol hadn't realized was that she'd stolen a fraction of their joint assets, as Dexter had been slipping money from their account into a safety-deposit box for months. The safety-deposit box was the only sure way Dexter knew of making things stay hidden. It was a method he intended to keep throughout the rest of his illustrious career.

When he stepped out of the front door in his new disguise and wearing a new suit, he felt more confident and in control than he had for a long time. Today he was going flat hunting, but only in a place from where he could safely complete his goals. He got on a bus to West London where there was a flat that had just become available around Richmond that looked particularly desirable for his needs. It was expensive, but Dexter wasn't bothered—money was no object, providing it was in the apartment block that he needed to be in. Money didn't matter—all that mattered was being close to him, the person who had all the answers to his problems—the one who was going to create the environment that would enable Dexter to get Detective Machin off his back for good.

CHAPTER 69

Carol Barnes," Roberts said, looking at his computer screen. "She was murdered with a kitchen knife, and the house was torched to add to the confusion. The chief suspect in the murder is a man called Dexter Blackstock, her husband, who disappeared around the time of the murder."

"And this was in Manchester?"

"Yes. In Baguley three years ago. The police have no leads as to where Blackstock is, as the man's completely disappeared off the radar." Roberts printed out a sheet with the crime details from the Greater Manchester Police.

Machin read the police report. Neighbors and friends of the couple reported that Blackstock had obsessive, compulsive tendencies, and the time span fitted some of the missing dates in Rivers's past. Machin had to admit it had possibilities. Cowley had given Machin and Roberts permission to drive up to Manchester to check it out. They had photos of Rivers from the film set that Machin intended showing to people who knew Blackstock to see if Rivers and Blackstock were one and the same man.

"Good work, Sergeant," Machin said.

Roberts was a good organizer, she thought. His dogged determination enabled him to find things that others couldn't. She rang Nick and said that she'd be staying in Manchester overnight so wouldn't be around for a couple of days. Nick was disappointed. His city job was stressful and all-consuming. Making love with her was a wonderful release for both of them. She promised to call him the moment she returned. Nick was the first good relationship she had been involved in for a long time.

But thoughts of Nick would have to wait.

As they headed north, she kept thinking of Rivers. She rang the South Wales police for a progress report, but they hadn't found him. That didn't surprise her in the least—he must have left the area. When DI Evans told her they would be keeping a guard on Debbie Duncan indefinitely, Machin was relieved. In Manchester, she needed to talk to the people face-to-face who'd been around Blackstock and Barnes. Some things you just couldn't do on the computer. She needed to look into their eyes and see if Rivers's ghost was lurking there in the guise of Dexter Blackstock. Machin hoped that Manchester would fill in some of the gaps and have some of the answers. As they sped along the motorway in the afternoon sun, they passed a road sign, which read: *MANCHESTER 50 MILES*. She hoped that a lot of the answers to the mystery that was Peter Rivers were waiting in the Baguley area of Manchester, fifty miles away.

CHAPTER 70

Debbie had insisted that she wanted to go home to Guildford to be near her mother.

The police weren't happy about it and had wanted her to remain in Wales for a few weeks while the hunt for Peter Rivers was in full swing. Debbie sat in her mum's front room, drinking one of the endless cups of tea that her mum seemed to produce for her. Her mum meant well and tried to comfort her in her sad, bumbling fashion, but this was one ordeal that Debbie couldn't be comforted from. She couldn't sleep, as visions of the attack wouldn't leave her head.

It wasn't just the raw desolation of the rape that was getting to her, it was also the fact that the police hadn't captured Rivers and he was still out there. There was a police guard outside her door. It was meant to reassure her and show that the police took Rivers's threat to her safety seriously. It was as she dozed in her chair after dinner one afternoon that she awoke to find Paul Rome and her mum standing over her.

"Mr. Rome has come to see you, Debbie darling," Mrs. Duncan said.

"Please call me Paul," Rome said.

Mrs. Duncan said she would and then went to make them tea. After she left, an uncomfortable silence enveloped the room. Finally, Rome said, "I wasn't sure whether to come and see you, but I had to come, Debbie, I'm worried about you."

He wasn't the only one. Debbie was worried about herself with psycho Rivers out there somewhere. The police had left her a two-man guard. It should've reassured her, but it still left her wondering whether two men would be enough?

She'd never seen such hate and loathing in a man as she'd seen that night. It was as if a mask had suddenly slipped, and Rivers's true evil had been revealed.

"Thanks for coming," Debbie offered somewhat weakly, not sure if she wanted Rome there or not.

Mrs. Duncan brought in the tea and then left them alone to talk. Rome tried to make conversation.

He tried to take Debbie's mind off of recent events by talking about the film. He told her that Thompson had put everything on hold until Debbie was ready to film the final scenes.

"I wish I'd done more about Rivers," Rome said. "I thought there was something strange about the man, he was always trying to goad me because he knew I liked you. The incident in the hotel toilets should've told me there was something not right about him."

"I should've known, Paul. I was close to him, and I should've noted the warning signs."

Rome didn't know what to say—only Debbie, being Rivers's lover, could've known if there were any warning signs.

"He fooled everybody, Debbie. Thompson and the rest of the crew thought he was normal."

"But you didn't."

"No, Debbie, I didn't. There was always something about him I found strange.

When you were seeing him, I never said anything because I thought you'd just class it as the rantings of a jealous love rival." Rome regretted the fact he hadn't pushed it. He would always wonder whether or not it would've made a difference.

Debbie had seemed to be besotted with Rivers, so much so that Rome was surprised when Debbie said, "The night of the attack, I told Rivers that I didn't want a relationship after the movie, and it was over between us."

Rome let her statement sink in. He thought that Debbie and Rivers were a couple, but what he was being told, now, confirmed otherwise. "Thompson looked up Rivers's employment records, and there are big holes in his employment past. Up to two years ago, nobody seems to know much about him."

The police had told Rome a certain amount but not everything. They hadn't revealed Rivers's stint in the mental institution. There was a lot the police hadn't told the film crew, so as not to make them any more jittery than they already were. Sam, the makeup girl, had told the police of sporadic acts of violence she'd witnessed from Rivers during their brief relationship. Rome thought that if Debbie had only spoken to Sam earlier, then maybe she'd have ended her relationship long before she did. Regrettably, nothing could now change the chain of events, and Debbie would have to live with it.

Rome tried to comfort her, but he could see that the only comfort she was going to get was via the passage of time and the fading of her memory. When he left, he felt that his visit had achieved nothing. Debbie barely nodded after him as he shut the front door and went back to his Mercedes. As he drove away, he was lost in thought, so much so that he didn't notice a dark presence hidden behind him. As the cold Beretta pistol barrel pressed into his side, he finally noticed someone was there. Alas, for Paul Rome, Hollywood legend, the moment he noticed was already too late.

CHAPTER 71

Carrie Iverson was a small mousy woman. Her eyes didn't help dispel that image as they seemed unable to focus on you and continually darted around you. It was only after she'd carefully examined Machin's badge for a few moments that she finally released the security catch on the door, and let Machin and Roberts enter her house. Her cramped living room smelled of cat. Machin and Roberts sat uneasily down on the magazine-strewn sofa then explained why they were there. Machin noted a fear in Iverson's tired-looking eyes when Machin mentioned the fire and the murder of Carol Barnes.

"I never did like Dexter," Iverson finally offered. "There was always something about him that didn't strike you as quite right. I used to hear him shout at Carol. He was always bullying that poor woman. Why she put up with it until he did what he did, I'll never know."

Machin wanted more and pressed for details. Iverson told her what she knew.

She explained about the domineering attitude Blackstock had toward Barnes—it sounded similar to the story that Sam, the Regal makeup girl, had told. It was a carbon copy of the story Douglas had been told by Sparshot during her time with Rivers. Iverson's story sounded so similar that, when Machin showed Iverson a couple of pictures of Rivers, she was not surprised when Iverson confirmed that Peter Rivers, alias Trevor Slater, was, in fact, Dexter Blackstock.

After the interview, Machin sat in the car and faced her many demons. This was the second murder that they knew about. That murder, combined with Tracy Sparshot's murder, meant that they now knew that Rivers was responsible for at least two murders. If they hadn't gone to the hotel that night to arrest him, Machin was convinced that Rivers would also have murdered Duncan and Thompson.

"A serial killer, ma'am," Roberts said, stating the obvious.

It somehow seemed worse when Roberts said it, Machin thought. Up until that moment, she had been in a state of denial. Now that Roberts had said it, she couldn't deny it any longer. The bodies were starting to pile up—it was reminiscent of the worst excesses of Bundy and Gasey. How many more were out there, waiting to be discovered? It was a question that Machin wasn't sure she wanted to know the answer to—because where there were bodies, pain and misery wouldn't be far behind. Machin had found in her job over the years that pain and misery had a habit of seeping into your soul and leaving nothing but a dull ache in your head.

CHAPTER 72

DI Machin and DS Roberts stood at the edge of the cliff top and stared at the crumpled Mercedes down below. This craggy stretch of Sussex coastline with its meandering cliffs and easy access to the public was known as Suicide Alley by the locals.

Machin, staring over the edge at the sheer drop, could see why, if you wanted to kill yourself quickly, one leap of faith from the dewy grass down into the abyss would be enough to guarantee an instant death on the jagged rocks below. They'd found the body of Paul Rome in the crumpled Mercedes. Paul Rome, egomaniac film star, as far as Machin was concerned, was definitely not the suicide type.

"The media will be all over this, ma'am," Roberts said.

They certainly would be, Machin thought. They were already hounding the police over the Debbie Duncan attack, and, when they found out that Hollywood heartthrob Paul Rome was dead, the media interest would go through the stratosphere. Then there was the fact that Duncan's attacker was now confirmed as a lunatic serial killer. Machin was already getting a headache thinking about the flak that Cowley and the press were going to give her.

Seeing as there was nothing they could do here, they went back to the car, sat, and made calls on their mobiles. Rome's body had been found in the car and identified at the crime scene. There could be no doubt it was him. At the moment, they weren't sure whether Rome was already dead when the car hit the rocks or whether he'd died as a result of the fall. Machin would wait until the autopsy confirmed the cause of death, but in her head, she had no doubts after what they'd discovered up north, that Rome's death was murder, and Peter Rivers was the killer. She rang HQ and ordered another guard to be put on Debbie Duncan.

Rome had visited her at her Guildford home a few hours before he'd been found dead. In the police interviews with Debbie Duncan and Paul Rome, the police had established that Rome and Rivers were love rivals, a rivalry that had recently come to blows. As Machin perceived it, Rivers—the jealous, possessive serial killer—had eliminated a love rival.

It was horrible and, yet, it was good. Horrible that Rome had been murdered, but good that it showed that Rivers was still hovering around Debbie Duncan—an obsession with her that Machin hoped would lead to his downfall. Rivers must've been nearby watching the Duncan household when Rome had visited earlier today. He must've waited for Rome to return to his car and then pounced, she surmised. She checked with Rome's nearby hotel, and nobody had seen him there since he'd left in the morning, confirming that her appraisal of events was probably true. She drove to the Duncan house and sadly told Debbie the grim news.

"I'm ruling out suicide," she stated coldly.

"Paul Rome was full of life, there's no way he would've killed himself," Debbie said, her mind already lost in the terror and despair just thinking about it.

"The stretch of cliff the Mercedes went off at can't be reached by car without breaking a padlock to open a nearby gate. There's no doubt that the Mercedes going off there wasn't an accident, the fall was deliberate."

Suddenly alarm registered on Debbie's face. "It was him, wasn't it?"

"Until the autopsy, we can't be sure, but if you want my opinion, I think Rivers murdered Rome."

"My God!" Debbie cried. "He must've been out there watching the house when Paul arrived."

"I've increased the guard outside, Miss Duncan," Machin offered feebly.

The dismay that now showed on Duncan's face indicated she wasn't going to be pacified.

"I want to be moved to a safe house," she pleaded.

Machin wanted to move her to a safe house, too. She couldn't. There were overriding reasons that, if she told Debbie Duncan, she'd never understand. The plain and simple truth of the matter was that Peter Rivers seemed obsessed with Duncan and would keep coming after her, something you could never tell Duncan. You could never tell her the fact that she was being used as bait. "With the extra guards, you'll be safe here," Machin promised.

"That madman is out there—I want to be moved!"

"If we move you, Debbie, he's still going to be out there. If we move you, your mum will still be in danger."

"I want Mum moved with me!" Debbie insisted.

Machin sighed. "If we move you, then you're going to be forever worrying about Rivers. Until we capture him, even in a safe house, you'll never feel truly safe with Rivers forever out there—he'll always be haunting your dreams."

"You're meant to reassure me," Debbie said.

"With a killer out there on the loose, I can't afford reassurance. If I'm going to protect the public, I need action." The detective decided not to mention the fact that they now had confirmation Rivers regularly switched identities and was a serial killer.

A door suddenly opened in Debbie's mind. The look of horror that, she knew, had previously been fixed on her face was nothing to the terror that must now reside there. "You're using me as bait," she yelled.

The silence that now engulfed the room told Debbie she was right. Machin finally said, "I wouldn't call it bait, I'd call it more a reason for Rivers to stay in the area. If we move you, then he's got nothing to stay near here for, and it'll probably mean that we lose his trail for good."

"Don't play that game with me, Inspector!" Debbie rounded angrily. "Don't try and make me feel guilty if I ask you to move me and Mum for our own safety."

Machin didn't know what to say. Already she'd said too much. Admitting to a recent rape victim that they were for using her for bait was definitely not in the police's manual for the way to handle victims. "I'm not trying to make you feel guilty, Miss Duncan, I'm just asking you to face up to reality. How long, with limited police resources, do you think we'll be able to keep a three-officer guard on you? You've seen how resourceful Rivers is, there's no way that we can guarantee a safe house will be completely safe for you."

Debbie stared blankly out the window, lost in thought. Machin could see that she finally realized how vulnerable her position really was. Debbie now saw many demons through her window, demons that wouldn't be expunged by simply moving. "So what you're, in effect, saying, is that I've got no choice."

"There's always a choice, Miss Duncan. If you want,

I'll get on to the relevant people to arrange a safe house. Personally, I'd advise against it, if Rivers is hanging around the area because he's obsessed with you, then that obsession isn't just going to end because you've moved. Staying here means you have a chance to put an end to this and an opportunity to finally get this monster out of your life."

Debbie had problems concentrating on anything since the attack. Visions of the nightmare that Rivers had subjected her to in that hotel room wouldn't leave her. Was Machin offering her a chance to expunge those demons, or was she offering her death?

Debbie didn't know. Nobody could know. Debbie was being asked to make a decision here that could irrevocably change her life. If the police didn't capture Rivers, she was forever going to see him out there. Did she want to spend the rest of her life in a state of nervous exhaustion, always with the expectation he might come calling on her? She decided she didn't, quickly concluding that she had no other option other than to become Machin's worm.

CHAPTER 73

It was a nice riverside apartment. Dexter stood on the balcony overlooking the meandering Thames, tired after his hectic day's exertions. Paul Rome, Hollywood legend and ego-obsessed film star, was dead. Rome had quickly found out on that Sussex clifftop that death could quickly become a reality in the real world and not just a passing nuance in another one of his action movies. A forensic examination would quickly discover the drugs in Rome's system, the position of the injection prick in the back of his neck would rapidly prove that he hadn't injected them into himself.

Debbie would now know Dexter was out there and hadn't forgotten her. How could he ever forget her? How could he forget this woman who had spurned his advances? The fact that she now knew, and that terror would be throbbing through her veins, suitably inspired him. Dexter would now take time for his planning and preparation. Everything was now moving back in the direction he wanted.

He was back in control. Debbie Duncan had momentarily upset the equilibrium of his life, but that disruption would soon be over with her death, and then he could start anew.

A chill wind cut through him off the gray-green river. Dexter slipped back into his plush, well-decorated living room and sat on the shiny leather sofa. He was paying a fortune for living in this exclusive corner of London, a corner that was only three miles from where he'd killed Tracy. It might as well have been the other side of the world as far as the blundering efforts of the police manhunt for him were concerned. He switched on the TV news—there were some breaking stories of the mysterious death of Hollywood legend, Paul Rome, in a car crash in Sussex. Dexter laughed. The only crash had occurred after Dexter had pushed the Mercedes off the clifftop with an unconscious Rome inside. It had certainly crashed when it hit the rocks below, which reminded him of the moment of exhilaration felt as he'd stood and watched Rome die. It was an exhilaration he'd long ago decided he couldn't live without.

He looked at his watch. It was six p.m., and the last fading vestiges of daylight were turning to dark black night. He stood out on the balcony, from where he'd watched his new specimen for several days, and now was about his time to return from work. As the smart-suited man stepped out of the cab below, he had no idea that Dexter was watching his every move.

His new specimen would never know that their first meeting was going to be anything other than chance.

These were the moments—the moments when every sense in your body was heightened with the expectation of what lay ahead. Dexter quickly left the balcony and hurried out the front door. When the lift opened, and Dexter's prey stepped out of it, Dexter bumped into him.

"Sorry," Dexter apologized, "I should be more careful."

"No problem," the man said.

Dexter seized the moment. "You live next door to me. I'm Giles Perkins, your new neighbor."

They shook hands. It was a manly shake, firm but respectful. "I'm Nick Spiller," Nick said.

You most certainly are, Dexter thought. *You're Nick Spiller, city trader, thriving city businessman. You're a Tory voter, and you went to school at Eaton. In 2008, you were divorced from Tania Lucock, who's now married to an accountant called Simon and living in Hertfordshire.*

There wasn't much that Dexter hadn't researched about Mr. Nick Spiller. Of all the things he'd looked up, discovered, highlighted as an area of potential weakness, there was one thing that stood out from all the others, which meant Mr. Nick Spiller's days on this planet were numbered.

Nick Spiller had the misfortune of being the boyfriend of DI Machin. Rather regrettable for Nick Spiller's welfare, she was the detective inspector who was proving to be too much of a thorn in Dexter's controlling life plan.

CHAPTER 74

Thompson didn't know what to expect. Debbie was in a hell of a state after the rape when she'd returned home to her mum. Now, with Rome dead, she was likely to be much worse. For the first few minutes of his visit, he stood and held her in the center of the living room. It caused an uncomfortable moment for Mrs. Duncan, who stood there in silence after showing Thompson into the room. Any thoughts Thompson had, about Debbie not being in his life and remaining at a distance, had now ended as he stood in this room, holding her tight, knowing that she was a woman that he needed as a friend and one he wanted to protect from life's ills. Finally, they separated as Mrs. Duncan coped with the trauma of the situation in the only way she knew how, and that was by making tea.

After it was made, Mrs. Duncan laid the tray on the oak coffee table then left them alone. They both ignored the tea and talked. "He's still out there after me," Debbie told Thompson nervously.

"Did he kill Rome?" Thompson asked.

That question had been bugging him since he'd

heard news of Rome's death. He knew enough about Rome to know that Paul Rome wasn't the suicide type.

"There's no evidence yet to prove for certain, but DI Machin thinks so."

In Thompson's meeting with Machin, he'd found her clever and efficient—if she thought that Rivers had killed Rome, then he believed he had. "I'm going to stay here with you until they capture him," he told her, reassuringly.

"Thank you," she said. A few months ago, the fiercely independent Debbie Duncan would never have agreed to this, Thompson thought. It showed how much the rape and the aftermath had badly affected her psyche that she'd said yes in an instant.

"The police will get him, Debbie," Thompson tried to reassure her. But with the police's poor performance in the manhunt to date, he was far from certain of that scenario.

"He must've been waiting for Paul when he left here, as the time of death, according to the police estimate, was a couple of hours after Paul left me yesterday," Debbie said, remembering how considerate Paul had been on his visit. He'd come to see her because he genuinely cared. His reward for his kindness had been death.

"Until the police capture him, I'm sticking to you like glue," Thompson promised.

He held her again, and Debbie decided, locked in his strong arms, that she felt the safest she'd felt in a long time.

After Thompson was settled, Debbie went for a bath, while Mrs. Duncan was busy making dinner. Thompson got his travel bag from the car, telling the police guards that he'd be staying there for a while.

When he returned to the house, he thought about the guards' camaraderie when he'd told them and wondered if the guards would've been so welcoming if they'd known what was in his bag.

In the living room, Thompson laid his travel bag on the sofa then went over to the window and pulled the curtains across. After making sure the Duncan women were both occupied, he went back to his bag and fumbled underneath the clothes to the bottom. As his hand brushed against the cold metal, it sent a shiver down his spine. In a recent movie called, *Downgrade* about Glasgow crime gangs, Thompson had met some of society's less savory characters. One of those characters had been ice-cream baron and Glasgow crime overlord, Archie McFadden.

With his rough housing estate upbringing, Thompson had found he seemed to hit it off with the McFaddens of this world. He, himself, had lived among the unwashed, knew the social conditions at close hand that created criminals like McFadden. It meant that, when Thompson had made his request to McFadden, he had been most willing and able to supply it.

Thompson studied the Sig Sauer pistol as he took it from the bag, the name sounding like Tom Sawyer's Swedish cousin. But one look at the fine cut of the metal and the lethal box of shells McFadden had supplied with it, and Thompson could see that, in the hand of the right man, this handgun could be a weapon of brutal destruction. He tried holding it and aiming it at the door, wondering if he was capable of using it. He'd never killed anyone. He wasn't sure if he could kill even a reptile like Rivers. When he thought about what Rivers had done to Debbie and the murder of Paul Rome, as he hid the gun back among his clothes, Thompson could feel dark, menacing forces stirring inside him. It was at this moment, he had his answer, and that answer was yes, in the case of Peter Rivers, Thompson was sure he could pull the trigger.

CHAPTER 75

It had been a long crappy day. Machin stared at the information boards in the incident room, with all the relevant information about Rivers posted there, and concluded that they were no closer to finding him than they had been at the start of the day. She needed a couple of hours' downtime solace to take her mind off this current stage of the disaster that was the manhunt for Rivers. She told Roberts and the team that she was stepping out for a couple of hours and would return by midnight. Nobody begrudged her a break—she was the hardest working member of the team, which earned her their respect. The fact that she was the last person on the team that day to take some downtime showed their respect for her wasn't misplaced.

A clear sky meant the first whiff of winter was in the air as she stepped into her car and called Nick on her mobile.

"I want to come over for a couple of hours," she told him.

"I'll be waiting," Nick said. "I'll just get rid of Giles—"

"Who's Giles?" she asked, not recalling the name in Nick's list of acquaintances.

"Giles moved into the flat next door a few days ago. He's a university teacher, a very nice man."

Machin's alarm bells were ringing. "What does he look like?"

"Does it matter?"

"Just tell me, Nick," Machin pushed.

"If you must know, he's about six foot with strawberry blond hair and a beard," Nick said.

The alarm bells started dissipating, even so, she wanted to meet the guy and make sure. She told Nick she'd be there in a minute and would like to meet this man who was Nick's new best friend. He said he'd keep him there until she arrived. She wondered if she was becoming paranoid. Rivers was getting inside her skin, making her doubt everything around her. In all her years in the force she'd never conducted a hunt for a serial killer. It was unchartered territory, was bound to have some mental repercussions.

She picked up a Chinese take-away she thought would suitably fortify her for the long night ahead. When she went back to the incident room, God only knew when she was going to resurface again. This case had taken over her life and would encompass all of her being until the monster was captured. Then there were Rome, Debbie Duncan, other endless complications. She needed to be held in the loving arms of her boyfriend for a couple of hours.

It was times like this that she was glad she wasn't alone.

As she stepped out of her car outside of Nick's luxury Richmond apartment block, she quickly noted everything around her. She double-checked that her car was locked. After what happened to Rome, she couldn't afford to take any chances. The pathology lab had gotten back to them—there were traces of barbiturates in Rome's system and a needle mark on the back of his neck. She now had no doubts that Rome had been murdered and had warned her team to be careful. Rome's and Sparshot's murders showed how dangerous Rivers could be.

Then there was Carol Barnes. After talking to witnesses in Manchester, and all of them confirming the picture of Rivers as the man they'd known as Dexter Blackstock, it left yet another murder to lay at Rivers's door. Machin wondered where it was going to end, as she stepped out of the lift and knocked on Nick's door.

Nick was warm and welcoming as he opened the door. They hugged and kissed. It was at moments like this that she realized that this man was everything to her. As they stepped into the living room and she saw Giles Perkins, her alarm bells were suddenly on full alert.

When Perkins fired the silenced Beretta 92FS twice at Nick, and her boyfriend crumpled to the floor in front of her, Machin knew that her realization had come too late for Nick.

CHAPTER 76

DS Roberts was sitting at his desk looking over CCTV footage from traffic cameras in the area near the Duncan house. It was a long, soulless task with so far nothing of any relevance found to make his efforts seem worthwhile. It was as he stopped for a moment to have a swig of his coffee and was quickly thumbing through the messages on his mobile phone, that he noticed the message that had come in a short while ago from DI Machin. She said she'd found some new information, had a new lead. She told Roberts that she was going to Luton to follow it up and that she'd ring him later.

Roberts was baffled. Machin had gone to her boyfriend's for some downtime. How could she have found a new lead on the way there? It didn't make sense. He rang her, but all he got was her voicemail which probably meant she was driving. He tried to think of any significance of Luton to the investigation but could think of nothing the team had been investigating that would lead in that direction. He needed to speak to her. He'd try her mobile again in a short while and keep trying till he got an answer. If there was a startling new development in the hunt for Rivers, then Roberts wanted to be in on the kill.

Roberts wasn't one for waiting—a fact he proved by ringing her three more times before a half-hour was up. It was not normal for Machin not to involve Roberts. This was very out of character for her. He went back to looking at the security camera footage. If she wasn't answering her phone, there was nothing he could do until he finally spoke to her.

In a few minutes, he'd show the others the text message and ask them if they'd encountered any reference to Luton in their search for Rivers.

Roberts could only surmise that it might be a link to Rivers's past, but, until he spoke to Machin, he could only guess. He rang her again and left another message. He couldn't hide the irritation in his voice, all he could think as he was speaking was, *Pick up the bloody phone, Inspector.*

CHAPTER 77

Machin was tied to Nick's double bed. The knots were expert, couldn't be moved, the knots of a monster who was used to tying up his victims. Rivers had gagged her and momentarily left the room. He returned carrying one of Nick's sharp kitchen knives, he'd put the gun in his pocket. It looked like it wasn't going to be a quick kill. He stood beside the bed and stared at her, seemed to be savoring the moment. Meanwhile, Machin was thinking about Nick lying dead on the floor in the other room, and tears formed in her eyes. There would be no reprieve from the cavalry. The monster had laughed as he informed her that he'd just texted her colleague to inform him she'd gone to Luton to follow up a lead.

Dexter looked at the supreme specimen before him. A fully ranked police inspector was the ultimate prize. DI Machin had magnificent grit and determination. He needed to see how far he could mentally strip her before the kill. The body of her boyfriend in the other room meant she was hurting, in her cornflower-blue eyes he could see an intense mixture of loss and hatred. It meant she was ready for his ultimate mind game. He went to the living room, dragged the body of Nick into the bedroom, and plonked him on a chair near the bed. The specimen needed a constant reminder of what he'd done to her, how Dexter had ended all her hopes and dreams.

Dexter couldn't see an engagement ring on Machin's finger. He was disappointed, as an engagement ring would have meant that they'd made a lifelong commitment, that he'd taken away everything that encompassed her future life. With the knife, he gently cut off Machin's blouse buttons. As the last button pinged, she stared at him with fear and loathing.

Dexter liked the fear of women, their realization that they'd made it in a male-dominated world. Yet, the position that Machin now found herself in meant that, inevitably—for all her protestations of work success—her current predicament proved that, in fact, she was the weaker sex.

He stood back and admired her helplessness. She was a woman in charge, a detective always used to working methodically and being in control of a situation. Dexter couldn't imagine the thoughts that must be racing through her head, as she realized that her job, and the fact that it had brought Dexter to the door, had inevitably caused Nick's murder. Dexter needed time to work, time without distractions. Debbie Duncan was his Achilles heel. Until she was dead, he couldn't hope to enjoy new experiences.

"I'd like to give you my full attention, Inspector, but first I've got unfinished business to take care of." Dexter laid the kitchen knife on the window ledge, intending to leave it there to tantalize her thoughts while he was away.

People didn't escape from Dexter's bonds. The Internet was a wonderful tool, and Dexter had experimented with all kinds of rope knots over the years, via the web, until he'd decided on several of the unbreakable variety.

He took some bullets from his pocket and reloaded the Beretta. He went out on the balcony and stared at the night sky and the rain that was starting to pour. Rain was a cleanser, a washer, but—unlike Dexter—t wasn't the means to wash away the sins of Debbie Duncan and DI Machin.

CHAPTER 78

Thompson awoke from his uncomfortable doze on the lumpy sofa. In his semi-conscious state, he'd heard something. He listened intently for a few minutes. When he didn't hear anything further, and after he'd glanced out the front window and seen nothing, he decided he'd imagined it and went back to sleep.

Outside, Dexter remained still, in the undergrowth, deciding he'd made too much noise when he'd trodden on the fallen branch. After fifteen minutes and with no guards coming to investigate, he continued his slow journey through the undergrowth. The cop in the car had been easy, had made Dexter's kill simple by leaving his front passenger window open enough for Dexter to fire his silenced Beretta point blank into the side of the cop's head.

There were two of them left. One stood near the front door, the other was around the back. Dexter crept through the undergrowth, approaching the porch, under which the armed officer was sheltering from the rain. As Dexter got near, his eyes were completely focused on the Heckler & Koch that was slung in front of the guard's hands, so much so that Dexter didn't notice the horror and exasperation in the guard's eyes as the two fatal shots from Dexter's Beretta thudded into the guard's head, causing an explosion of the guard's brain dura and immediate death. As Dexter stood over the dead man, the guard's radio crackled to life, as the guard from the back of the house checked in. Dexter had to move quickly, the other guard would expect an immediate reply from his partner. When none was forthcoming, he'd instantly smell a rat.

Dexter didn't panic. When you panicked, you made mistakes and lost control. As the other guard's radio messages became more frantic, Dexter did the only thing he could, or any sensible man could do under the circumstances, and that was, he took his clothes off.

CHAPTER 79

Roberts rang Machin's mobile phone again and still he couldn't get an answer. In desperation, he rang her boyfriend, Nick's, home number. When Nick didn't answer, Roberts was starting to get concerned. It was after midnight, so even if Nick had gone out for the evening, by now, he'd have surely returned. Roberts made a quick decision, grabbed his coat, and headed for his car. He would go to Nick's apartment and see if he knew where Machin had gone to. It was ten past twelve, and she still hadn't replied to his many messages. It was very unlike her, worryingly unlike his boss.

With such an important manhunt taking place, he couldn't understand why she seemed to have taken herself out of phone contact. If she'd gone to Luton, she'd be there by now and would've had an opportunity to call in. Maybe Nick would know the answer, could put an end to this mystery. Roberts had left DC Thomas in charge and told him to ring him immediately if there were any developments. So far their trawl through the Guildford CCTV network had found nothing. Rivers was clever, a very dangerous adversary, the chances were that there wouldn't be anything. To kill Rome like that in an area with a heavy police presence took either a lot of balls or it showed how much of a head case Rivers was. It meant that Rivers was so far lost in the realms of insanity that he could no longer appreciate risk.

Roberts was worried, which made the fact that he couldn't get hold of Machin even more alarming. He'd never known his boss text and not ring, as all good detectives knew when a person changed their routine it was suspicious. Whatever it was, the answer wasn't sitting here waiting for the call that never seemed like it was going to come.

Nick would know the answer as he was the last person to see her before the text. He wouldn't be happy when Roberts knocked on his door this time of the night. He didn't care, he simply wanted answers, and decided that the only way he was going to get them was via a visit to Nick Spiller.

CHAPTER 80

Police arms unit member, Sergeant Craig Davis, was worried as he couldn't get hold of Foster for their regular half-hourly check-in. He frantically tried again and still got no reply. He tried his colleague in the patrol car, but couldn't raise Munroe either. Munroe was their back up, should have answered immediately when Davis called. Something was badly wrong. He unfastened the safety catch on his weapon. His hand was shaking and his palms sweating. He wondered where the fuck his colleagues were.

He moved away from the back door, as standing there, he was an open target.

Now was the time to follow his training. He crouched low and ducked into nearby bushes. In the damp saturated bushes, he froze and listened. In the misty rain, he could see bushes moving around the side of the house as he realized that someone was edging toward him. He aimed his Heckler in the direction of the approaching figure, a figure he could barely make out in the murk.

As the figure got closer and he could see the unmistakable outline of a police uniform and Foster's Heckler, he stepped onto the slippery grass.

"Why didn't you answer the radio?" Davis snapped irritably at his partner.

"Because I'm afraid that I'm dead," Dexter said and fired his silenced Beretta point blank into Davis's forehead.

Davis clattered to the soggy ground, his face locked in an uncomprehending death mask. Dexter dragged Davis's body into the clammy bushes out of view. Foster had encountered a similar fate after Dexter had stripped him.

From his pocket, Dexter took out his set of skeleton keys. He thought of Debbie lying asleep inside and considered the moment when she realized that he hadn't forgotten her and he was in her room. As he unlocked the back door of the Duncan house and quietly entered, he could feel his phallus hardening. These moments of fear and tension were what he lived for, gave him a sexual buzz that nothing else in his life could.

He imagined the moment when the specimen opened her eyes and saw him standing by her bedside, thought of the look of terror and anguish as she realized the police weren't there to protect her. These were the moments Dexter craved—the moments he couldn't live without, he decided, as he cut the phone line for the hall phone and then slowly started to climb the stairs.

CHAPTER 81

Machin thrashed violently on the bed. She could feel the ropes burning into her wrists. They were never going to give. The metal headboard was another matter. As the wobbly headboard started to waver, she thanked God for Nick's shoddy DIY skills.

His landline phone shrilled several times during her struggle. She knew it was Roberts. He was a good detective. He would've reacted to the absurdity of Rivers's text message—a message supposedly from Machin about Luton.

She rocked harder, and the headboard began slipping out of its mountings. As the board finally snapped and sprang free, she could feel the release of tension in her tightly strung arms. Her numb hands could barely move, and her blood circulation was seizing under the cruel tightness of the ropes. If she didn't act soon, she'd be unable to do anything.

Her bound hands were still attached to the loose headboard as she stretched them toward the window ledge where the kitchen knife lay temptingly. No matter how hard she stretched, she couldn't reach it. Her senses were alive to every creak and groan of Nick's apartment as she shook with fear at the thought of the monster's return. Listening to Rivers's rantings before he'd left, about seeing to Debbie Duncan, Machin was sure that Rivers had gone after her.

She rocked the bed back and forth, and now she could feel it starting to slide on the carpet. The knife was creeping closer as the bed edged nearer to the ledge. She rocked harder. The bed slid a couple more inches. She stopped and stretched again, the tips of her fingers touching the knife handle's cold steel. She wildly rocked the bed one last time, and it slid an inch closer. Her hand locked around the knife handle, and she turned it slowly around.

As she sliced through the rope, she cut her hand. Blood and severed rope finally dropped to the floor as her hands sprang free.

She cut the rest of her bonds, slowly clambered to her feet. As her numb legs straightened, they buckled under the strain, and she fell to the floor. She sat, helpless, on the floor while blood slowly pumped back into her hands and feet. She stared at the lifeless figure of Nick sitting in the chair near the bed and thought about his hard masculine body close to hers. As she finally felt some life in her body, she stumbled to her feet. There was no time to grieve as she hurriedly put on her clothes.

Debbie Duncan and the police team guarding her were in danger. A quick search of pockets made her realize that Rivers had taken her and Nick's mobile phones. She hobbled into the living room, was about to snatch up the landline phone and call for help when the doorbell rang.

She looked through the front door peephole and saw Roberts. When she opened the door, she collapsed into his arms.

Roberts held her a moment. "What's happened?"

"Rivers has killed Nick. He tied me to the bed—" Machin coughed violently as the tension was finally released. When her coughing had subsided, she said, "He's gone to kill Debbie Duncan. We need to call the Duncans' house."

Roberts called the police team at the Duncan household. Nobody answered.

He called the Duncan household landline and couldn't get an answer. As they bundled into Machin's car and sped off toward Guildford, she didn't like the dark thoughts that were rolling through her head. She put on the siren and rammed her foot to the floor. The fact that they couldn't get hold of Duncan's guards told Machin that Rivers had arrived and that the lives of all the Duncans and those of the police team who protected them were in the greatest possible danger.

CHAPTER 82

Dexter stood on the landing outside Debbie's room, listening silently to the sound of her rhythmic snoring. He allowed himself a brief moment of reflection—things could've been so different between them. He fingered the Beretta gently in his hand. Now it had come down to the brutal reality of a quick kill, but he'd do his best to savor the moment. It would be easy to ram the gun in the side of her head and pull the trigger. A shot to the temple would do it. One quick shot to the temple, and the complex problem of Debbie Duncan would be over.

If only it could be that easy. Alas, such luxuries weren't available for Dexter.

He needed to see the fear in her eyes, experience the hate and loathing as he made the kill. The ceremony of death was something that couldn't be taken lightly. He moved closer to the bed, sat on the corner beside her, and watched her as she slept. She moved restlessly in her sleep—a sixth sense, as if she felt his presence. He studied her porcelain-white face. She looked as beautiful in sleep as she would in death.

Dexter's heart bled when he thought of what he could've done with this woman.

Without the mental torture or the months of molding her the correct way, her death, although necessary for his personal closure, seemed an irrelevance. He held his hand over her smooth, soft lips. She awoke with a start. There was the moment of recognition, as fear and helplessness overwhelmed her when she saw the gun.

"I've come back for you, Debbie, darling. You must know that our business isn't done."

Debbie was frozen with fear. The silenced Beretta was inches from her head, one wrong move and she knew he wouldn't hesitate to kill her. Questions were racing through her mind, where were the guards? Thompson? Her mum? The fact that Rivers was wearing one of the guards' uniforms told her the guards were dead. Rivers saw her fear and smiled. He gently stroked the Beretta across her face and was pleased when a mixture of nervous sweat and tears began running down her smooth skin.

"Your mum's asleep and alive in the other room," Dexter stated coldly. "If you do as you're told, I promise I won't kill her."

Dexter slowly removed his hand from her mouth, Debbie wanted to scream but knew it was pointless. With all her guards and Thompson dead, nobody would be coming to save her. "Why did you kill Rome?" she asked, in a desperate bid to distract him and buy precious time.

"I needed to act. I warned him once about coming near my property, but he wouldn't back off."

Debbie thought of the fight between Rivers and Rome in the hotel toilets, how it had all been part of this possessive psychopath's warped game. Rome was dead, Thompson and the guards were dead, now there was nothing left for Debbie apart from cooperation with the monster so she could save her mum. Debbie wanted to fight, but she knew from his previous attack at the hotel that he was too strong. There was no hope left, she concluded, and wondered if she co-operated with him, if she could rely on him to keep his promise not to kill her mum.

"Please don't hurt Mum," she begged.

Dexter could feel inside him the depths of joy as he heard the once-mighty Debbie Duncan begging him for mercy. That one act of emotional weakness and contrition proved to Dexter, once and for all, that Debbie Duncan's spirit was broken. He decided to be magnanimous in victory. "This isn't about your mum. Now you're broken, I've no need to hurt her."

He was starting to rant, just as he did when he'd attacked her in the hotel room.

Debbie could sense that it was almost over. Everybody was dead, and it wouldn't be long before he killed her. With her death, she could only hope that he'd be satisfied and leave her mum alone.

It was as she thought of the horror that shortly awaited her that she saw it—it was faint and darting, only a flicker of movement, but it was a movement behind Rivers, nonetheless.

CHAPTER 83

Machin entered Guildford with her police lights flashing, siren wailing, and her accelerator foot rammed to the floor. She skidded as she hurtled through a red light and almost hit a taxi coming the other way. Roberts was talking to headquarters on his mobile. They couldn't raise anybody at the house, and the nearest patrol car was five minutes from the Duncan house. It looked like Machin and Roberts were going to be the first to arrive. Roberts took his pistol from his shoulder holster. He knew that Rivers was armed, armed and extremely dangerous. This was the reason why he'd signed out the gun that he was weapons trained to use.

When they were a few streets from the Duncan house, Machin turned off the siren, not wanting to alert Rivers to their presence. The wipers flapped away, rain beating on the windscreen, a reflection of them in the rearview mirror showing Machin that both their faces were etched with tension. She was unarmed so she would have to stick close to Roberts when they entered the property. She didn't like it. Rivers was not a man you wanted to confront without a weapon.

"Don't take any chances, Sergeant, this is a shoot-to-kill situation." Machin didn't want any hesitation. Hesitation with a psycho like Rivers got you killed.

When they were close, Roberts checked his weapon one last time. He was an expert marksman on the range, rarely ever missed. Shooting a man, compared to shooting a target, was a whole new ballgame, especially when the man was a deranged killer who'd be shooting back. When they arrived, they found Munroe with his head caked in blood dead in the backup car. Machin grabbed Munroe's weapon from his shoulder holster and checked that it was loaded. She smiled as she decided that the detectives' survival odds had now dramatically improved.

At the house, they separated. Roberts would go in the front and Machin would enter around the back. It was a classic pincer movement that would block Rivers's avenues of escape.

As she jumped a mossy, wooden fence and clambered through the undergrowth, she found Davis's still warm body. Rivers had arrived. He would show no mercy, she concluded, leaving Davis's body and edging toward the house. As she closed on the back door, she could feel a shiver run down her spine. Her mind and body were alive to the tension—she felt the clammy presence of the grim reaper hovering in her mind in the darkness. Machin was ready. After Nick's murder, she was determined that Rivers wasn't going to escape from their trap, and that, either with him dead or captured alive, the Peter Rivers manhunt was going to end here.

CHAPTER 84

The gun felt wrong in his hand. Thompson had never fired a handgun before, and he wasn't sure he could hit what he aimed at. He noted Debbie's position to Rivers who was standing over Debbie as she lay in bed. Alarmingly, she was too close to Rivers. If he fired with them being so close to each other, there was a very real chance he could kill Debbie. He concluded that using the gun was his last option.

As he was almost on top of Rivers, the man suddenly became aware of Thompson's presence and spun around. He was quick, but not quick enough to avoid the butt of Thompson's gun, smashing into his jaw and breaking it. The force of the blow caused Rivers's grip on his Beretta to loosen. The gun fell from his hand and clattered across the carpet. As Thompson turned his gun on him, Rivers grabbed Thompson's gun arm and pointed the barrel away from him. Both men lost their balance and crashed to the floor locked in a desperate arm wrestle for control of the Sig Sauer. In the melee, Thompson felt his grip on the gun weaken as Rivers's psychotic strength was winning the battle. Just before Rivers could wrestle the Sig

Sauer free, Thompson dropped it on the floor, and they both frantically grabbed for it.

Thompson locked Rivers in a Judo hold. Rivers's arms flung wildly. The gun was within a foot of them on the floor. Rivers slipped an arm free and stretched toward it.

Thompson was struggling to hold him, but Rivers could see he was going to make it, and his hand gripped the barrel with a last supreme effort of psychotic energy. As he turned, the gun toward Thompson, Debbie's teeth bit hard into his gun hand. He screamed in agony and dropped the gun. Debbie yelped as Rivers ripped his hand from her mouth.

It bought Thompson microseconds of time—time enough to drag Rivers away from the pistols. As Debbie picked up the Sig Sauer, Rivers finally slipped free of Thompson's grip.

When he saw Debbie aiming the pistol at him, he ran. As he hurtled along the landing, Debbie stumbled after him. When she reached the top of the stairs, Rivers was plunging down them.

Debbie aimed the pistol in the direction of Rivers's rapidly descending back and fired. Before the shot reached Rivers, he had turned at the bottom of the stairs heading for the back door.

As Debbie saw where her wild shot had landed, her face registered horror. Roberts, who'd just come through the open front door, fell forward, wounded. As she heard the back door thump open, it was like a door to all her nightmares opening. In a few moments, Rivers would be lost in the dark, encompassing blanket of the night. Somehow, the gods had given Debbie a chance to end it, and, as she hurried to the side of the wounded policeman, she sadly realized that she'd blown it.

CHAPTER 85

When Machin heard the gunshot, she was suddenly filled with fear and tension.

The one overriding thought pounding through her head was that she needed to get inside to help her colleague, and she needed to help him fast. She hurried across the damp lawn, the wet saturating her trousers. As she approached the dark foreboding house with her pistol prone, the wind whipped rain across her face. Roberts, the Duncans, and Thompson were the innocents inside. There was too much collateral, inside the house. Machin knew she'd have to show caution, though a desperate Rivers would show none.

When she was twenty yards from the back door, it suddenly burst open, and Rivers stood in front of her. He saw Machin and the gun pointing at him and knew immediately that, after what he'd done to Nick Spiller, she wouldn't hesitate to shoot him if he didn't give himself up.

Dexter smiled. He was facing a lifetime in prison—prison would be a chance to work some reverse psychology on all the psychologists that were sure to swarm around him. Dexter accepted the fait accompli—it was time to move on to another avenue in his life. "I'm unarmed, Inspector." Dexter raised his hands in the air. "I give up."

Machin surprised him and smiled. Dexter didn't like it. He thought that, with the murder of Nick Spiller, he'd broken her, that he'd left her a quivering wreck back at Spiller's apartment.

"Nick was also unarmed," Machin stated coldly and then fired her pistol three times into Dexter's midriff, fatally ripping apart his lungs and kidneys. Rivers's face registered the shock he was unable to mask, as he stumbled forward and fell to his death in the wet grass.

As Machin stood over the body, she sensed someone watching. When Thompson stepped out the back door onto the grisly scene, she wondered how long he'd been standing there and how much he'd witnessed.

Any thoughts of future repercussions from the kill ended when Thompson said, "Well done, Inspector," and then surprised her by hugging her.

They slowly separated as the circus arrived. When they went back into the house, they found out that Roberts's injury only needed minor surgery, and Debbie and her mum would be taken to the hospital for observation. As the crime scene team were busy around them, Machin and Thompson sat in the living room, quietly sipping brandy.

"Thank you for killing him," Thompson said.

"I thought he was armed. He left me no choice," Machin said weakly in defense.

Thompson shrugged. "I'd have done the same. If I could've been in the position you were in with the guy who murdered Jodie, then I know, Inspector, that I'd have done exactly the same."

Thompson's hints and veiled references to the kill

left Machin in no doubt that he had seen her execute Rivers. Machin had always thought of herself as a good copper, but the events of the last few hours had shown her otherwise. Her killing of Peter Rivers/Slater/Blackstock —whatever the hell his name was—had been motivated by something other than upholding the law. Her murder of Rivers had been motivated by one overriding human emotion that made even the most normal citizen do alarming things. Revenge was a dirty word for a cop to use, but, Machin decided, it was the only appropriate word here.

Could she remain in the force after all that had gone on tonight? Could she ever look at a case objectively after tonight's events? In the future, tonight's events would always leave her open to self-doubt, make her wonder if her actions meant that she would not be able to continue in her role as a copper and a strict upholder of the law. She had gone to a dark, menacing place at Nick's flat, and at the Duncan house—a dark place where thoughts of revenge seemed to override everything. She wasn't sure what she'd found inside of her tonight, but one thing was certain—whatever it was, she didn't like it.

CHAPTER 86

Thompson sat with Debbie Duncan in directors' chairs outside his trailer on the set of *The Valley of Dreams*. As they stared down the valley at the weak, wintry sun making the dewy grass sparkle, both were contemplating the end of the film and all the misery that the curse of this film had brought on everybody. They'd finished the last few scenes involving Debbie, and Thompson had somehow managed to incorporate them into the rest of the movie.

With Paul Rome dead, they had had to change the final scene. The joint scene with Rome and Debbie, in a bout of soul-searching concerning the state of their marriage, was regrettably no longer possible. Today was the last day on the set before everything was dismantled. Today was the last time that Debbie Duncan and Clay Thompson would see each other for a while.

"The worst part in all this, Debbie, is this wonderful movie is now only ever going to be remembered for Rome's death, your rape, and all the misery that has followed it."

Debbie decided that, after her brutal rape, no matter

how good the movie was, she'd always remember it with a heart full of hate. But, after what they'd gone through that night at the Duncan household, there was now a special bond between the two of them and a lifelong friendship that, Debbie decided, would never be broken.

The last day of seeing her friend wasn't a day of reflecting on the film's demons. "I'm glad things are going well for you with the police inspector," she said, and she genuinely meant it.

"We've both lost partners in a similar way, and that suffering has created a bond between us, enabled us to talk openly about our loss. Sarah's a wonderful woman."

Thompson wouldn't tell Debbie how sometimes Sarah woke up screaming in the night when she thought about Nick, or about how he was equally emotionally damaged when he thought about Jodie. Some things were best left unsaid. With Debbie's recent nightmare, Thompson was sure that hearing about other people's miseries was the last thing that she wanted.

They'd come a long way since he'd first signed her up after that local play that Jodie and Thompson had seen her in. Thompson sometimes thought that if he hadn't signed her up, then this whole nightmare would never have happened.

But it wasn't always a good thing to reflect too much. "Just take things nice and slow, Clay. Promise me that you'll take things slow."

Debbie stood as her chauffeur-driven car arrived to take her back to Guildford. They hugged, and Thompson kissed her on the cheek. At that moment, he knew that, regardless of what had gone before, their friendship would last. The more Thompson dated Sarah, the more he felt that there was something special between them. It was going to take time, as such a tragic loss was not something that could be overcome in an instant.

As Debbie's car became a pinprick on the horizon, he thought about Rivers, of what and who he'd been. There was so much they'd uncovered, unspeakable things like a collection of rings kept in a tin that he'd taken from the fingers of his murdered girlfriends and wives. In Peter Rivers, they'd all looked inside the eyes of madness, and as far as Thompson was concerned, one thing was certain, *The Valley of Dreams* was always going to be a film synonymous with that madness. *The Valley of Dreams*, after the final edit, was a movie that Thompson would never watch again.

The End

About the Author

Paul Howard was born in the Garden of England, in East Kent, and educated at Castlemount Secondary school, a school that closed thirty years ago. He's always felt lucky to be surrounded by such a wonderful coastline and has fond memories of days spent on the beach as a kid. His deceased father, Mike, was a seaman, who often used to regale him with tales from his overseas trips, including catching strange fish in New Zealand and of his friend, Vic, who used to bare-knuckle fight at fairgrounds in Australia.

Howard lives with his partner, Anna-Maria, a German woman, whose great uncle was Max Brauer, a former prime minister of Hamburg. In the 1930s, Brauer was involved in trying to stop Hitler from coming to power. The resultant success of the Nazis meant that he had to flee Germany for Manhattan before he was arrested. Howard's partner's family has an interesting past, with her deceased English father, a special forces commando in World War Two, receiving commendation letters from Winston Churchill for his bravery in the conflict.

In the 1980s, Howard worked for Hoverspeed at Dover International Hoverport. At the time, he never appreciated what a unique job it was. Because of the huge fuel costs, hovercrafts are far too expensive to run these days. The possibility of having passenger-carrying hovercrafts again is something the world will never see. Since 1989 until recently, Howard worked for Royal Mail as a postman, but his partner's disabilities—Ehlers-Danlos Syndrome, and other associated conditions—meant he has had to give up work to become a home-care-giver.

In his years of working for Royal Mail, he found a sense of community and a level of camaraderie among postmen that you wouldn't find anywhere other than the armed services. Unfortunately, due to his circumstances, it was time to move on, so, alas, he had to leave many friends behind, look to the future, and focus on his writing.